BBC
DOCTOR WHO

AT CHILDHOOD'S END

Sophie Aldred

with Steve Cole & Mike Tucker

BBC BOOKS

3 5 7 9 10 8 6 4 2

BBC Books, an imprint of Ebury Publishing
20 Vauxhall Bridge Road,
London SW1V 2SA

BBC Books is part of the Penguin Random House group of companies whose
addresses can be found at global.penguinrandomhouse.com

Penguin
Random House
UK

Storyline by Sophie Aldred, Steve Cole and Mike Tucker

Doctor Who is a BBC Wales production for BBC One.
Executive producers: Chris Chibnall and Matt Strevens

First published by BBC Books in 2020

www.penguin.co.uk

A CIP catalogue record for this book is available from the British Library

ISBN 9781785944994

Publishing Director: Albert DePetrillo
Project Editor: Steve Cole
Cover design: Two Associates
Production: Sian Pratley

Typeset in 12/15 pt Albertina MT Std
by Integra Software Services Pvt. Ltd, Pondicherry

Printed and bound in Great Britain by Clays Ltd, Elcograf S.p.A.

Penguin Random House is committed to a sustainable future for
our business, our readers and our planet. This book is made from
Forest Stewardship Council® certified paper.

MIX
Paper from
responsible sources
FSC
www.fsc.org   FSC® C018179

TABLE OF CONTENTS

To the three men in my life who ARE my life;
you anchor me and yet allow me to fly.
Vince, Adam and William – this one's for you.

PRELUDE

As far as Justine was concerned, it was almost as if she had been scooped up from her old life and deposited on some remote alien world – just like the girl in that corny old film *The Wizard of Oz*. Except that it was no magical Technicolor kingdom in which she now found herself, it was central London in January, and that was about as far from magical as you could possibly get.

It had been raining constantly for nearly three days now. The coat that she was wearing purported to be weather-proof, but she doubted that the manufacturers had ever expected it to be worn continuously for day after day as she had been doing, and with no chance of it drying out. Her boots were starting to suffer as well, and she didn't want to imagine how uncomfortable she was going to be if she had to start trudging through the streets with wet feet. Thankfully she had managed to wedge herself into the doorway of a closed and shuttered newsagent during the worst of today's downpours, so at least the spare clothes that she had bundled up in her rucksack would still be dry.

There were much better places to shelter from the rain, of course, but recent experience had taught her that the bigger and more sheltered the storefront, the more aggressively the security staff would move her on.

She sighed. When she'd imagined her escape to the capital it had seemed so vibrant and exotic, the images on her television showing her nothing but happy, smiling people hurrying through the dazzling displays of twinkling lights as they went about their Christmas shopping. Those lights were all gone now, and if there ever *had* been any happy smiling people thronging the streets then they had all been replaced by morose impostors. She had lost count of the number of times she had been shouted at or shoved out of the way in the last few days.

Still … it was better than being back at home. She'd take the sullen strangers over Adrian any day.

Adrian was her mum's boyfriend. He said that he was involved with construction in the film industry – a carpenter or plasterer or something – but it hadn't taken Justine long to realise what he *really* was. Every time they were alone he'd sit close beside her, make salacious comments that made her skin crawl. Justine had told her mum, but Mum refused to believe it: 'You're jealous. Trying to spoil this for me …'

Their house in Bristol had always been a sanctuary for her, a safe place where she could shut out the outside world, and surround herself with the things that made her happy. Adrian's arrival had changed all that, and now, every time that she returned home to find his big, black SUV parked outside, the house seemed like the most dangerous place in the world.

Better the streets on her own than back there with him.

That had been over three weeks ago now. Pulling up the collar of her sodden coat, she heaved her rucksack higher onto her shoulder and set off through the sea of people hurrying though the rain-soaked streets. She wondered for the thousandth time if anyone was looking for her. Every day she was afraid of being sighted, and just as scared of staying lost.

It'll get easier, she told herself, wondering if she'd ever really believe that.

She made her way east along the Strand, the crowds thinning out as she left the theatre district behind her, trudged past the law courts on Fleet Street and entered the quiet calm of the City of London. The financial district was bustling with people during weeknights, but at the weekends it was virtually deserted, and that suited Justine just fine.

She hurried on past the huge, historic buildings that still dominated this part of London – St Paul's Cathedral, the Bank of England, the Royal Exchange – and made her way into the tangle of narrow passageways that wound their way through Cheapside. The ancient stone buildings now gave way to modern structures of steel and glass, and the Portacabins and heavy machinery of the construction sites that littered the roads at the foot of each.

She turned into another alleyway, ignoring the 'road closed' and 'diversion' signs and making her way towards the steel fence that had been erected at the far end. Checking that there was no one watching, Justine quickly scaled the fence, dropping nimbly onto the freshly laid tarmac on the other side. She hurried across the deserted building site, splashing through huge shallow puddles of rainwater to where a huge pile of air-conditioning ducting sat swathed in tarpaulins at the base of a towering construction crane.

With one last look around to check that she hadn't been spotted, Justine lifted up the edge of the tarpaulin and ducked inside. This had been where she been sleeping for the last week. Most of the local construction sites were impossible to get into, but in the five nights that she had been here Justine had only seen one elderly security guard. She assumed that there must be some delay with the construction project as she hadn't seen a single worker, or noticed any movement or goods either in or out. Whatever the reason she was just glad to have somewhere safe to sleep. The length of ducting wasn't warm, but at least it was dry and relatively clean. The only real downside was that she occasionally heard rats scurrying across the top if it, their claws clattering on the metal.

Shrugging off her rucksack, Justine crawled further along the length of metal tube towards a bundle of blankets. They'd been handing them out at a church in Soho, and Justine had accepted a couple gratefully. The material was harsh and scratchy, not at all like the blankets on her bed at home, but at least they helped keep out the worst of the cold.

Outside she could hear the rain intensifying, the tarpaulin starting to flap noisily in the wind. Shivering, she pulled the blanket tighter around her. So long since she'd slept in a proper bed, so long since she'd eaten a proper meal, so long since she'd had a shower … Three weeks of rain, and cold and rats.

As if on cue, there was the clatter of claws on the metal of the ducting.

A wave of despair threatened to overwhelm her. Justine had never felt so unloved and pathetic in her life …

Suddenly there was a tremendous cracking noise, like a bundle of twigs being snapped, but so loud that it shook the metal of the ducting. Instantly, Justine was on her feet, trying to work out where the sound had come from. Her heart leapt at the sound of footsteps from the yard outside and moments later there was the rustle of plastic as the tarpaulin covering the mouth of the ducting was pulled aside.

Justine snatched up her backpack as two figures wearing filthy, hooded tops stepped into the tube.

Oh, God. She felt herself freeze, terrified.

'No need to be scared, dearie.' The leading figure's voice was rasping and hoarse. 'We're not going to hurt you.'

Justine backed away as the intruders started to advance along the pipe towards her. 'I haven't got any money,' she said quickly.

'Money?' The figure gave a wheezing laugh. 'It's not money we're after.'

'Got no use for it,' chipped in the other. 'It's a donation, we want.'

'A what?'

The first one giggled. 'Charity begins at homeless.'

Justine had heard enough. The two were trouble, clearly off their heads. She turned to run, knowing that there was a way out at the other end of the ducting, but as she turned, her foot caught on the hem of her blanket and she crashed heavily to the floor.

Immediately the two figures pounced, gripping Justine's arms and legs. With a scream of rage, Justine kicked out, her heel catching one of her assailants on the side of the head and sending him sprawling.

Snarling with anger, the other pinned her to the floor. Justine gave a gasp of horror. Beneath the hood there was something terribly wrong with her attacker's face. The eyes were big and dark, the features misshapen.

With a hiss, the thing opened its mouth, baring teeth like rotten spikes. A vile animal spray splattered onto Justine's face. She groaned, revolted. The smell was overpowering.

As blackness engulfed her, all she could hear was the chittering of rats ...

PART ONE
2020

CHAPTER ONE

Dorothy McShane jolted from her sleep, lashing out at the creature that was reaching for her. But there was no creature. She was alone in her bedroom, her attacker nothing but a phantom from a nightmare.

With a groan, she slumped back onto the bed, the sheets rumpled, her arms and forehead slick with sweat. She closed her eyes again and lay motionless in the cool dark for a moment, trying to control her breathing and slow her heart rate. It had been the same story every night this week. The same nightmare, the same moment of sudden awakening, the same conviction that she was fighting for her life.

It was becoming tiresome.

As with all the previous occasions, she tried to recall the exact events of her nightmare, hoping that some remembered detail might provide a pointer to what might be triggering these dreams.

They always began in exactly the same way: feeling herself being drawn out of her body, watching her sleeping self recede into the distance as she rose higher and higher until she was floating far above the city, looking down on the patchwork of roads and buildings, lights blazing into the night. Then things tended to kick up a gear and she found herself moving faster, gaining altitude until London was no more than a smudge of light below her. Soon the planet itself was revealed – a globe of brilliant blue against the blackness, before that too receded, and she was flying through nothing but stars and blackness.

Dorothy always enjoyed this bit – she'd always enjoyed the sensation of speed. Bikes, cars, planes; she couldn't get enough of them...

As dreams went, there was little that was unusual so far; dreams of leaving the physical form behind and of flying were common enough. Indeed, given her own past history, it might also be considered inevitable that she would have dreams of this type, but it was what happened next that was troubling her.

The exhilarating flight was always brought to an abrupt halt in the same place – a vast dust-scoured desert littered with razor-sharp rocks and shards of broken crystal, stretching out seemingly forever beneath a sky the colour of vomit. Every breath that Dorothy tried to take in this barren place seemed to sear the inside of her lungs, and with every step she took, the edges of the rocks threatened to slice though the soles of her shoes.

All around her she could see other figures making their painful way across the hostile sand, too far away to make out their faces, but close enough to hear their anguished cries. There were scores of them; men, women, children, all making their way towards a huge building on the horizon.

The structure was vast, its cracked and crumbling walls seemingly made out of rough, dark pumice. Huge chimneys rose from its centre, belching thick, oily smoke into the sick-looking sky and the sound of grinding engines reverberated from within. Fingers of lightning constantly tore from the clouds that roiled above it, and cracks of thunder echoed across the barren landscape.

It was a vision of hell itself.

Dorothy tried to force her subconscious to remember something useful, some face that she recognised, or a detail about the building that seemed familiar, but any memory that might help unravel the cause of her nightmare was always drowned out by the appearance of … the creature.

The event that tore her from her sleep each night was never exactly the same, but it always started the same way. The boiling clouds started to thicken and swell, the pale yellow of the sky darkening to a deep pus-like orange. Deep in the clouds a huge dark shape started to solidify.

All around people started to flee, and Dorothy fled with them, not knowing what it was she was running from, but knowing instinctively that it was the right thing to do. The razor edges of the rocks tore at her feet making her cry out in pain with every footfall. She dared not think what damage they would do to her hands and face if she lost her balance and fell.

From behind her there was a sudden crack of thunder, immediately followed by the sound of hoarse, animal breathing as something unseen bore down on her.

And every night Dorothy turned to face whatever the horror might be, only to find a fast, scabrous talon, its fingernails cracked and dirty, reaching out for her, engulfing her, snatching her off her feet and lifting her towards a face so terrible, so monstrous that she woke literally believing that she was fighting for her life.

Dorothy took a deep breath and opened her eyes. Her mouth was dry, and she knew from experience that there was little chance of her being able to get back to sleep. Pushing aside the sweat-soaked duvet she swung her legs to the floor and stood for a moment, naked in the dark, curling her toes in the thick pile of the bedside rug, luxuriating in the air-conditioned calm of her room. Reaching down, she snatched up a robe from where she had discarded it on the floor the previous night. She'd never been tidy as a teenager. Things hadn't changed.

There was a rustle from the far side of the room and a black cat appeared, sauntering across the polished wooden floor towards her, its expression leaving Dorothy in no doubt that her exertions had woken it from its sleep.

'Yeah, Sorin,' muttered Dorothy. 'Like you never have bad dreams ...'

Sorin hopped up onto the bed, sniffing at the rumpled sheets disdainfully before curling up in a fold of the duvet. Dorothy gave him an affectionate rub behind the ear, then shrugged into her dressing gown, tied it and made her way down the stairs that led to the rest of her apartment.

As with every other morning, the view from her apartment lifted her spirits. The floor-to-ceiling windows, coupled with the fact that she was 18 storeys up, gave her an unparalleled view over London, and on a clear day she could see as far as the Chilterns. She always felt that early morning was the best time to see London. A scant few hours when the craziness of the clubbers and partygoers was over, and the different craziness of the morning commute had yet to begin.

In the summer she liked to watch as the first rays of the rising sun caught the spires of the churches and lit up the dome of St Paul's Cathedral, rising above the rooftops, making the grime-blackened stone shine as if glowing with an inner light. But this was January, and sunrise – if the sun did indeed manage to shed any light through the ponderous grey clouds – was still hours away. London would be dark for a good while yet.

Crossing to the window, she peered down at the ancient buildings that formed the Tower of London. Choosing this location for the headquarters of A Charitable Earth had amused Dorothy. She had been quite adamant about it when the building had been commissioned, despite the fact that there had been immediate and vociferous opposition to its construction.

She had known all too well what the basis for that opposition was, of course, and it had nothing to do with environmental concerns, or visual pollution, or any one of the other dozen or so reasons that had been put forward to try and impede the building's construction.

The truth was that, nestled in the foundations of the Tower of London, had been the UK control centre for UNIT – the UNified Intelligence Taskforce – a first-line defence against alien incursions. No one had been prepared to admit that publicly, of course, and so the legal team that Dorothy had employed successfully overcame every other objection to the building's construction, and now an elegant tower of glass and steel loomed over the ancient walls of flint and stone.

Dorothy's reason for locating her headquarters here had been simple: it provided a clear view down onto the private roadway that led to UNIT headquarters. Being able to track the number of vehicles going in and out had given her early warning of any possible unusual activity. She had never imagined that just a few years later the entire organisation would be mothballed on the orders of Whitehall. The official protests from Geneva went on, but the fact remained that UNIT was over and the Earth less defended.

If Brigadier Bambera had stayed in charge of UNIT then perhaps things would've gone differently. But poor old Winifred was still listed as 'missing in action' following a Sea Devil attack on a classified military listening post just off the South Wales coast. Dorothy had set up a search protocol on her computer for any report mentioning Bambera by name, but if the brigadier had been located, then someone was keeping it quiet.

'I should've set up in Cardiff,' Dorothy muttered.

Turning away from the window, she made her way to the well-equipped open-plan kitchen and turned on the kettle. As soon as the water had boiled she made herself a cup of strong, black coffee, snatched up the remote that was sitting on the counter top and started to flip through channels on the wall-mounted TV.

It never ceased to amaze Dorothy that television companies could turn out so many hours of utter trash. It was hardly surprising that this stuff was relegated to the small hours of the morning schedule. As she clicked from channel to channel in search of something that could keep her engaged for an hour or so, a familiar face appeared on the screen and Dorothy gave a groan of despair.

Kim Fortune was a conspiracy-theory nut who hosted his own podcast – *Kim Fortune's Mysterious World*. How the hell had he managed to get himself a broadcast slot, even on one of the less reputable cable channels? Ordinarily, Dorothy wouldn't have given him the time of day, but Kim had proved himself to be a better investigative journalist than even *he* suspected, and several months ago one of his podcasts had got worryingly close to the truth. He'd suggested that there might be a connection between several unexplained events and herself – the elusive CEO of A Charitable Earth – and so Dorothy had agreed to be interviewed, figuring that if he was going to broadcast stories about her, then she might as well have some level of control over their contents.

To a certain extent that strategy had worked, and so far she had managed to steer his research away from the events of her past that might prove complicated to explain and into areas that were far less contentious. The downside was that he now took her willingness to be interviewed as a taciturn approval of him and his journalism, and barely a week went by when he wasn't trying to contact her to present his latest theory about aliens, or government projects, or the Loch Ness monster ... He'd even turned up at reception last month before security had politely and firmly informed him that Dorothy wasn't available to meet him and escorted him from the premises. Even then he'd hung about on the street for nearly an hour before leaving. Dorothy was tempted to let him know about the former UNIT base under the Tower; that might divert his attention for a while ...

Kim's TV show appeared to be much the same as his podcast – with schlocky music and added dodgy CGI. He was presenting an exposé about alien abductions in the UK. There were interviews with parents claiming that their children had been abducted, and teenagers telling the stories of their lucky escapes. Dorothy was about to change the channel but then stopped as one of the interviews caught her attention.

The girl that Kim was interviewing must have been about 13 or 14. Flanked by her grim-faced parents, she described how aliens came to her house and tried to abduct her. Ordinarily Dorothy would have dismissed the claims as pure fantasy but, as the girl continued to relate what had happened to her, Dorothy began to realise that it was uncannily similar to her own dream.

Fascinated now, Dorothy turned up the volume and sat on one of the breakfast bar stools, sipping her coffee and listening intently to the girl describe her experience. It was extraordinary. The out-of-body experience, the sensation of flight, the hostile, searing desert … It was all exactly the same.

The real gut punch, however, came right at the end of the interview, when Kim revealed that the events had taken place in Perivale, no more than a few streets away from where Dorothy had spent her early years.

As the programme finished and the credits started to roll, Dorothy sat back, her mind racing. Not only was the girl's experience virtually identical to the nightmares that she had been having, but the fact that it happened in Perivale made it virtually a carbon copy of what had happened to her when she was 16 – scooped up in a time-storm from her old bedroom in 1987. At the time she'd naively thought that it had been the result of her juvenile meddling in chemistry, only much later learning it was the work of an ancient evil entity, Fenric.

Was the same thing somehow happening to other people? Her own experiences could've made her sensitive to these storms in time, whatever they were.

Why? she thought miserably. *Why is it happening again?*

CHAPTER TWO

Shutting off the TV, Dorothy made her way into the sitting room, dropped down onto the couch and flipped open the laptop that sat on the huge glass-topped coffee table that dominated the room.

Tucking her legs underneath her in an almost yoga-like pose, Dorothy placed her coffee on the table, slipped on her reading glasses and began to search for anything connected with reports of alien abductions in the West London area. The search parameters that she set were wide ranging, but her laptop was no ordinary PC, and the powerful software loaded onto it was capable of searching a far wider set of databases than was strictly legal – not just conspiracy websites and dark web forums, but police reports, military communications, government memos …

In less than 15 minutes she had managed to find at least a dozen instances of missing persons in the West London area and, whilst there was nothing that correlated with any official government reports indicating alien activity, each of them did match with accounts of strange 'cracking' sounds.

Five of them were in Perivale.

Dorothy knew that she really had little choice other than to investigate further.

That was going to upset a lot of people.

She closed the laptop and glanced at her watch. 5.30am.

'Well,' she murmured, taking off her glasses, 'nothing like getting an early start.'

Uncurling herself from the sofa, Dorothy made her way back upstairs, took a brief shower and then changed into plain black leggings, a vest top and a thick, high-necked pullover. As she sat on the edge of the bed lacing up her boots, she glanced over at the badge-festooned jacket that hung on a stand against the far wall.

She paused for a moment, contemplating it. 'Why do I even keep you?' she said aloud.

Whatever was going on, whatever monsters from her past might be rearing their heads, she needed to face them as the woman that she was now, not the girl that she used to be.

Snatching a leather jacket from the wardrobe, Dorothy gave Sorin a brief scratch behind the ears then hurried back down the stairs, crossed the room and unlocked the door that led directly into her company office. To her surprise, Sanaul was seated at the desk.

Dorothy tutted. 'Don't you ever sleep?'

Her business manager turned to her with an apologetic smile. He was in his early sixties, dressed in an immaculate three-piece suit, his silver-grey hair and beard a stark contrast to the deep chestnut hue of his skin. 'It seems that neither of us has been able to sleep, Miss Dorothy. You, I assume, have been rudely awakened by your troubling dreams again, whilst I find that can never stay in my bed when I know that there are unfinished accounts to be dealt with.'

Dorothy grinned. Sanaul was more than just a colleague; he was her partner-in-crime, her confidant, and her friend. She had met him during the relief operation after a catastrophic cyclone had struck the Indonesian coast about five years ago. He had been coordinating the emergency response teams, while Dorothy had been there with her own team setting up a temporary hospital structure and arranging for the delivery of medical supplies.

Over the two weeks that they had been thrown together Dorothy had watched him with growing admiration as he coped with crisis after crisis, setback after setback, always with unflappable good humour and meticulous attention to detail. He in turn saw her as something of a kindred spirit and the two of them had become good friends.

Once the disaster was finally under control, Dorothy had flown back to Kerala with him, taken him out for a meal and offered him a job. To her surprise, he had accepted without hesitation and since he had joined the management team A Charitable Earth had never been run more efficiently.

There was only really one slight hiccup, and that was in over five years she had still not managed to get him to call her by her first name at work. He'd spent his first year addressing her as Miss McShane, which set Dorothy's teeth on edge. In the end they'd agreed to compromise on 'Miss Dorothy'. As far as Sanaul was concerned that was still respectful enough for him to be happy with it, and it amused Dorothy because it made her sound like one of Basil Brush's sidekicks.

Sanaul's smile faded as he noticed what she was wearing. Boots and leggings weren't exactly standard office dress for a Chief Executive Officer.

'Are you going out, Miss Dorothy?'

Dorothy nodded. 'I think that there's something going on that needs checking out. I'm off to visit an old friend in Perivale.'

'So I can only assume that you've forgotten that you have a meeting with Jane Thackeray at the World Ecology Bureau at 10.00 and another with the Disasters Emergency Committee at 3.00?'

Dorothy said nothing.

'You've not forgotten, have you?' Sanaul tried but failed to hide his disapproval. 'You want me to go in your place. Again.'

Dorothy held up her hands. 'What can I say? Something's come up ...'

'But that only gives me –' Sanaul checked his watch – 'four hours to prepare!'

'Yeah.' Dorothy started to edge towards the main doors. 'There are some notes in my desk diary that might help. Top drawer. I'll try and get back for the second meeting if I can. Oh, and I want to you to find out which production company is behind the Kim Fortune documentary series that went out on Channel 19 this morning.'

'Priorities, Miss Dorothy!'

'You're right – do that first. I need to speak to the girl Kim interviewed who says she was abducted. See you later.'

With a grin and a wave, Dorothy closed the doors on Sanaul's cries of protest and hurried across the lobby, stabbing at the lift call button. To her relief the lift was there waiting and the doors slid open immediately. She stepped inside and pressed the button for the garage level. As the indicator lights started to blink their way from eighteen to zero, Dorothy felt a tingle of anticipation that she'd not felt for many, many years. At the same time she felt a pang of sadness that she didn't have the Doctor alongside her to share this with.

'Seems as though there's still work to do, Professor.' She shook her head, felt the old anger bubble with surprising heat. All the times they'd overthrown evil, brought down heartless regimes – on Terra Alpha, Segonax, Colostro Minor – they'd sparked revolutions in a day and tripped merrily away in the TARDIS to somewhere new. But Dorothy knew now that the real danger began when the empires toppled: rebuilding was everything. If you walked away and just left people to it, you could be abandoning them to any of a hundred worse ways forward.

Did we really do any good? How many times had she asked that of the shadows in her silent penthouse. *If we went back to those worlds we thought we'd saved, what would we find?*

20

She thought of the pile of reports waiting for her to read, of the sheer volume of planning and admin required to bring aid to the people who needed it, to spend the funds where it mattered; the little details and the little people to coordinate so that the right changes came about.

'Yeah, there's work, Professor,' Dorothy muttered. 'And I'm doing it my way.'

There was a soft chime as the lift reached the lowest level of the building and the doors slid open. Triggered by the movement, banks of LEDs blinked into life, bathing the garage in a soft white light.

Dorothy's moment of melancholy was lightened by the sight that greeted her. Sanaul always referred to the garage as 'Miss Dorothy's Toy Box' and he wasn't wrong. The two Honda Fireblade motorcycles alone were enough to lift her spirits but it was the sleek vehicle parked beside them that was her real pride and joy.

The Hypergreen, prototype of an ACE-funded start-up in Malaysia, looked like a classic sports car and could go from zero to 90 miles an hour in just over 3 seconds – and yet it was every bit as green as its name and paintwork would suggest. The car was parked on a pad on the floor that charged it wirelessly; with a full charge, the liquid-cooled solid-state battery gave the car a range of over 400 miles.

Unlocking the Hypergreen, she slipped into the driver's seat and grinned as the electric motors hummed into life. Using the paddles on the steering wheel to put the car into gear, she pulled out of the parking space then accelerated up the ramp out of the garage and into the chill morning air.

'Wicked,' she murmured. Then bit her lip and eased up on the accelerator. What was she, 16 again?

Even at this time in the morning, traffic was already starting to build up. In another hour it would be nose-to-tail and by 8am central London would be virtually gridlocked. Although that was a downside to where she had chosen to build her headquarters, it did at least give her a cast-iron excuse to give Sanaul as to why she couldn't make it back in time for that DEC meeting …

Turning onto the Victoria Embankment, she made her way alongside the Thames for a short while before snaking her way up through Covent Garden and Holborn then up past Regent's Park and onto the Westway heading out of London. As soon as she reached the elevated section by Paddington Station, the temptation to just floor the accelerator was almost too much to resist. She restrained herself.

Crikey, I must be getting old …

The first time that she had ever driven anything had been on this stretch of road. Her friend Flo had been dating a plumber who, for some reason that she couldn't recall, was nicknamed Darth Vader. One Sunday Darth had decided that he was going to teach Dorothy how to drive and, after an hour or so grinding the gears of his beaten-up transit in the carpark of B&Q, they had headed out onto the Westway.

Dorothy could still recall the exhilaration she had felt as the battered old van had picked up speed, and the needle on the speedometer had crept higher and higher – 60, 70, 80 … She remembered the screams of her friends in the back as they had begged her to slow down. Darth hadn't let her drive his van again after that. In fact he'd never really looked at her the same way ever again, realising, perhaps, that he had unwittingly awoken a side of her that had been dormant until that point, a yearning for speed, for excitement, for danger … That need was still there.

Under control, thought Dorothy. *You keep it under control.*

CHAPTER THREE

Before long the elegant Art Deco frontage of the Hoover Building came into view, and soon after Dorothy turned off the main road, making her way through the residential streets of Perivale before pulling to a halt outside an ugly low-rise block of flats.

Locking the Hypergreen, she made her way up the concrete stairs to the top floor. She knocked loudly on a door painted a monstrous shade of bright pink. After a few moments there was a muffled curse and the sound of movement from inside. The door opened and an attractive blonde in a very short bathrobe appeared, squinting blearily in the early morning light.

'Oh, no …' she groaned as she realised who had woken her.

'All right, Squeak …' said Dorothy looking in amusement at the tousled hair and smudged makeup. 'Blimey. Getting to be a bit old for clubbing on a weeknight, aren't we?'

'Thirty-seven isn't old!'

Dorothy gave her a look that she hoped said, 'Who do you think you're kidding?' and pushed her way inside, making her way to the tiny kitchenette. The place was a total tip, unwashed plates and takeaway pizza boxes piled on every worktop, the sink full of mugs and wineglasses. Dorothy extracted two of the mugs, rinsed them and then filled the kettle.

'Looks like it was a good night.'

'Yeah, well, I didn't expect to be up at some god-awful time of the morning, did I?'

Dorothy cast an enquiring eye towards the bedroom door. 'I'm not disturbing anything am I, Squeak?'

Squeak raised an eyebrow. 'No, you're not – *Ace*.'

'All right, point taken.' Dorothy had asked people to stop calling her Ace a long time ago, and knew she should really return the favour. 'OK, Chantelle, I'm sorry.'

Dorothy had known Chantelle since she'd been born. She'd baby-sat her a couple of times at school when her mum had been working late. The truth was that Chantelle wasn't actually her real name either, it was Abigail, but on her 15th birthday she had apparently decided that she wanted to be an actress and that Abigail wasn't a 'showbizzy' enough name, and so had insisted that everyone started calling her Chantelle instead.

To be fair, she had actually achieved her childhood ambition and, after a brief stint modelling clothes for Henrik's online store, had picked up a couple of bit parts in some of the soaps, before landing a reasonably large role in a low-budget horror film. That in turn had led to a successful modelling career for a high-end fashion house. The downside was that it had also attracted her a legion of dedicated male fans – most of them trouble. Dorothy had never met anyone who had dated as many lowlifes and losers as Chantelle.

What continued to impress Dorothy, however, was that despite the reasonable success that her career had brought her Chantelle had stayed close to home. Getting herself a flat in the same block as her mum and her gran, shopping in the same local stores as she always had still, drinking in the same pubs … In fact the only way you'd have known that she was famous at all was from the covers of dozens of glossy fashion magazines featuring her that hung framed on virtually every wall.

It wasn't just the fierce family loyalty that made Dorothy want to keep in touch with her. Chantelle had used some of her earnings to set up an anti-knife crime initiative in the area, putting money into youth centres, skateboard parks and libraries. Dorothy had actually tried to get her to join A Charitable Earth on several occasions, but Chantelle kept turning her down. She liked her modelling career and, despite the man-trouble, she liked the party-girl lifestyle that went with it.

This morning, however, she was looking like she might be regretting that last part. Dorothy spooned a heaped teaspoon of instant coffee into each of the mugs, filled them both with boiling water and then handed one to Chantelle.

'Here. I get the impression you might need it.'

Chantelle grunted something unintelligible and made her way into the lounge, pushing aside a pair of discarded Louis Vuitton jeans and slumping down on the elegant sofa.

'What are you doing here, anyway?'

'I need a bit of info,' said Dorothy, following her.

'Info that couldn't wait until a civilised time of the morning?'

'Given that your idea of a "civilised time" is gone noon, no.'

Chantelle glared at her. 'You know, you only ever get in touch when you want something, Miss CEO. You never just want to go out for a chat or a drink any more.'

'Can't keep up with you, can I?' Dorothy said breezily. 'Please. It's important.'

'It always is …' Chantelle sighed. 'OK … What is it you're after?'

Dorothy told her about the programme she had watched, about the alien abductions, the missing girls, the strange noises and the research that she had done linking a large number of those events to Perivale.

She had expected Chantelle to be dismissive, angry at being dragged from her bed because of claims made in some far-fetched, conspiracy theory documentary, but instead, her friend listened carefully to what she was saying, a frown beginning to crease her forehead.

As Dorothy finished, Chantelle put down her coffee and leaned forward. 'It's weird. I did hear a strange noise a few nights ago.'

'Oh? What sort of noise?'

'I dunno. Like firecrackers, or a bunch of twigs snapping. I thought it was a car backfiring, or kids mucking about. Didn't really take much notice. I've had more to worry about with all the rats that we're getting around here these days.'

'Rats?'

'Yeah. Really big ones. I'd never had a problem with them round here before. I guess it's all the food bins left out these days.' She paused. 'There's another thing ... You're the second person to come around here asking about this.'

'Really?' Dorothy's ears picked up. 'Who else has been asking?'

Chantelle shrugged. 'I've not seen him myself. But Gina said that she caught a bloke poking around late at night in the alleyway behind her house. Her Malcolm chased him off.'

Dorothy felt a sudden surge of expectation. Could the Doctor be back in Perivale investigating things too?

Before she could question Chantelle further her mobile suddenly rang. It was Sanaul. She hit answer. 'Hi. Something up?'

'*I suggest that you turn on the television.*'

Dorothy frowned.

'Problem?

'*It'll be easier if you just see for yourself.*'

Dorothy snatched up the remote from the table and switched on the vast flat-screen television hanging on the wall. Every channel had the same story – breaking news about a mysterious object that had suddenly appeared in orbit around the Moon. The image that all of them were showing of the ship was indistinct – it appeared to be a slender elongated cone, with a series of coral-like growths at one end. Dorothy felt a sudden shiver run along her spine. There was something horribly familiar about this...

She flipped to the BBC News channel, which seemed to have slightly more information about the incident.

'The UFO appeared in Moon orbit at 7.10 GMT. Both NASA and the ESA have confirmed that there had been no prior detection of its approach, stating that the object just appeared on their scanners from nowhere. Military sources from all major powers on Earth are saying that the arrival of the UFO without warning is not automatically being seen as an act of aggression; however, if it makes any attempt to approach the planet without further communication as to its intent, then action will be taken. In the meantime it is understood that missions are being prepared by NASA, the ESA, Russia and India to intercept the UFO in Moon orbit, and unconfirmed reports suggests that China might have a rocket ready to launch within 24 hours.

'We now go over to our Manchester Studios where Science Correspondent Jonathan Amos is talking to Professor Brian Cox about what the arrival of the alien spacecraft might mean...'

Dorothy shut off the TV and unmuted her phone.

'Sanaul?

'Yes, Miss Dorothy?'

'You'd better clear my diary for a few days.'

Without waiting for his confirmation, she hung up and slipped the phone back into her pocket. On the sofa Chantelle was looking concerned. Dorothy couldn't blame her. Something about that UFO had unnerved her. It was nothing specific – she was certain that she'd never seen anything like it before – but there was something ... Something that was starting to gnaw away at the back of her memory.

'This isn't good, right?' said Chantelle. 'I mean, you come here talking about alien abduction and then this thing shows up … Surely that's not a coincidence.'

'I don't think so,' Dorothy sighed.

'So what are you going to do now?'

'Go and get a closer look at that UFO.'

'How?' Chantelle frowned. 'You got a big telescope?'

Dorothy smiled. 'Better that that.'

CHAPTER FOUR

Dorothy's sports car blasted out of London along the A40 at nearly 90 miles an hour, the powerful electric motors barely making a sound. If the speed cameras flashed her, let them; she had to get things moving as fast as possible. She needed to reach that UFO before anyone else did, and there was only one person who could help her do that.

She slid her phone into a docking slot on the dashboard and a 'hands free' notification came up on the screen above the speedometer.

'Phone Will Buckland.'

The phone gave a beep and a mobile number flashed onto the screen.

Will was another old friend. Well, more than that. He might have been the first British man on the Moon if the ESA funding hadn't been cut, but Dorothy was cool with that: with him earthbound, she'd dated him for nearly a year. They had met at a fundraising event in the City, hit it off immediately and embarked on one of the longest, most intense and, above all, fun relationships that Dorothy had ever experienced. But then he'd wanted more, all her old trust issues had reared their stupid heads, and she'd ended it – over six months ago now. Even so, Will remained one of the few people on the planet whom she felt she could trust.

He was also currently the Director of the British Space Defence Centre at Devesham.

The phone had only rung twice when her call was answered.

'Dot, what a nice surprise.'

Dorothy grinned at the sarcastic tone of his voice. 'Don't call me Dot, you muppet. I just thought, it's been a while, might be nice to catch up.'

'Really? So, this surprise call out of the blue has nothing whatsoever to do with the fact that an alien spacecraft has just appeared in orbit around the Moon?'

'OK, it might have something to do with that.'

'You know how to wound a man.'

'Look, Will, I need a favour. You're going to be sending up a probe to take a look at this thing, right?'

'You know that any information that I might have about that is going to be classified.'

'And I know that the very fact that you won't tell me means that you are. So, listen. I want to be on that probe.'

'I beg your pardon?'

Dorothy could picture his incredulous expression. Damn, he still looked hot. She shook her head, hit the brakes as she took a corner. 'I'm serious, Will. If you're sending up a probe than I need to be on it.'

'And I'm telling you, Dorothy, that it's impossible.'

'So you *are* sending a probe?'

'I didn't say that …'

'Look, neither of us have time for this.' Dorothy played her trump card. 'So, what if I could get us into lunar orbit in a matter of hours?'

There was silence on the other end of the line for a moment.

'You can't be serious.'

'You know me. I promise you that I can bring something with me that will guarantee that your probe will reach that UFO nearly two days before even that Chinese rocket gets there. But that offer comes with conditions ...'

'If you're serious about this then you'll have a place on the team ...'

'No team,' she said firmly. 'Just the two of us. No one else gets involved or the deal is off.'

There was another long pause.

'You know, if you really wanted us to go out on another date then you could have just asked.'

'You wish.' Dorothy smiled. 'Now, I'll be there in a couple of hours. You'd better be ready for me. Call end.'

With a tingle of warmth inside her, Dorothy sped up, the grey, industrial sprawl of London soon giving way to the green fields and rolling hills of Buckinghamshire. As she passed through the gap in the Chiltern Hills that marked the boundary with Oxfordshire, she turned off the motorway. After a few miles she turned again, taking a narrow, single-track road signposted Kirkwood Farm. The road ended at a large, imposing-looking decorative iron gate. After a brief pause, the gate slid open and Dorothy drove down the long, sweeping driveway that led to the farm itself, admiring the sleek, thoroughbred stallions that stamped and snorted in the damp morning air in the fields at either side.

Kirkwood Farm was primarily a horse stud, although in recent years it had also become a popular wedding venue, the impressive tithe barn in the grounds proving ideal for both ceremonies and receptions. The owners had also started renting out plots of land for business units and shipping container storage, and Dorothy had now had a contract with them for several years.

The driveway forked as it neared the farmhouse, and Dorothy took the branch that led into the business area, tyres crunching on the gravel as she made her way past the 40 or so shipping containers that were lined up in neat rows on either side of the yard. Her own containers were at the far end of the site, their red-and-white paintwork a little cleaner than the others.

She pulled up outside them and turned off the ignition, nodding in satisfaction as the Hypergreen's batteries immediately started to charge, drawing power from the electromagnetic induction pad hidden beneath the gravel surface.

Getting out of the car, she crossed to the end container, tapping her password into the digital padlock that secured the doors. With a quick glance around the farmyard to check that she was alone, Dorothy heaved open the heavy steel door and slipped inside.

'Lights.'

At her voice command a dozen or more wall-mounted lights sprang into life, illuminating a huge open space. Unlike the other containers stored at the farm, these had been specially designed, the internal walls capable of swinging up so that instead of a series of individual storage spaces, a large flexible workspace could be created, in virtually any configuration. From the outside, however, there was no indication that they were anything other than standard shipping containers, and that suited Dorothy just fine.

She had developed them as a means of providing temporary buildings in disaster situations – hospitals, barracks, emergency shelters – but they had also proved to be ideal in providing her a base away from London, far away from prying eyes – her own personal 'batcave'.

Securing the door behind her, she made a quick inspection of the workshop, checking that it was still secure and that everything was where she had left it. Although she had no reason to believe that anyone suspected that what was being stored on the farm was anything more than emergency aid supplies, assets of A Charitable Earth, Dorothy was paranoid about what might happen if Torchwood ever caught wind of her storage facility, and she certainly didn't want anything in here falling into the wrong hands.

The walls of the workshop were lined with cupboards and racking, some with familiar tools and machinery, others with strange, unearthly shapes; alien technology that Dorothy had acquired over the years.

At the far end of the workspace, sealed off behind an airtight plexiglass screen, was a sophisticated laboratory. The aptitude for chemistry that Dorothy had shown as a teenager hadn't left her and, whilst she still spent more time than she considered healthy refining the formula for her old Nitro-9 explosive, she was also having considerable success in developing a compound capable of breaking down plastic with minimal waste. At the moment she was referring to it as 'anti-plastic', but she'd have to come up with a better name if she was going to try and patent it.

Along the opposite wall were her workbenches, each of them witness to another project started and left half-finished as some new natural disaster descended and took over her life. She sighed as she caught sight of a disassembled motorcycle, its engine in pieces next to one of the benches. She'd embarked on the restoration of the Triumph Bonneville T120 last year, with the intention of having it finished by the summer. That seemed like a vain hope now ...

Running a hand over the bike's fuel tank, she turned and crossed to the centre of the workshop, and to the device that was her reason for coming here. Despite its alien design, the machine that dominated the room was clearly a single-person aircraft of some kind, the dull grey metal of its fuselage shimmering and moving like oil on water. If she could get it working again this was going to revolutionise her ability to travel – not just on Earth but off it as well. The problem was it was knackered, and despite her best efforts, she'd not managed to make much headway in repairing it.

The other problem was she had no idea which race was responsible for its manufacture. That at least might have given her some starting point for her repairs. It had been pure fluke that she'd been able to get her hands on it before the authorities – a case of being in exactly the right place at exactly the right time.

She'd been on a climbing holiday in the Lake District – a rare break between crises – when she'd gotten word from Sanaul that UNIT were tracking a UFO coming in fast over the Scottish coast and heading her way. Despite objection from UNIT headquarters in Geneva, two Typhoons had been scrambled from the Quick Reaction Alert station at RAF Lossiemouth with orders to intercept and destroy. In order to minimise any collateral damage, the pilots had been ordered to shoot down the intruder over Cumbria.

Snatching her night-vision binoculars from her rucksack, she'd scrambled out of her tent, and begun scanning the clear night sky. To her surprise she had spotted the UFO almost immediately, a brilliant pinpoint of light moving low and fast over the peaks of Wasdale Head, the Typhoons in close pursuit. With a thrill, Dorothy had realised that she had a ringside seat for the imminent engagement.

The lead fighter was virtually level with her when it unleashed the first of its Advanced Short Range Air-To-Air Missiles, the infrared seeker locking on to the UFO and streaking away into the night with a blaze of flame. Triggered by its proximity fuse the warhead exploded, the detonation sending shockwaves racing across the surface of the lake. Dorothy had shielded her eyes as flaming wreckage cascaded down from the night sky, the bracken on the hillside bursting into flame as each piece made contact. Then she'd caught sight of something else plummeting towards the ground. Using the falling debris as cover, a smaller craft was making a powered descent. Fascinated, Dorothy had watched as it arced away from the main debris field, hugging the side of the scree slope and vanishing beneath the dark waters of the lake. It had been using the fallout from the explosion as camouflage, presumably banking on the fighters' infrared instrumentation being overwhelmed by the fires that now blazed on the fells.

Dorothy had known that UNIT would be searching for every single piece of the downed UFO. That was fine with her. What she wanted was the tech they didn't know about.

She wanted the pod.

It had been nearly three weeks before the last of the military trucks finally departed and the area was opened to the public once more. Sanaul had made a big show of announcing to the press that A Charitable Earth was testing a new generation of inflatable boats and specialised diving equipment for use in remote areas of Malaysia and India that were increasingly being affected by catastrophic flooding due to rising sea levels.

Given the depth of the lake, Sanaul had been sceptical of finding anything. It had come as something of a surprise, therefore, when the experimental underwater search-and-rescue drones located the pod on only the second night of searching. It had come to rest on an underwater ledge, only ten metres or so below the surface. Scans showed that it was empty; the pod must have misfired as the mother ship suffered huge systems damage.

After loading their prize into the back of a Range Rover, Dorothy had headed back south to her workshop at Kirkwood Farm, leaving Sanaul to wrap up the testing that had formed their cover and dispel any suspicions that their arrival might have caused. Her hope had been that the pod would be in a fit state to fly – her wealth allowed her to afford the best forms of transport that Earth had to offer, but sometimes she just wished that she had access to something more.

As far as she had been able to tell, the entire ship was powered by a small, spherical device, humming softly to itself. Having located what she assumed to be the links to the engine controls, she was about to start dismantling it when a low, burbling chirrup from deep inside the workings of the ship made her stop.

The links weren't just mechanical, they were *alive*. Connecting the power unit to the controls of the ship was some kind of semi-biological entity, a symbiotic engineer.

'A squidgy gadget,' Dorothy murmured, looking at it now. '*Squidget*.' She reached out a tentative hand to the creature, just as she had when she'd first discovered it. The thin, pulsing tentacles shimmered at her touch.

Of course, she was no closer to finding out how it worked than she had been on day one. The power source seemed inexhaustible, and adaptable to virtually any scenario – she'd been using it to power all the lights and equipment here at the batcave for years, and as far as she could tell the thing was barely ticking over.

The one thing that she had discovered was that the Squidget responded to voice control and that had made what she was about to do at the Space Defence Centre an awful lot simpler.

'Power down and disconnect,' she said sharply. There was a chirp from the Squidget and the hum from the power source stopped. With the briefest of flickers from the lights, the backup generators took over. Dorothy had several projects in the laboratory that required constant refrigeration, so whilst the alien power supply took care of most of her needs without drawing to attention to what she was doing here, there were occasions when she needed more conventional generators.

In a blur of motion the Squidget withdrew its tentacles, clinging to the side of the sphere like some kind of strange coral growth. Dorothy lifted the propulsion unit from its housing and transferred it to an aluminium flight case, the Squidget giving an unhappy burble as she closed the lid.

With a last look around the workshop, Dorothy hoisted the flight case into her arms and crossed back to the door.

'Lights off.'

Securing the door of the darkened workshop, she unlocked the car, opened the boot and placed the flight case containing the propulsion unit and the Squidget next to the overnight bag already nestled there. She went nowhere without being prepared these days. Slipping back into the driver's seat, she made her way back down the snaking drive and before too long she was back on the motorway heading west.

CHAPTER FIVE

It was approaching noon when she finally pulled into Devesham, the village as picturesque as she remembered it, despite the drab winter weather. As she drove through the village square with its battered stone cross and old-fashioned phone box, she glanced over at the Fleur de Lys pub with a wistful smile. She'd stayed there with Will during her first visit to the Space Defence Centre just after they'd started dating. It had been a good couple of nights.

She turned into the private road that led to the Defence Centre, the low, concrete buildings and towering radio telescope dish in stark contrast to the chocolate-box charm of the village itself. Dorothy smiled to herself. Only the British could decide to locate a state-of-the-art space facility within walking distance of a sleepy, rural hamlet.

As she approached the main gate, a security guard emerged from his hut, eyeing the Hypergreen with undisguised admiration. As soon as he had confirmed that Dorothy was expected, he directed her to a car park space that had been reserved for her outside the main building. As she pulled into the space, the twin glass doors to reception slid open and Will emerged, making his way towards her with a huge grin on his face.

He was every inch the *Boy's Own* comic book cliché of what an astronaut should look like – tall, blue-eyed, with a floppy fringe of dark hair and a toned physique that would make a professional tennis player envious. As Dorothy stepped out of the car, he swept her up in an enormous bear hug, and she got a whiff of expensive cologne. She really *had* enjoyed dating him.

'It's good to see you, Dorothy.'

She kissed him on the cheek. 'You too, Will.'

'You made good time.' He glanced at the Hypergreen. 'I guess your new wheels helped with that.'

Dorothy smiled. 'Play your cards right and I'll take you for a ride.'

Will raised an eyebrow at that. 'You're the one who wants the ride, if I recall …' He frowned, looking at the tiny boot on the sports car. 'And I thought that you were meant to be bringing something with you?'

'Do I ever disappoint?' Dorothy opened the boot and carefully lifted out the box containing the propulsion unit and the Squidget.

Will jerked back in alarm as the thing in the box gave a loud chirrup.

'What the hell …?'

'Before you ask, it's easier if I just show you.' Dorothy grinned. 'Now where's this spaceship of yours?'

Obviously fighting back his curiosity Will ushered her in through the sliding glass doors and led her through the building to the launch facility at the rear of the complex. As they stepped through the air-tight door into the hangar, Dorothy looked up at the gleaming shape of the SDC probe and gave a whistle of admiration.

'Behold, the *Virgil*.'

Dorothy had followed the design and construction of the probe with interest. She knew that *Virgil* was the most sophisticated and successful British spacecraft ever built. Built as a successor to the ill-fated XK-5 space freighter, it was a two-stage, medium-lift, reusable launch vehicle, the lift stage separating after lift-off, returning to Earth and landing vertically, whilst the three-man probe itself was capable of re-entering the atmosphere and landing like a conventional aircraft.

As they made her way across the hangar towards the launch gantry, a woman in a white lab coat emerged from the shadows at the base of the spacecraft. Dorothy turned to Will angrily.

'I thought I said that no one else was to be involved or the deal was off!'

Will stopped and frowned, taken aback by the tone in her voice. 'And if you think I'm capable of launching a state-of-the-art space vehicle into orbit single-handed then you're sadly deluded.'

Dorothy looked away, took a deep breath. 'I'm sorry.'

'The world doesn't work the way you seem to want it to. You might think that you can go it alone, that you don't need anyone else, but sometimes you do. Sometimes you just have to trust people.'

Trust! Dorothy just stared at him, aware that any further words at this point might not come out the way she intended. He knew more about her life than most people but even he didn't know all of it.

To her relief, he said nothing further. He just gave her a sad smile and then shifted his attention to the woman approaching them

'Dorothy, this is Sam O'Connor. She'll be acting as Mission Controller on this little jaunt. Sam, this is Dorothy McShane.'

Sam shook her hand firmly, her smile warm and genuine. 'Nice to meet you. Will's talked about you a lot.'

'Once,' Will countered with a grin.

'Or twice.' Sam smiled back at Will. 'He doesn't seem to have a bad word to say about you.'

With an unexpected pang of sorrow, Dorothy realised that the two of them were far more than just co-workers. 'Yeah, well, he's easily fooled,' she said, forcing herself to sound far more flippant than she was actually feeling. Fortunately, Sam was far more intrigued by the box that she was carrying.

'So this is it?' Sam raised an eyebrow. 'This is what's going to get us to the Moon before the Chinese?'

Dorothy nodded. 'Oh yes.'

Sam shot a quick glance at Will, then shrugged. 'You'd better follow me then.'

She led them across the hangar to a service lift that ran up the side of the support gantry. The three of them squeezed inside and they were whisked 80 feet into the air to where the probe sat on top of the first-stage booster.

A tool station sat on the metal gantry next to the probe, and Sam had already removed several plates from the outer hull of the probe, revealing the tangle of fuel pipes and coolant systems of the second-stage engine.

'I've assumed that we intend to launch conventionally and only engage your device once *Virgil* is in orbit,' said Sam. 'I'm guessing there's no point in advertising to the rest of the world that this is anything other than a standard Moon-shot.'

'Even so,' said Will, 'the rest of the world is going to realise pretty quickly that something's up if this thing goes as fast as you say it does.'

Dorothy said nothing. The truth was that it wasn't just the rest of the world that she'd wanted to keep this hidden from; it had been UNIT, Torchwood, the Countermeasures Group and a dozen other government agencies that would be breathing down her neck if they knew what she had ...

'OK,' she murmured. 'Let's do this.' She placed the box down on the gantry next to the open panel and unsnapped the clasps.

'Oh, my God.' Will took an involuntary step back as the lid opened and he caught sight of what was inside.

'I don't believe it.' Sam's eyes widened and she leaned forward to get a closer look as Dorothy gingerly lifted out the alien drive system and its symbiotic engineer. 'How on earth do you intend connecting that … thing with *Virgil*?'

'Earth has nothing to do with it,' said Dorothy, reaching inside the open hatch and placing the alien machine amongst the gleaming metal thrusters.

She stepped back, snatching a cloth from the tool station and wiping the grease from her fingers.

'Interface,' she barked.

The Squidget exploded into life, thin hair-like feelers erupting from every pore on its body, its skin virtually glowing with energy. Chirruping excitedly to itself, it began to extrude itself into every nook and cranny of *Virgil*'s engine compartment, the tendrils thickening and hardening as they went, engulfing the metal and plastic of the probe with slick alien flesh.

'Dorothy …' The alarm in Will's voice was clear.

'Sometimes you just have to trust people.' She looked at him and found she had to force the smile. 'Remember?'

'It's unbelievable.' Sam was staring in amazement at the schematic readout on the laptop sitting on top of the workstation. 'It's taken that thing less than a minute to bypass the entire ignition subroutine and hardwire itself into the propulsion control systems.' She looked at Dorothy in astonishment. 'How is it doing it? Its size seems to increasing exponentially. Where is it getting the additional mass?'

'Dunno.' Dorothy gave her an apologetic shrug. 'Bigger on the inside? Come on, we'd better get up to the control cabin. The Squidget is pretty intuitive when it comes to our technology, but it does occasionally get some of the fine details wrong.'

Will shot her a look. 'The fine details?'

'Yeah. When I first got it, I hooked it up to one of my motorbike engines. Worked pretty well, but it got confused as to which control was the brake and which was the throttle. Made for an interesting test drive.'

'Great.' Will sighed. 'I'm the one who has to drive this thing, remember?'

'All the interface connections look pretty good to me,' said Sam looking up from her laptop. 'But we should do a full diagnostic check of the controls before we go any further.'

'Agreed,' said Will firmly.

The three of them re-entered the lift and ascended the final 20 feet to the probe's nose-cone, ducking in through the airlock and squeezing into the cabin. The slick, vine-like tendrils from the Squidget were visible everywhere, integrating themselves with *Virgil*'s control systems.

Will swung himself into the centre of the three padded seats, Sam sliding into the seat next to him and they began to run through the diagnostic checks. Knowing better than to try and assist on a process with which she had no experience, Dorothy stood to one side, watching as the two of them went through what was obviously a well-rehearsed routine. They worked well together, calmly anticipating what the other was about to do, responding to instructions quickly and without fuss. They made a good team. She supposed that they were an equally well-matched couple.

As if aware that she was thinking about him, Will suddenly turned and looked straight at her. Dorothy felt her cheeks flush, but Will was too hyped-up to notice, his eyes wide with excitement.

'It's incredible, Dot, this thing of yours has managed to hook itself in to every one of our systems. It even seems to be capable of taking direct instruction from the flight computer.'

'So it's got the brakes and throttle the right way round this time?'

Sam nodded. 'You said that the Squidget was intuitive; well I'd go further than that. It seems to understand the fundamental basics of this vehicle so well that I'd go so far as to suggest that it has some mild empathic or telepathic ability.'

'Intuition,' Dorothy said.

'Well, I'm basing that on observations of—'

'I was talking about the Squidget. Might just be highly intuitive.' Dorothy clapped her hands together in anticipation. 'Anyway. If everyone's happy that things are in working order, let's get going.'

'Now, hold on just one minute,' said Sam firmly. 'You're a 50-year-old woman who has never been into space before.'

Dorothy gave Will a cool glance. 'So when he talked about me, it was about my age?'

'I just mean, you're not going anywhere until you've had a full medical assessment.'

Dorothy opened her mouth to argue, but Sam interrupted her before she could speak, her expression making it perfectly clear that this wasn't open for negotiation. 'So as long as I'm Mission Controller then you'll do things the way I want them done. That means a full medical before I declare you as fit to fly, understood?'

'Fine.' Dorothy nodded. 'Understood.'

From across the cabin, Will was grinning like a Cheshire Cat.

Dorothy just wanted to smack him.

Over the next hour, Dorothy went through the most thorough medical examination she could ever remember. Heart rate and blood pressure were checked and rechecked, blood samples were drawn and sent for instant analysis, she was prodded and probed with all manner of sinister-looking instruments; brain function, liver function, kidney function … While those results were being collated, she'd undergone a hearing test, an eye test, a lung-capacity test.

Now she was on a treadmill, sensors taped all over her forehead and chest, an ECG beeping away alongside her, her breathing being monitored and regulated via an oxygen mask over her nose and mouth.

She was aching, irritated and exhausted.

To make matters worse, Will had been at one side of her briefing her in the details of take-off procedures, landing procedures, emergency evacuation procedures, whilst Sam had been on the other questioning her about her diet, how much exercise she took, how much sleep she was getting…

To cap it all, the television screen on the wall had been running a news story about how the Chinese were almost ready to launch their own intercept craft – the *Long March 5B*.

Finally her patience came to an end and she stopped running, bringing the treadmill to a halt.

'What's wrong?' asked Will, concerned. 'Are you feeling OK?'

'Yes,' snapped Dorothy, tearing off the oxygen mask. 'I'm fine. I was fine before, and I'm fine now, and my ability to survive a crash landing on the Moon is not going to be affected by whether I'm currently getting my five-a-day. In the meantime the Chinese appear to be getting ready to start fuelling their probe so shall we just make a decision? Am I fit to fly or not?'

She stood there, breathing heavily, sweat soaking her shirt as Sam and Will stared at each other in silence. Then Sam nodded.

'You're fitter than women half your age. There's nothing that indicates you will have any problem with the stresses of either lift off or re-entry. I'm going to instruct the flight team to start pre-launch checks. We should be good to go in about two hours.'

Dorothy gave a grateful sigh. 'Then I'm going to go and have a shower.' She snatched up a towel from the bench where Will was sitting. 'You'd better have a spacesuit in my size for me to pick out when I get back.'

Chapter Six

Chantelle sat in front of the mirror in her bedroom, putting on her make-up and trying to summon up some enthusiasm for the evening out with the girls that she'd agreed to last weekend.

If she was honest, she could do without it. She'd been out three nights this week already and, despite the irritation that she'd felt towards Dorothy when she'd pointed out that 37 might be too old for this kind of lifestyle, there was some truth in it.

She put down her lipstick and stared at her reflection. She didn't look her age, did she? Was she still kidding herself that she was the same happy-go-lucky kid that she'd been in her 20s? Perhaps it was time to stop all this fashion nonsense. She'd been irritable at work all day, so much so that the creative director had actually pulled the plug on the photo shoot early, telling everyone that they'd start again from scratch on Monday.

She sighed. Perhaps it was time to get a proper job like her gran wanted her to. Maybe she should take Dorothy up on that offer of a job at A Charitable Earth after all ...

No sooner had the idea popped into her head than she was angry about it. Dorothy McShane wasn't the solution to her problems, she was the cause of them. Chantelle had known Dorothy – Ace – for as long as she could remember and, when she'd been little, had always considered her something of an older sister. Then, suddenly and without warning, Ace had vanished from her life, and no one had been able to explain to Chantelle where she had gone or why.

That was probably something that she could have come to terms with, except that, a few years later, Ace had suddenly appeared again, and bad things had come with her – things that looked like cats, but were in fact something far more alien. Chantelle had been too young to understand everything that had gone on that summer, but old enough to know that Ace had bailed on her again.

Then she'd heard talk that Dorothy McShane had come into money – an inheritance, or a big investment come good, or a lottery somewhere – whatever, she'd not spent a penny of it on her old mates, just invested it in that 'ACE' charity of hers.

It was so many years later that Chantelle finally found out for herself. She'd walked into her usual pub in Perivale one Friday night and Dorothy had just been sitting there at the bar, looking like she belonged there; like she had never left. There had been a teary, wine-fuelled reunion and the two of them had talked into the early hours of the morning, the conversation continuing at Chantelle's flat long after the pub had thrown them out.

And so, Dorothy had re-entered her life, and had been a constant, if unpredictable presence ever since. This morning was typical – she'd turn up out of the blue, ask about something weird, then vanish again, with no explanation of what was going on. What was even more irritating was that she was right about there being something odd going on in the area. How did she *know*? Just for once Chantelle would like to find something going on that Dorothy McShane *didn't* know about. Well perhaps she could surprise her. If there *was* something going on in Perivale then perhaps the girls would have some gossip that could give her a lead to something.

Feeling her gloom lifting, Chantelle finished doing her make-up, pulled on her huge, fleece-lined puffer jacket, snatched up her handbag and keys and made her way out of the front door. The grey clouds of the day had lifted, and the night sky was clear and full of stars. There would be ice on her car windscreen in the morning. Thank God it was the weekend and she didn't have to be at the studio at 6am. She stood on the walkway outside her flat for a moment, letting the cold January air clear her head. She was about to make her way down the concrete stairs that led to street level when a noise made her start.

She peered into the darkness. Was that a figure moving in the alleyway that ran along the rear of the flats? A muffled curse and the flash of light from a torch confirmed it. There was someone there! It must be the creep that Gina and her boyfriend had disturbed the other night.

Determined to have some useful information of her own that she could impress Dorothy with Chantelle pulled her phone from her bag, turned on the camera and gingerly made her way down the steps. As she crept across the yard to the gate that led into the alleyway, wet newspaper and discarded sweet wrappers catching in her toes at every step, she immediately regretted her decision to wear shoes that favoured style over practicality.

Listening carefully for any sound of the intruder she eased open the gate and peered into the alleyway beyond. At the far end she could see the figure of a man rummaging around the bin bags and recycling bins. If she could just get close enough to get a clear photo of him …

Keeping to the shadows she started to make her way along the alleyway, finger poised over the button on her phone. As she drew nearer it suddenly struck her that confronting the man in such a narrow location with no real means of escape other than the way she had come probably wasn't the wisest of decisions.

Fortunately the man was far too engrossed in what he was doing to notice her approach.

She reached the end of the alley and ducked down behind one of the huge plastic bins that the man had pushed to one side. The entire recycling area was bathed in the sickly yellow glow from half a dozen sodium lamps at the perimeter. Unfortunately the light just served to cast the man's face in shadow, and if her photo was going to be of any use then she needed a clear shot of him.

She was about to manoeuvre her way around to the far side of the recycling bin to try and find a better angle for her photograph when there was the pattering of claws and something warm and furry scampered over her exposed toes.

She jerked backwards, clasping her hand over her mouth to stifle the scream that would give her away, but her elbow caught the edge of the bin and it rolled forwards on clattering castors.

At once the man's torch swung in her direction and there was a panicked cry of alarm. 'Who's there? Who is that?'

With a groan, Chantelle realised that she recognised the voice from the television. It was that podcast guy that Dorothy had been going on about this morning. The guy from the documentary. What was his name? Kim Fortune or something …

She stepped out from behind the bin, shielding her eyes from the dazzling torch beam with her arm. 'Stop shining that thing in my face!'

'Who are you?' Kim Fortune lowered the torch and came bustling forward, his initial surprise rapidly turning to irritation. 'What are you doing here?'

'What am *I* doing here?' growled Chantelle. 'I live here, mate, you're the one who needs to explain what they're up to.'

Kim puffed himself up importantly. 'I'm conducting vital research.'

'Research? Poking around in the recycling bins. What do you expect to find? Little green men getting rid of their kitchen waste?'

Kim glared at her. 'There have been reports—'

'Yeah, I know there have been reports,' Chantelle interrupted. 'Most of them about some idiot with a torch poking around where he shouldn't be, disturbing people's sleep!'

Kim looked so crestfallen that Chantelle immediately softened her tone.

'Look, you're freaking people out, OK? You don't want anyone to start thinking that you are involved with the disappearances of those girls, do you? Besides, I don't think Dorothy is going to be too happy with you trampling all over her patch.'

'Dorothy?' Kim's ears pricked up and Chantelle immediately regretted her words. 'Dorothy McShane has been here?' An exultant look came into his eyes. 'Well, now I *know* that there's something strange going on!'

'She used to live here,' Chantelle began quickly – but broke off at a deafening 'CRACK' from the far side of the recycling area.

'Oh my God,' gasped Chantelle, spinning around in alarm. 'What was that?'

'That,' said Kim, 'was what I was waiting for!' He set off across the yard towards the source of the noise.

'No, wait …' Chantelle tried to catch his arm but Kim brushed her off. Cursing her shoes again, she set off after him, her high heels threatening to trip her at every step. What the hell was she doing? She should be in the club by now, drinking two-for-one margaritas with Becky and Gina, not picking her way through garbage in pursuit of some UFO-obsessed madman.

When she caught up with Kim, he was crouched behind a clothes-recycling bin, peering into the dark alleyway beyond. As she approached, he waved his arms in alarm. 'Be quiet, or they'll hear us!'

Biting her lip to stop herself telling him exactly what she thought of him right now, Chantelle ducked down next to him. '*Who* will hear us?'

Kim pointed towards the shadows at the far end of the alley-way. Chantelle peered into the gloom. To her surprise there *were* two figures there, lurking next to the fence that ran along the rear of a line of council properties. Both of the figures were small and wearing what appeared to be filthy hooded tops.

'You see them?' hissed Kim.

'I see a couple of kids.'

'Not kids.' Kim shook his head vigorously. 'It's them. I know it. They must be planning another abduction.'

Chantelle had had enough now. 'Oh for God's sake. They're bored kids! They're either out here smoking ciggies they've stolen from their parents or they're spray painting their stupid tags on the fence.'

She stood up, snatching the torch from him and pointing it down the alley. 'Oi! You two! Haven't you got better things to be doing on a Friday night, because I know that I ...'

As the two figures were lit up by the torch beam they turned in Chantelle's direction, and her voice dried in her throat as she caught a glimpse of the faces beneath the hoods. Sharp features pushing from matted hair. Large, dark eyes ...

From behind her she heard a sharp intake of breath from Kim. 'Oh, God. It's them! It's really them.'

Abruptly the two diminutive figures turned and fled.

'No. Wait!'

Grabbing the torch from Chantelle's hand, Kim raced off in pursuit. Chantelle didn't move, shocked by what she had seen; what-ever had been staring back at her, it hadn't looked entirely human.

From the darkness ahead of her there was a sudden anguished cry. Jolted from her stupor, Chantelle suddenly remembered that the alleyway down which Kim and the two strange creatures had vanished was blocked at the far end. The things had fled when discovered, but if they were cornered ...

Snatching up a length of wood from the floor, she ran after Kim fast as her heels would allow. As she reached the end, she could see him running from one side of the alleyway to the other, the torch beam waving frantically. Of the things he had been chasing there was no sign.

'Where are they?' asked Chantelle brandishing her makeshift club. 'Where did they go?'

'I don't know!' cried Kim peering desperately over the fences into gardens and backyards. 'I was right behind them. I was so close …'

Chantelle turned in a slow circle, searching for anywhere that the two creatures might be hiding, but the alleyway was deserted.

She let the length of timber drop to the floor, making Kim jump at the sound.

'Well don't just stand there!' he snapped. 'There must be a loose section of fence. Help me find it!'

'Not a chance.' Chantelle shook her head. 'I'm cold, my feet are wet and I've just seen something that's going to give me night-mares for weeks. I'm going down the club and I'm going to get drunk.'

Ignoring his pleas, she turned and started to make her way back along the alleyway towards her flat and the bustle of Perivale high street.

As she did so she noticed with disgust that, watching her from the undergrowth, there were dozens and dozens of rats.

CHAPTER SEVEN

The British space exploration vehicle *Virgil* sat in its launch cradle, incongruous against the backdrop of the English countryside, the slow, mechanical countdown that boomed from the Tannoy system a sharp contrast to the distant, barking cries of foxes and the mournful hooting of owls as they hunted mice and shrews in the fields

Inside the cockpit, Dorothy watched as Will performed the launch status check, responding methodically to the tasks Sam gave him over the radio.

'*Start automatic ground launch sequencer.*'

'Check.'

'*Retract orbiter access arm.*'

'Retracted.'

'*Start auxiliary power units.*'

Will reached out and closed a set of switches, and immediately a low hum filled the cabin.

'*Crew members close and lock their visors.*'

Will pulled down the clear visor on his helmet, glancing over at Dorothy to see that she was doing the same. Dorothy had to admit that she'd been impressed with the spacesuit and helmet that she'd been given. She'd been expecting something bulky, uncomfortable and difficult to move in, but the full suit only weighed about 20 pounds, considerably lighter than the launch-and-entry suits worn by space shuttle astronauts. The suit's patented material let water vapour escape but kept air inside, cooling the suit without compromising safety. The helmet had been incorporated into the suit, rather than being detachable, and the gloves were touch-sensitive. In fact, Dorothy was so impressed that, if she ever managed to get her space pod operational, she'd have to see she if could convince Will to part with one of these ...

'*Transfer from ground to internal power.*'

Sam's voice was loud in her ear now.

'*Ground launch sequencer is go for auto sequence start.*'

The countdown was now at less than 15 seconds.

'*Activate launch pad sound suppression system.*'

Dorothy felt a surge of anticipation. She was about to go back into space after years of being Earthbound.

'*Activate main engine hydrogen burn-off system.*'

Will turned and smiled at her. 'As dates go, this one should be memorable.'

Before Dorothy could come up with a pithy reply, the cabin was swamped with a deafening roar. She could barely hear Sam's voice over the earpiece.

'*Main engine start. Lift-off in five seconds, four, three, two, one ...*'

Dorothy was thrust back into her seat as *Virgil* blasted off from the pad. She felt as if a giant hand was pressing down on her. The acceleration was incredible. She wanted to scream with delight but the G-forces were so intense that it was all that she could do to draw breath.

After what seemed like an age the crushing pressure started to ease, and Dorothy was able to move in her seat once more. Will shot her a quick look.

'You OK?'

She nodded. Satisfied that she'd survived lift-off intact, Will leaned forward, preparing to detach the probe from the lifting stage.

'Mission Control, all lights are green on my board, trajectory looks good.'

'*Roger that, Virgil, main engine throttling back, stand by for booster-stage separation in 20 seconds.*'

As another countdown started to cycle its way towards zero, Dorothy turned her head and stared out of the cockpit window. The curve of the Earth was clearly visible below them now and the stars were more brilliant than they ever looked from the surface. God, she had missed this ... She lifted an arm, feeling the almost-forgotten sensation of weightlessness.

The countdown in her earpiece reached zero and there was a shudder as the first-stage booster detached from them, beginning its return journey to Earth where it would make a powered landing at Devesham airfield ready to be reused on the next mission.

'*First-stage detachment complete,*' confirmed Sam. '*Orbital insertion accomplished. She's all yours, Will.*'

Will slid his chair forward and adjusted the flight controls. 'Roger that, Control. Intercept course to UFO laid in. Stand by.' He turned to Dorothy. 'Right. This is it. Do I need to do anything to activate this Squidget of yours? Any special command phrases, stuff like that?'

Dorothy shook her head. 'No, just operate the ship as usual, the Squidget will do the rest.'

'OK,' he said dubiously. 'If you say so.'

As he reached for the controls, Dorothy laid her hand on top of his. 'Will, just take it easy on the throttle, OK?'

Will nodded, then took a deep breath.

'Mission Control, this is *Virgil*. Initiating prototype propulsion system on my mark. Five, four, three, two, one. Ignition.'

Time seemed to stop.

There were none of the vibration or acceleration effects that had accompanied the take-off, no G-force or suffocating pressure; the probe just transitioned from being stationary to suddenly moving very fast.

Very, very fast.

The stars became a blur – streaks of brilliant white against the blackness. On the rear-view monitor Dorothy could see the Earth receding at an astonishing rate. Will's mouth dropped open, the astronaut scarcely able to believe how fast they were travelling.

'Oh, my God ...' His voice was barely a whisper.

Dorothy could only imagine how he was feeling. Even she was staggered by the power that the propulsion system was generating, and she at least had already experienced something of what it was capable of. All around them the thin tendrils from the Squidget were glowing with a deep indigo light, brilliant pinpricks of sparking energy pulsing along each strand.

Through the cockpit window Dorothy could see the pitted grey shape of the Moon getting larger by the second.

'Will ... Will! You might want to think about slowing us down a bit.'

'What?' Will looked up from the controls, his eyes widening at the sight of the cratered surface looming in front of them. 'Holy ...!'

He eased back on the throttle and, miraculously the ship was suddenly stationary again. In her earpiece Dorothy could hear the frantic voice of Sam back on Earth.

'Virgil! Virgil! This is Mission Control. Respond, please. Will, we've lost you from our scopes. Will! Will, come in, please!'

Dorothy glanced across at Will. He was ignoring the radio and was obviously in a state of shock. 'Sam, this is Dorothy.'

'Dorothy, thank God.' The relief in Sam's voice was palpable. 'Are you two OK?'

'We're fine. Will's just going to need a moment to process a few things, that's all.'

'*Where are you? You simply vanished from our detectors!*'

'Your detectors might be looking in the wrong place. We're in Moon orbit.'

'*That's impossible ...*' There was a long pause then a gasp. '*I don't believe it! You've just travelled almost 400,000 kilometres in less than a minute.*'

Dorothy grinned. 'I told you I'd get you here before the Chinese.'

There was another long pause and then, to her credit, Sam returned to the matter in hand.

'*Can you see the UFO?*'

Will too had finally recovered from the culture shock of the journey. 'Sam, it's Will, I'm getting a mass reading 300 metres off our starboard side. I'm going to roll us over, see if we can get a view through the cockpit window.'

'*Roger that. Attitude thrusters only please, Will. Now we know what that Squidget is capable of I don't want you two ending up in orbit around Saturn.*'

Will grinned and started to make the preparations to turn the ship. There was a brief burst of power from the thrusters and they started to roll. Dorothy craned her neck, eager to catch a glimpse of the alien vessel out of the starboard window.

Slowly the dark, unsettling, thigh-bone shape of the alien spacecraft slid into view. As when she had first seen it on the television in Chantelle's flat, Dorothy felt a ripple of unease wash over her. There was something about the ship that felt horribly familiar, like some half-forgotten nightmare ...

'Are you getting this, Control?'

Will had activated *Virgil*'s cameras and every screen was now filled with close up images of the strange, silent behemoth.

'*We're getting it, Will. Can you put some light on it?*'

Will pressed a control and searchlights suddenly lit up the alien ship's hull. The surface was unlike any material that Dorothy had ever seen. It was less like metal and plastic and more like flesh; dark, twisted rolls of slick, oily flesh. It made her stomach churn.

'*We're getting nothing from your sensor readings that make any sense, Will. Is there any sign of a hatch or entranceway?*'

'Nothing that we can see. Do you want me to get closer?'

'*Affirmative, Virgil. Confirm that we'd like a slow fly past. But no heroics.*'

Engaging the manoeuvring thrusters once again, Will started to edge Virgil towards to the alien vessel. As they got closer, Dorothy suddenly felt a cold sweat prickle on her skin and she had to supress a surge of panic. She felt like she was going to be sick.

'*Dorothy, are you OK?*' There was concern in Sam's voice again. '*Your vital signs just spiked.*'

'I'm fine.'

'*That's not what my instruments are saying.*'

'I said I'm fine,' she snapped.

There was a sudden cry of excitement from Will. 'I think I've found something!'

Grateful for the distraction from the nausea she was feeling, Dorothy looked to where Will was pointing. There was a depression, a dark shadow on the side of the hull, the strange skin-like surface puckering and stretching around the edge. As they glided closer, it became obvious that it was an entranceway of some kind.

'Is that big enough to get the ship inside?' asked Dorothy.

Will studied the instruments for a moment then shook his head. 'Tolerances are too close. If we get stuck then we might never get back out again.'

'Then I guess we're going in on foot.'

'*Now hang on a minute,*' said Sam firmly. '*I passed you as fit to fly, not to go on an improvised EVA.*'

'And if we're not going to make a proper investigation of this thing then what the hell are we doing out here?' said Dorothy angrily.

'I have to agree, Control,' said Will. 'There's only so much we can do out here, and you can be damn sure that when the Russians and the Chinese arrive they're not just going to sit and look at it.'

Dorothy nodded at him, grateful for his support.

'OK ...' Even over the radio, it was clear that Sam was far from comfortable with the decision but was aware that there was no other option. *'But I want the two of you in constant radio contact, and if there is so much as a hint of trouble, you will get the hell out of there, understood?'*

'Understood,' agreed Will. 'No heroics.'

'Then you'd better get going. I'm sending data to the autopilot that will match Virgil's orbit with the UFO, but if that ship starts to change trajectory then you'll need to get back on board pronto.'

'Roger that control.' Will turned to Dorothy with a grim smile. 'So, fancy a stroll outside?'

CHAPTER EIGHT

Dorothy had forgotten just how disorientating a spacewalk could be; the lack of a clear sensation of up or down, the inability to judge scale or distance, the total absence of anything solid to cling on to ... Will had insisted on tethering them together before they had stepped out of *Virgil*'s airlock and, although she had protested that it was an unnecessary precaution at the time, she was now grateful that he had refused to take no for an answer.

She choked back bile as another wave of nausea washed over her, unsure if it was still the strange effect that the ship was having on her or the mere fact that she was floating, weightless, with nothing but infinity below her.

Determined that she was simply *not* going to disgrace herself by throwing up in her expensive spacesuit, she focused on the strange, puckered entranceway to the ship towards which they were heading. Will controlled their approach with bursts from a hand-held thruster unit.

Up close, the alien ship was even more unsettling than it had been when viewed through the cockpit window. The flesh-like hull seemed to possess a strange life of its own, ripples occasionally passing along its length in slow waves, as if the entire ship was reacting somehow to some unseen stimulus.

As they neared the entranceway, Will brought them to a halt and the two of them hung in the vacuum, contemplating the dark passageway ahead of them. Whilst there appeared to be no discernible hatchway or airlock of any kind, Dorothy could see some sort of membrane separating them from the ship's interior, its surface shimmering and iridescent, like a soap bubble.

'What do you think?' Will turned his head to look at her. 'Force field of some kind?'

'Only one way to find out.'

Before Will could stop her, Dorothy reached out, her gloved hand passing through the oil-on-water surface of the membrane.

At once she could feel a suction drawing her forwards and before she had a chance to contemplate the wisdom of her impulsive decision she was pulled bodily into the interior of the ship.

Immediately she could tell that there was gravity on the other side, her boots sinking slightly into the soft, spongy floor of the passageway. There was a breathable atmosphere too if the instrumentation in her suit was to be believed, although she would be checking those readings before doing anything else rash, like removing her helmet.

She turned to see Will floating on the other side of the membrane. His mouth was moving soundlessly and she realised that radio communication between the two of them was being blocked somehow.

She held out her hand, indicating that he should do the same. Tentatively he reached out towards the membrane. The instant that the fingers of his glove made contact there was a wet, sucking noise, and he was suddenly standing alongside her, the voice in her earpiece indication that radio communication between them had been restored again.

'You don't change, do you?' said Will, clearly annoyed about her impulsive decision to enter the ship. 'Charging into things without thinking. What happened to no heroics? Anything could have happened to you!'

'Yeah, well nothing did, did it? I got us on board the ship, which was the point of our little spacewalk, wasn't it?' She knew Will disapproved of her impetuous nature. He had always been the one who insisted on planning everything meticulously, working out the pros and cons of any situation rather than just making decisions made on gut instinct. It had been one of the reasons they had split up. 'What're you going to do, grass me up to Mission Control?'

Will glared at her. 'Communications with Sam are down. We're on our own.'

'Good. We'll get more done that way.'

Will's smile returned at that. He looked around the interior of the ship in fascination. The walls seemed to be constructed from the same skin-like material as the exterior hull, the twisted glistening surface occasionally broken by thin, semi-transparent buttresses, their glassy surfaces streaked with grime, like dirty fingernails.

'Have you ever seen anything like this before?' asked Will with a shudder.

Dorothy frowned. She'd encountered bio-mechanical technology before – the dragon from Iceworld, Zygons, Axos, to name but three – but this was subtly different to all of them. There was still something frighteningly familiar about it all, though. Something that hovered right on the edge of her conscious memory. 'It feels as though it's something that I *should* recognise …' She shook her head in frustration. 'Every time I think I remember something, it goes again.'

'Then stop *trying* to remember. It'll come to you.'

'OK.' Dorothy gave his arm a squeeze. 'Have you seen the atmosphere readings?'

Will checked the screen in his helmet, cocking an eyebrow in surprise at the readout. 'Breathable ...' He shot her a nervous glance. 'I suppose you want to risk it and open our visors?'

Dorothy shrugged. 'It'll save our oxygen reserve, and at least I won't keep worrying about chucking up in my helmet.'

'Charming ...' He sighed. 'OK. But me first, this time ...'

Without giving her a chance to argue, Will reached up and unclasped the seals on his visor, sliding it back and drawing in a tentative breath. Dorothy watched him carefully, ready to reseal his helmet at the first signs of any adverse reaction.

Will exhaled. 'It's fine. Smells damp ... like a forest after a rain shower.'

Dorothy unsealed her own helmet and sniffed the air, Will was right. It did have that wet soil smell, but other than reminding her of the fields around Kirkwood Farm, the smell triggered no useful memory.

Will disconnected his helmet and swung into its harness on the back of the suit. Dorothy did the same.

'Shall we take a proper look around?'

Will gave a mock bow and gestured down the passageway. 'After you.'

The two of them made their way deeper into the interior of the ship. To Dorothy's concern the passageway didn't widen out or lead to any open areas as she had hoped; if anything it seemed to get narrower, with openings to even smaller shafts appearing either side of them with increasing frequency. After a minute or two of walking they reached a T-junction, the tunnels to the left and right of them seemingly identical to the one they had just traversed. Dorothy was beginning to get the impression that the ship might not have been built to carry passengers at all.

Will was obviously having the same thoughts. 'It feels almost as though we're inside some kind of machine ...' he mused.

Dorothy had to agree. The passages *did* seem to be laid out like cable runs, or circuit lines ...

A sudden chill ran down her spine again and she shivered.

Will looked at her curiously. 'Are you all right?'

'Yeah, there's just something about this place ... déjà vu kind of thing.' She shook her head. 'I'm just getting spooked, that's all. Come on, which way do you think we should go?'

Will looked around, then pointed towards the left hand passageway. 'This way.'

'OK.'

They made their way along the musty-smelling corridor. After a few metres it began to widen, a light shining from the far end.

Will and Dorothy emerged onto a wide platform looking out onto a vast, cavernous chamber that looked as though it stretched the entire length of the alien ship, the far ends vanishing into hazy darkness. Long, wide galleries lined the walls, connected by narrow walkways that crisscrossed the abyss.

Dorothy began to make her way along the gallery, knowing that she was searching for something but unsure as to what that something might be. A sudden difference in the texture of the walls made her stop and suddenly she found herself removing her glove, reaching out to a patch of hull with a distinctly different feel.

As her fingers made contact, there was the same wet sucking sound that she had heard when Will had entered the ship and a section of the wall in front of her suddenly opened up, slick flesh sliding apart like the iris of a camera lens.

As she stepped through intro the space beyond, three startled faces turned to look at her. Two of them – a man and a woman – appeared to be in their late teens, while the third was an older, grey-haired man in a smart leather jacket. But it was what stood beside them that took Dorothy's full attention and almost took her breath away.

It was a battered, blue police box.

The TARDIS. Unashamedly incongruous, and possibly the most beautiful thing Dorothy had ever seen.

The seconds passed and, as the breath returned to her body, she turned to the boy. 'Where is he?'

The boy stared at her in bemusement. 'Where's who?'

'Are you one of the crew here?' the girl asked.

Impatient now, Dorothy took a step towards the TARDIS, bellowing through the doors. 'Oi, Professor! Come on out!'

The older man stepped across the doors, blocking her. 'Believe me, love, there's no one called the Professor in there ...'

'They know me as the Doctor.'

Dorothy turned at the sound of the warm, Northern tones to see a tall, slim, blonde woman in a long, grey coat standing inside the door. Her grin was as bright as the stripes of colour across her top. And it was a smile of recognition.

Dorothy, for reasons she couldn't comprehend, felt a wave of emotion.

'Who are you?' she demanded.

'It's me, Ace! Different body, but the same brilliant brain and much better hair.'

'You're the Professor?' Dorothy could barely bring herself to believe it. 'No way.'

'Come on! Regeneration! You remember ... When a Time Lord's body gets old or damaged ... yadda, yadda.'

Dorothy could feel the rational part of her brain dismissing what she was hearing, and yet there was something so familiar about the woman in front of her. She could feel her eyes beginning to blur with angry tears.

'Prove it. If you're the Professor, prove it.'

'All right! You support Charlton Athletic cos your favourite uncle lived in Plumstead. You love motorbikes – although I never let you ride one. You taught yourself to speak proper cos you wanted to sound like a *Blue Peter* presenter. You can't see a Dalek without feeling a twitch in your baseball-bat hand, you learned to love jazz, and you think being tall is overrated. Oh, and you hate clowns.'

'She sounds pretty awesome,' said the boy, smiling, while the girl and the older man swapped baffled looks.

'She is.' The Doctor's grin grew wider. 'It's good to see you again, Ace.'

Dorothy felt the warm rush of surrender. 'Blimey, Professor. It really *is* you.'

INTERLUDE

1990

'This is wicked, Professor!'

Ace scrambled to the top of a rocky outcrop on the edge on the barren plateau where the TARDIS had landed. Stretched out in the valley below her were the ruins of a city; for as far as the eye could see, huge, curved walls of white-grey stone were crumbling into the desert floor, columns and buttresses that must once have arched in soaring, elegant curves above the city streets reduced to no more than dust-covered rubble. It looked more like it had melted than collapsed.

'It's like Athens designed by that surreal bloke with the pointy moustache.'

'Salvador Dalí, yes,' said the Doctor thoughtfully. He leaned on his umbrella, both hands clutching the curved red wood of its question mark handle. 'It is somewhat reminiscent of *Gradiva Finds the Anthropomorphic Ruins*.'

'You what?'

'It's a painting.' His lined, quizzical face softened with a smile. 'By Dalí!'

'If you say so. I was thinking of that one with the melting clocks.' Ace remembered that Manisha had liked that painting, and had hung a print on the lounge wall of her flat. Before she'd been burnt out, that was ...

'Ah. *The Persistence of Memory*.' The Doctor's voice stopped her going down a dark series of thoughts.

'Yeah, right.'

The Doctor locked the door of the TARDIS and swung the key into his waistcoat pocket with a theatrical flourish. 'Shall we go and take a stroll through some memory lanes, then?' he said, peering up at her expectantly.

Grateful that the Doctor was always able to offer distractions just when she needed them, Ace bounded back down the slope and hooked her arm through his.

The two of them started to make their way towards the city, following an ancient path that zigzagged down the mountainside. The path had obviously not been used for some considerable time, and there were several occasions where they had to detour around huge boulders that blocked their way, or find alternative routes where the track had eroded to nothing.

Eventually they stepped down onto the valley floor. At ground level the city was even more impressive. Ace hadn't appreciated the sheer scale of the place. Even in their ruined state, the curved buttresses that she had spotted from the mountainside towered over them.

'Who built this, Professor?' she asked, running a hand over the wind-scoured surface. 'And what happened to them?'

'Ah ...' He gave a deep sigh, a pained look creasing his features. 'This was the home of the Astingir; an ancient race of poets, explorers and inventors. This city was their proudest achievement. It was also the final battleground in their war with the Wraiths.'

'A war that they lost, I'm guessing?' said Ace grimly, staring at the devastation around her.

Before the Doctor could reply, there was a low, grating rumble and the ground beneath their feet started to shake. Ace stepped back from the towering buttress in alarm as dust and rocks clattered down around her and from somewhere in the distance a shattering roar heralded the final collapse of one of the already precarious buildings.

Ace looked to the Doctor for reassurance but the little Time Lord was hurrying off along one of the wide, rubble-strewn avenues, peering at the digital readout on his pocket watch and muttering worriedly to himself, oblivious to the masonry crashing down around him.

She jogged after him, suddenly suspicious that their arrival on this planet was, as usual, not as random as she had initially thought. She caught up with him at the doorway of a low, domed building; more intact than most of the others around it. The earth tremors had started to subside now and the Doctor was peering down a steep flight of steps that led down into the gloom of the building's interior.

'All right, Professor. What's going on?' demanded Ace. 'We're here for a reason, aren't we?'

'Unfinished business, Ace,' said the Doctor, his piercing blue-grey eyes regarding her.

'It always is with you,' said Ace accusingly. 'It's something to do with that war, isn't it?'

He nodded. 'The Wraiths had all but destroyed the Astingir; driven them to the very edge of extinction. But those who had fought so hard had done so for a reason. They were giving the people in this building a chance to finish creating something. Something that would end the war. Something terrible.'

Ace stared down the steps into the darkness, unexpectedly feeling the skin on the back of her neck prickle. There was a power here. She could feel it. 'It's still down there, isn't it?'

The Doctor nodded. 'Shall we go and take a look?'

He pulled a box of his everlasting matches from his pocket, struck one, and the two of them made their way down the steps, the sound of their footfalls echoing off the walls. The entire building was of a different construction to the rest of the city, hewn from some crystalline substance that seemed to suck in the light from the match, sending strange lightning-like patterns flashing through the walls.

'The place looks completely untouched,' said Ace, her voice reverberating eerily. 'How come this building escaped when everything else has been destroyed?'

'Because the Wraiths did not dare touch this place,' said the Doctor grimly. 'Partly because once they learned of what it contained they wanted it for themselves, partly because they feared what might happen if it was damaged.'

'But what *was* it, Professor?' Ace was beginning to lose patience with him. '*What* did this building contain?'

'That.' The Doctor pointed with his umbrella.

The stairs had ended at the entranceway to a vast, circular chamber ringed with columns made from the same glassy material as the corridor. In the centre was a pit, and from the pit rose a twisting, spitting column of blazing, luminous energy.

The Doctor entered the chamber, hurrying to one of six, tall, cylindrical control consoles that stood like sentinels around the edge of the pit. Ace followed him, staring up in awe at the energy column, feeling her skin prickle all over as she neared it, but getting no sensation of heat despite the brilliance of the light. As she stepped forward to get an even closer look, she felt a gentle pressure holding her back. She looked down to find the crook of the Doctor's umbrella hooked around her arm.

'Let's not get too close,' he murmured. 'Not until I've made a few checks at any rate.'

Ace returned her gaze to the swirling vortex. 'What is it, Professor?'

'Incredibly dangerous,' said the Doctor, studying the readouts that flickered on the control console. 'The Astingir called it the Quantum Anvil.'

'And this is what they used to win the war?'

'Yes. A kind of temporal possibility engine.' The Doctor nodded. 'The Astingir drew the Wraiths to this planet and then used the Anvil to fracture the time stream of each and every one of them into infinite potential outcomes, leaving them unable to interact with the real world. They truly are wraiths now; ghosts created by the machine.'

Ace couldn't tear her eyes from the madly thrashing maelstrom. There were strange shadows dancing through the ribbons of energy. 'And you knew it was here?'

'Whenever the TARDIS passes within a few star systems of the Quantum Anvil, I can feel it in my bones. On occasion, I've even navigated by it.' The Doctor nodded grimly. 'If this device ever malfunctions, it will corrupt huge tracts of space-time. I check in on it every now and again, just to make sure that it isn't leaking.'

In normal circumstances Ace would have been frustrated at that revelation, annoyed with him for pretending that their landing here was purely random, but she was certain now that she could see dark, sinuous shapes weaving at the edges of the light which were somehow mesmerising.

With the Doctor now totally focused on the readings on the console, Ace stepped closer to the Anvil to get a clearer look at the strange phenomenon. As she did so, another series of tremors shook the building, much larger than the previous ones.

Dust and grit rained down from the domed ceiling, and the ground heaved beneath her feet. Ace threw up her hands to steady herself.

And her arm slipped inside the column of energy.

Time stopped.

For the briefest fraction of a second Ace felt she could see everything – literally everything – from the tiniest microbe to the largest supermassive black hole, all overlaid. The sensory input was so great, so overwhelming that she could barely endure it. A gasp of pain and helplessness burst from her lips as she felt her mind and body shutting down at the onslaught on her senses.

Mercifully the vision ceased as suddenly as it had started and Ace found herself drifting through the memories of a baby – warm and calm and safe. Without knowing how, Ace knew that these were memories of being in the womb.

There was a sudden burst of light and pain and time started to speed up again, racing through the life of the child as she grew from baby to toddler to teenager. With a jolt of surprise, Ace realised that it was her own life she was witnessing – no, not just witnessing, reliving. She winced as the tide of memories washed over her: every school lesson, every fight with Mum, every friendship, every kiss, every betrayal, every regret.

Swamped with conflicting emotions, she tried to pull back, but the Anvil had her in its grasp, and it wasn't finished with her yet.

With shocking suddenness, the bombardment of remembrance ceased and she found herself face to face with a female figure, her face hidden in shadow. Already knowing what would happen, Ace raised her hand in greeting and the figure standing in front of her did the same. This was no image in a mirror; the Anvil was showing her herself, as she was here and now.

Abruptly the figure shattered, fragmenting and reforming into multiple Aces – two, then four, then eight, then sixteen … The Anvil was extrapolating every possible path that she could take from this point in space and time.

Ace's mind filled with jumbled, fleeting glimpses of those possible futures …

Travelling with the Doctor forever, growing old by his side as they fought monsters and saved worlds. Dying in an explosion, killed by her own Nitro-9 at ground zero. Laughing as she danced with Sorin – or someone who looked like Sorin. A son? No. An ancestor! Screaming at the top of her lungs as the gun in her hand punched round after round into a squad of advancing Daleks, the flames as they blew apart reflected in the mirrored lenses of her sunglasses. Standing beneath the orange skies of Gallifrey, an ornate collar shielding her face from the heat of the midday sun, her robes billowing around her as she strode towards the vast, domed city of the Time

Lords. Drinking alien liquor with a dark-haired woman on board the TARDIS, flirting with a young man …

Living, dying, leaving, staying, laughing, crying … The visions came faster and faster, each revealing a different fate, each promising a different life that she could lead. With each fragmentation, the greater the possibilities, the more impossible the choice.

And yet …

With increasing frequency, a common theme started to become dominant through the disparate timelines that raced through her mind. Her own world, the Earth, slowly dying; a decaying world, orbing a decaying sun, its people broken and hungry, its surface caked with filth and pollution. A world where vile creatures rose up from the sea to prey on the living – Haemovores. Vampires.

She frowned. She knew this future. This was the future that Fenric had engineered. But she and the Doctor had changed that future, hadn't they? How could it still be a possibility?

The only worthwhile future is one where that future stays stopped.

No sooner had the thought flashed across her mind than a dark shape suddenly appeared at the periphery of her vision. As she turned to look at it, another appeared, then another and another. Soon the bright white light around her was stained with shadows, more and more of them, circling ever closer.

The shadow figures were more distinct now, their faces clearly visible; contorted with pain and anguish, their eyes burning, their voices pleading. With sudden realisation, Ace knew that these creatures were what remained of the Wraiths.

They surged towards her, a dozen or more grasping hands reaching out, smoke-like fingers passing through her flesh. Every nerve in her body exploded with pain. Ace cried out in agony. More and more of the creatures started to surround her, the pain intensifying with each desperate attempt they made to grasp hold of her. The light was almost gone now, extinguished by the tide of blackness that engulfed her.

Something suddenly gripped her arm, substantial this time, the fingers digging hard into her flesh. Ace began to struggle as whatever had hold of her started to drag her backwards, bellowing at the top of her lungs.

'Let me go!'

'Ace! It's me!' It was the Doctor's voice.

Her strength gone, Ace stopped fighting and allowed herself to be dragged back from the swirling storm of screaming shadows.

As she was pulled clear from the Anvil, her legs gave way and she collapsed in a heap on the glass-like floor, her limbs shaking from the shocks that the shadow creatures had inflicted.

'Ace, are you all right?'

'Yeah ...' she said weakly. 'Yeah ... I think so.'

The Doctor helped her to her feet. Agonising pins and needles shot through her arms and legs.

'Did they touch you?' asked the Doctor urgently. 'Did they make contact?'

Ace nodded, trying to rub life back into her limbs. 'They kept grabbing at me, like they were trying to tear me apart, but they couldn't get a grip.'

'Get a grip ...' He peered into her eyes for a moment, a concerned look flickering across his features. 'There shouldn't be any lasting damage.' He shot a look up at the Anvil. 'We need to get away from here.'

'Give us a moment, Professor. I feel as though I've just gone ten rounds with Frank Bruno!'

'There's no time, Ace!' snapped the Doctor. 'According to the readings I've just taken, those tremors were caused by the wash from the warp baffles of an Astingir cruiser coming out of hyperspace. They must have set up intruder alarms since my last visit and our arrival here has obviously triggered them.'

'So?' Ace was still trying to get some feeling back into her legs. 'You're just checking up on it. What's the problem?'

'The problem,' said the Doctor sternly, 'is that if they have even the *faintest* suspicion that we are here then they will shoot first and ask questions later. We need to get back to the TARDIS, and quickly.'

With that, he turned on his heel and hurried out of the chamber, making his way back up the steep, crystal steps to the surface.

'Hey! Hold up.' Wincing with the effort, Ace staggered after him, still haunted by the burning touch of the Wraiths – and the cold, growing certainty that there was something that Doctor wasn't telling her.

PART TWO
2020

CHAPTER NINE

Dorothy emerged from the TARDIS wardrobe room and hung her expensive SDC spacesuit on a familiar-looking hat stand near the door. She lingered in the doorway, thinking of her old bomber jacket hanging up at home, wishing she'd made the decision to wear it today after all. She'd found none of her old clothes here, and in borrowed jeans and a jumper she felt so ordinary. She watched as the Doctor darted to and fro around the central console that dominated the TARDIS control room.

It was difficult to believe that this was the same person that she had travelled with all those years ago ... She'd known about regeneration – the Doctor had explained it to her – but it was one thing to understand the theory, quite another to witness it first hand. There was nothing that even *remotely* resembled her Doctor. The hair was different, the manner was different, the height, the accent ...

Oh, and the fact that he'd regenerated into a woman, of course.

And it wasn't just the Doctor that had changed. The TARDIS was virtually unrecognisable from the ship that Ace had once travelled in. Gone were the clean white walls, with their softly glowing roundels, replaced with dark, perforated metal sheets, their upper edges swathed in misty shadows. Gone too was the sleek hexagonal console; the mushroom-shaped control centre that now dominated the room looked as though it had been hewn from hunks of crystal; the huge, quartz-like fingers that arched overhead glowing from within with a warm amber light.

The entire place was vast – far larger than it had been. Mind you, it had only been the two of them back then; these days the Doctor seemed to be travelling with a small army. She glanced over to where her three fellow human travellers were talking in hushed tones on the far side of the room. The older man, Graham, had seemed friendly enough, but the other two – Yaz and Ryan – seemed to be a little wary of her.

Ace couldn't blame them. She had always been very protective of *her* Doctor. She smiled as she recalled the outrage she had felt when Brigadier Lethbridge-Stewart had referred to her as 'the latest one'.

Weird, she thought. *I'm thinking of myself as Ace again...*

She regarded the Doctor once more. How many people had he ... *she* travelled with since their time together, she wondered? How many different faces since they had parted company all those years ago? Would she still remember the circumstances of their parting? Would she recall the details of their time together at all?

As if knowing that she was being scrutinised, the Doctor lifted her head, staring straight across the room at her. Ace felt her cheeks flush, but if the Doctor noticed she didn't say anything.

'So, are you going to give me the coordinates for this super-secret base of yours, or shall I just dig out an OS map of Oxfordshire and you can point?'

Pulling her phone from her jeans pocket, Ace opened up the maps app, typed in Kirkwood Farm then crossed to the Doctor. 'Try not to land on top of the Triumph.'

The Doctor took the phone and grinned at her. 'Smashing.'

As the Doctor started setting coordinates, Graham wandered over to Ace's side, a concerned look on his face. 'What about your mate?' he asked. 'Is he going to be all right on his own?'

'Will? He'll be fine.' Ace and Will had agreed that he would pilot *Virgil* back to Earth on his own, whilst she went with the Doctor in the TARDIS. Sam hadn't been overly happy about that arrangement but had reluctantly agreed that they needed to find out what information the Doctor had about the UFO as quickly as possible.

Will and Ace had returned to *Virgil* and collected a series of remote cameras and sensors, positioning them in key positions around the alien ship. That would hopefully give them advance warning if anyone else boarded, or if the ship did anything unexpected. Will was now making his way back to the shuttle to begin his return journey to Earth. As soon as he landed he was going to disconnect the Squidget and propulsion unit and rendezvous with the rest of them at Kirkwood Farm.

Ace felt a sudden pang of guilt. Unbeknownst to Will, whilst he had been occupied collecting the surveillance equipment from the shuttle's cargo hold, she had taken the opportunity to instruct the Squidget that as soon as *Virgil* had safely touched down at Devesham it was to shut down and only take further instruction from her.

She knew that he was going to be angry with her for doing so, but she didn't see that she had any choice. Will might have given her his word that he wouldn't make any attempt to investigate the Squidget any further, but she wasn't sure that Sam would give her the same assurance. She'd seen the gleam that had come into the mission controller's eyes when she'd got her first glimpse of the Squidget. Ace was in no doubt that Sam would almost certainly take the opportunity to make a thorough investigation of the alien technology and, given their relationship, who knew how easily persuaded Will might be to go along with her. The safest thing to do was to simply deny her the opportunity.

'He'll probably get back to Earth before we do!' said Ace with a breeziness she didn't feel. 'Given the Professor's track record of steering the TARDIS that is …'

'Oi!' The Doctor looked up from the console with a look of indignation. 'I'll have you know that I'm in perfect control of this machine. Now hold on, here we go.'

She threw a lever and Ace's heart leapt as a familiar wheezing, groaning sound filled the air. Moments later the room lurched alarmingly and Ace hung on to the console for dear life as the TARDIS pitched and rolled its way into the space-time vortex.

Ace looked at the Doctor in alarm at the violent take-off but, far from being concerned, she actually seemed to be enjoying herself. The others just held on to various handholds around the console room with expressions of weary resignation. Obviously this was normal for the TARDIS these days.

Mercifully the flight was a short one and soon the grating materialisation noise echoed around the room once more. The instant that it faded the Doctor flicked the switch that opened the doors.

'Right then,' she said cheerily. 'Let's have a look at your gaff, then.'

Still trying to come to terms with the enthusiastic personality of this new Doctor, Ace led the TARDIS crew out through the doors and into her batcave.

'Lights.'

As the lights came up, the Doctor gave an appreciative whistle. 'Ooh, very nice.' She started to scurry around the workshop, peering inquisitively at the objects that littered the shelves and benches, cooing appreciatively when she found something that she liked.

'Make yourself at home,' said Ace. 'I'll put the kettle on.'

Graham gave her a nod of approval. 'You see? Someone who's got her head screwed on. Someone who realises that you can go adventuring through time and space and still make time to get a decent cuppa!'

'Oh, don't start.' Ryan rolled his eyes.

Ace grinned and made her way over to the small kitchenette in the corner of the workshop, filling the plastic kettle at the small sink. 'There are some biscuits in the cupboard too.'

'Oh, you can definitely stay,' said Graham hurrying to join her and eagerly pulling open the cupboard door.

'Careful,' said the Doctor, amused. 'Feed him too well and you might never get shot of him.'

Ace made a show of busying herself making the tea, using the time to get a proper look at the Doctor's new travelling companions. She'd already made up her mind that she liked Graham. He was like an excitable puppy, although she sensed that some of it might be a front. There was a melancholy about him, a hint of underlying sadness.

Ryan seemed to be a fairly typical teenage boy, not unlike the kids that Ace had hung around with in her youth. He'd made a beeline for the dismantled Triumph Bonneville as soon as they'd landed and was examining the dismantled engine on the workbench in exacting detail.

Yaz was the one she hadn't quite got a handle on yet. It wasn't that she had been unfriendly, it was just that unlike the other two she seemed to content to watch rather than chat, and Ace could tell that she was watching *everything*. Unlike the Doctor, Yaz was making a slow methodical circuit of the workshop, as if mentally cataloguing its contents. That made Ace a little nervous.

'Well, now I know how you managed to get to an alien spacecraft orbiting the Moon in record time!' The Doctor was peering delightedly at the wrecked pod in the centre of the room. 'A Rintlekk emergency escape vessel.'

Ace picked up a two mugs of tea and crossed to the Doctor's side. 'I might have guessed that you'd know what it was just by looking.' She shook her head in disbelief. 'Three years I've been trying to hack into old UNIT files trying to find out where this thing came from. I should have just phoned you up and asked.'

'Yeah,' said the Doctor quietly. 'Always up for a phone call …'

There was an awkward pause as they sipped at their tea, each of them waiting for the other to say something more. It was the Doctor who broke the silence, turning her attention back to the pod.

'I seem to remember that these pods come with a wiggly, little silver interface thingy?'

'I call it the Squidget.'

'Squidget! Fab. I'm assuming that that's now inside the shuttle your boyfriend is piloting?'

'He's not my boyfriend,' said Ace firmly. 'At least not any more.'

'But you trust him?'

'Yes, totally.'

'Good.' The Doctor smiled. 'I look forward to meeting him properly.'

Determined not to let the Doctor start poking around in her private life, Ace changed the subject. 'So how did you lot end up on board that ship?' she asked. 'How did you know it was there?'

'I picked up a strange transmission whilst the TARDIS was in flight,' explained the Doctor. 'Unidentifiable, alien, apparently ancient. Had to come and have a shufti, didn't I?'

'Well it suddenly appeared out of nowhere as far as everyone on Earth was concerned, 24 hours ago. I'm guessing that it was cloaked and that someone switched that cloak off … You?'

'Ha! See, it couldn't have been me!' said Graham, hurrying over to join them. 'I was looking for a light switch, pulled a wrong lever-thing.'

'Of course!' the Doctor cried.

Graham looked vindicated. 'Of course it wasn't me?'

'Of course it *was*.' She frowned and nodded thoughtfully. 'But it suggests there must be time dilation moving through the station's circuitry. You switched off the shields and the effect was felt a day earlier. Verrrrrrry interesting ...'

'Yeah, the world's powers thought so too,' Ace said wryly. 'God knows how many probes they're preparing to send up right now, that's why me and Will had to move so fast. Did you find anyone on board?'

The Doctor shook her head. 'Deserted. And believe me, we spent *hours* wandering those corridors.'

'Yeah, coz Granddad here got himself lost!' Ryan had joined them beside the pod now. 'And we had to find him.'

'It wasn't my fault!' said Graham indignantly. 'All those corridors looked the same! I said we should have been roped together.'

Ace kept to the point. 'Any idea what it's doing here? Where it came from?'

The Doctor shrugged. 'As far as I could make out it's a huge collection and transmission relay station, but the technology is really, *really* complex. And clearly it's designed to harness time energy too ...'

'So what's it collecting?' asked Ryan.

The Doctor shrugged. 'Not a clue.'

'I might have an idea ...' Ace was slowly starting to piece things together. She quickly brought the Doctor up to speed about the missing girls, and the reports of strange figures on the streets of Perivale. 'Reports of alien abductions and an alien ship appearing in orbit around the Moon – surely that's more than just coincidence?'

The Doctor nodded. 'Yeah ... something weird is definitely going on here.'

Ace was about to tell her about the strange feeling that she'd experienced on the alien vessel, the impression that she'd been there before, when Yaz's voice rang out across the room.

'What's this?'

Ace looked up to see her lifting a semi-transparent sphere, about the size of a marble, from a box full of identical spheres on the laboratory bench.

Putting down her mug, Ace strode quickly across the workshop. 'I'd be a bit careful with that if I were you.' She plucked the sphere from Yaz's fingers and placed it carefully back in the box. 'It'll make quite a bang if you drop it.'

'Ace,' said the Doctor accusingly. 'Please tell me that you're not still making Nitro-9?'

'Nitro-90.' Ace grinned. 'Packs a bit more of a wallop than the stuff you're used to, Professor.'

'Explosives?' A frown crossed Yaz's face as she glanced at the other half-completed experiments dotted around the lab. 'You make explosives here?'

'I make lots of things here,' said Ace defensively. 'The explosives are just a hobby.'

'That's some hobby!' snorted Ryan.

'I tried making home brew once,' piped up Graham. 'That ended up being quite explosive. Bit of a shame, really. I was letting it ferment in the airing cupboard … Ruined all of your gran's pillowcases.'

Ignoring the look that Yaz was giving her, Ace closed the lid of the box and placed it in a tall, refrigerated cabinet alongside several other boxes. She was kicking herself for having left the box out and open. The problem with spending so much time working alone was that it encouraged bad habits. She would need to be more careful in future.

Before Yaz could ask any more awkward questions, Ace's phone rang. It was Sanaul.

'Hi Sanaul.' Ace answered it straight away, grateful for the interruption. 'What's up?'

'*Miss Dorothy, I've got that information that you wanted about the young lady from the documentary.*'

Snatching up a pen and paper from the laboratory bench Ace scribbled down the name and address. 'That's great, San. Good work.'

'*And the vehicles that Miss O'Connor requested on your behalf should be waiting for you. A couple of company Range Rovers.*'

'Thank you.' As soon as she'd realised that she'd be heading back to Earth with the Doctor in the TARDIS, Ace had asked Sam to get in touch with Sanaul and make sure they had alternative transport available.

'*If you could bring them back intact this time, it would help the figures for this quarter.*'

Ace grinned. She'd rolled a Range Rover during a mission in the Gobi desert a few months back, and he wasn't going to let her forget it in a hurry. 'I'll do my best.'

Slipping her phone back into her jeans, Ace turned to the Doctor. 'Right, we've got a lead. An address for the girl in the documentary who claims that she was the victim of a failed abduction attempt. Gotta be worth having a chat?'

'Oh, definitely!' The Doctor clapped her hands excitedly. 'Nice work, Ace!'

Ace gave an embarrassed smile, unsure how to respond to this warm, enthusiastic Doctor.

Her phone rang again. This time is was Chantelle.

'Hi Chantelle. What's up?'

'*I think that I had a little bit of a close encounter last night …*'

Ace glanced across at the Doctor. 'Hang on a sec, I'm going to put you on speaker.'

Tapping the speaker icon on the phone, she beckoned the Doctor over. 'OK, Chantelle, what's been going on?'

Chantelle related her encounter with the strange, hunched figures in the alleyway and their mysterious disappearance. The Doctor and Ace listened, not interrupting, until Chantelle had finished her story.

'*I should have called you straight away, but, to be honest, I was freaked out, so I went out with the girls and got more than a little bit tipsy. I tried to call you this morning, but you weren't answering your phone.*'

'Yeah, I was … out of town.' Ace wasn't about to explain to Chantelle how she had been to the Moon and back. 'Look, Chantelle stay put, OK? Either I'll come over myself or I'll send someone. In the meantime, stay out of that alleyway, all right?'

'*Oh, don't worry. I'm not going down there alone again in a hurry.*'

'I'll see you later.'

Ace hung up and turned to find the Doctor looking at her carefully. 'Perivale seems to be where everything is going on these days,' she said quietly. 'Missing girls and now this …'

'Well it's a good thing that you're travelling mob-handed these days, isn't it, Professor?'

The Doctor raised an eyebrow. 'Split up?'

Ace nodded. 'There should be two Range Rovers waiting for us in the yard. We can get to Perivale in under an hour. Someone can come with me to interview the girl, whilst everyone else checks out Chantelle's alien hoodies.' She raised an eyebrow at the Doctor. 'Do you want to be on Team Ace?'

The Doctor grinned. 'Wicked.'

CHAPTER TEN

Ace accelerated up the slip road onto the motorway, missing the effortless power of the Hypergreen. She had no doubt that Will was making the most of his temporary ownership of the sports car. She would be having words if it came back with so much as a scuff on it.

The M40 was its usual endless train of articulated lories heading towards London and the south coast. It was already getting dark and a light rain had started to fall, forming hazy haloes around the sickly yellow motorway lighting.

There was a loud squawk from the radio. Ryan was mucking around on the walkie-talkie in the other car, coming up with ludicrous call signs for them all. Ace turned down the volume, pleased to have a chance to talk to the Doctor on her own, but unsure as to where that conversation might lead.

'So, just like old times, eh, Professor?'

'Yeah …' The Doctor smiled wistfully. 'Just like old times, Ace.'

There was a long awkward pause.

'How have you been?'

'What have you been up to?'

The two of them spoke simultaneously, then embarrassed laughter broke the ice.

'You first,' said Ace. 'This new face of yours. Is it the only new one since I last saw you or have there been a few?'

'Oh, there have been a few,' said the Doctor, her smile fading. 'More than a few, in fact ...'

There was another long pause. Realising that she wasn't going to be drawn any further on that subject, Ace changed the focus. 'What about your crew? I suppose there have been more than a few of them since me, too?'

'Yeah ... I always seem to find someone daft enough to come along for the ride. Everyone always seems more than happy to leave the Earth behind them and head off into the wild blue yonder.'

'Not all of us have a choice about that, if you recall,' Ace reminded her. 'I didn't exactly choose to end up on Iceworld, you know.'

'No ... You didn't.'

Another pause. This was getting ridiculous.

'Professor ...' Ace took a deep breath. 'I think that whatever is going on has something to do with me, with that day that I was taken away from Earth.'

'Oh?' The Doctor looked at her curiously. 'Why?'

Grateful to have a confidante who wouldn't question the more extraordinary aspects of her story, Ace told her everything about her recurring dreams; about the feeling of being drawn from her body and launched across space, about the strange alien land-scape, about the cries of her fellow abductees, about the creature whose huge, terrible claws dragged her screaming back to consciousness.

The Doctor just listened, nodding to herself occasionally, her expression betraying nothing.

'And now it seems to be happening again,' said Ace more emotion in her voice than she had wanted. 'Teenage girls being whisked away from Earth, a huge, evil presence. If this is Fenric again ...'

'It isn't,' said the Doctor firmly. 'This is something different.'

Ace glanced over at the Doctor, suddenly wary by the certainty in her voice.

'You sound very confident about that.' A surge of old anger started to build. 'Please tell me that this isn't some scheme of yours?'

'It's not!'

'I'm not going to let you do this again, Professor!' Ace suddenly let years of pent-up rage burst out of her. 'If you think for one minute that you can just drop back into my life out of nowhere and start pulling the same old crud ...'

'Ace, I promise you, I have had nothing to do with any of this!' said the Doctor pleadingly. 'I know that we parted on bad terms, but I *am* sorry. For everything that happened ...'

Ace kept her eyes on the road. She wanted to believe her. She really did. But she knew what the Doctor was like.

'We're not gonna have this conversation now, Professor,' Ace said. 'Anything else, fine. But not this conversation.'

Instead, the two of them talked about things that had happened since they had parted company; the places they had been, the people that they had met. The Doctor was impressed at just how big Ace's charity empire had become, and at the projects that she had become involved with.

'But it must have cost a fortune. How did you raise the finance?'

'I've got you to thank for that, Professor,' said Ace, grinning to herself.

'Oh?' The Doctor looked puzzled.

'You remember that business in the 1940s? The Cybermen in the Blitz?'

The Doctor nodded.

'Do you remember that one day you really wound me up?'

'Um, no, not specifically,' the Doctor admitted. 'But then, I did tend to wind you up quite a bit, as I recall.'

'Yeah, well, I decided that I'd had enough, so I set up a contingency plan.'

'Oh?'

'I grabbed 50 quid in old money from your wallet when you weren't looking, found a bank that I knew would still be around in my time and opened a high-interest savings account.'

The Doctor just stared at her, saying nothing. Ace could tell that she was unhappy about that little revelation, but she didn't care. She had known at the time that it was breaking one of the Doctor's unwritten rules, but she had been so angry with him that that one act of rebellion had, in her mind, somehow helped redress the balance between them. He had been happy to manipulate her life for his own ends, so she'd felt it was only fair to manipulate his. Little had she known how useful that money was going to be all those years later …

They drove the rest of the way into London in silence. Fortunately the rush-hour was starting to build, so Ace had to concentrate on manoeuvring the big four-by-four through the dense traffic. Finally they pulled up at the address in Perivale that Sanaul had given them.

As they stepped out of the car, the Doctor looked around the estate and frowned. 'This looks familiar.'

'It should be,' said Ace pointing at the row of dark trees silhouetted against the clouds behind the houses. 'That's Horsenden Hill. Ring any bells? Cheetah people? Exploding motorbikes? The Master?'

'Ah …' The Doctor's expression darkened. This had been the site of an epic battle with the Doctor's arch enemy. A battle that had left its scars on both of them. That had had been 30 years ago for Ace. She wondered how long it had been for the Doctor …

Leaving the Doctor standing in the drizzle with her memories, Ace located the house where the girl and her family lived.

'It's that one.' She nodded at one of the 1930s semis on the other side of the street. 'How do you want to do this? Say that we're here from the Government? From the TV company?'

'How about we use this?' said the Doctor, snapping out of her reverie and pulling a small leather wallet from the pocket of her coat and flipping it open. 'Psychic paper.'

'You what?' Ace eyed the blank paper in the wallet suspiciously.

'Shows the reader whatever I want them to see. Saves a lot of time.'

'Very cool,' said Ace. 'I remember when you had nothing but a couple of spoons in your pocket.'

'Oh, I'm all mod cons these days,' said the Doctor proudly. 'Psychic paper, sonic screwdriver, mobile phone, Corby trouser press … I've got the lot.' With that she set off towards the front door of the house.

Wondering whether the Doctor might actually *have* a Corby trouser press magically secreted in her coat pocket, Ace hurried after her. She was about to suggest that *she* should do the talking when, before she could stop her, the Doctor reached out and rang the doorbell.

As the chime rang out inside the house, the curtains in the bay window twitched open and a man's face appeared for a second before vanishing again. Moments later there was the rattle of a security chain and the front door eased open a crack.

'Yes? What do you want?' The man they had seen at the window was peering suspiciously at them.

'Mister Eldon? I'm the Doctor, this is my friend Ace.' She held out the wallet. 'We were wondering if we could have a quick word with your daughter?'

Mr Eldon stared at the proffered wallet for a second, and then closed the door.

Ace groaned, mortified at the clumsy way that the Doctor had made their introductions. She might claim to be a different Doctor, but some things obviously didn't change.

She was about to say as much when, to her surprise, the door opened again and, with a brief look up and down the street, Mr Eldon beckoned them inside.

'Sorry about that,' he said shutting the door behind them. 'I had to check that you were official. We've had so many weirdoes wanting to talk to Kerry since that wretched documentary. Please ...' he gestured towards the door at the end of the hallway. 'We were just finishing our dinner.'

Impressed by the immediate effect that the psychic paper had had on the man, Ace followed the Doctor down the hallway and into the kitchen. It was virtually identical to the house that she had grown up in as a child. The same slightly outdated wallpaper, the same kind of knickknacks and pictures on the walls, the same smell ...

Kerry was sitting at a dining table, her mother clearing dirty plates into the sink. A baby monitor sat in the middle of the table. Both women looked around nervously at Mr Eldon as he followed the Doctor and Ace into the room.

'Andrew?' asked Mrs Eldon. 'Who are these people?'

'Kerry, Tracey, this is the Doctor and Ace. They're from NASA.'

Ace bit her lip, wondering if the Doctor's psychic paper might have over-exaggerated their importance just a tad. Her concerns seemed to be justified as Kerry pushed her chair back from the table, her eyes wide and frightened.

'She's not from NASA. And her name isn't Ace. It's Dorothy. Dorothy McShane. She's from that charity.'

'Smart girl.' Ace pulled up a chair and sat down opposite her. 'Ace is an old nickname. Only really old friends are allowed to call me that. It's why I named my company A Charitable Earth – same initials. And you're right, I'm not from NASA like the Doctor is, but I do help them out occasionally. You probably saw in the papers last year that I was going out with an astronaut called Will Buckland?'

The tabloids had made something of a big deal about their relationship. They'd even been photographed by paparazzi on a holiday they'd taken in Greece. Ace was hoping that it was the sort of thing that might stick in the head of a teenage girl. To her relief, Kerry nodded.

'Well, he introduced me to the Doctor.' Ace shot a look at the Doctor, making it clear that she wanted her to back up the lie. 'She's NASA's expert in extraterrestrial life.'

'Yeah, that's right.' The Doctor pulled up a chair next to Ace. 'Not much about aliens that I don't know. Love 'em.'

Ace mentally crossed her fingers and hoped that no one would question why an expert from NASA would have such a broad Northern accent. Fortunately Kerry and her parents just seemed relieved to be able to relate their story to what they assumed to be an 'official' investigator.

'We've heard that there have been some disturbances going on in this area for weeks – people seeing things in alleyways. Have you lot seen anything odd?'

The Eldons looked at each other, then nodded.

'Andrew thought he heard something in the alleyway round the back,' said Mrs Eldon. 'A "strange snapping noise", he said, like a twig being broken, but really, really loud.'

'When was this?' asked Ace.

'Last week, around 1am. I was just coming back from work.'

'Long hours at the moment?' queried the Doctor.

'New mouth to feed,' said Mr Eldon, looking pointedly at the baby monitor on the table. 'I've started doing late shifts and Tracy has gone back to working part time for the council.'

'Leaving Kerry here alone a lot the time,' mused Ace.

'I don't mind being on my own,' piped up Kerry. 'It's nice to get some time to myself without the baby screaming all the time.'

Tracy Eldon glared at her. 'I've told you, she's teething.'

'Well, does she have to scream about it?'

'Kerry!' snapped Mister Eldon. 'Don't shout. We've got guests!'

Ace winced, remembering similar exchanges from her own childhood.

Kerry sat back sulkily. 'Well, it's irritating. Almost as bad as the noise the rats make.'

'Rats?' Ace shot a look at the Doctor. 'You've got a problem with rats?'

'It's only just started,' said Mrs Eldon hurriedly. 'It's not like the house is infested or anything. Andrew is dealing with it.'

'They're having a deck put down in the garden a few houses over,' explained Mr Eldon. 'I think that a nest must have been disturbed or something.'

'Have you actually seen them?'

'No. But we can hear them … Scratching. Outside the door, under the floor.'

'It was the noise that the rats were making that woke me up,' said Kerry quietly. 'The night … the night it happened.'

'Why don't you tell us exactly what *did* happen?' said the Doctor gently. 'Start at the beginning. Don't miss out any detail.'

Kerry took a deep breath. 'It started with the dream.'

'*The* dream …' Ace leaned forward. 'So a dream you've had more than once?'

Kerry nodded. 'I've had it six or seven times. I'm lying in bed and suddenly I can feel something pulling at me, pulling me out of my body. It's like I'm floating, looking back down at myself …'

As Kerry related the details of her dream, a shiver ran down Ace's spine; the alien world, the screaming people … Kerry was describing the same event as her own dream. Every detail – only this time the ending was different.

'I can hear this thing chasing me. I never see its face, just hear its breathing.' Kerry's voice was beginning to sound panicky now as she relived her nightmare. 'I try to run, but the stones I'm running over hurt my feet. I turn around to see what it is behind me but it's so big. Then a huge hand grabs me …'

'And then what?' Ace urged her, desperate to know how her dream ended.'

I don't know!' cried Kerry. 'I can feel the hand crushing me, squeezing me. I'm screaming …'

She burst into tears, obviously still terrified by the memory. Her mum hurried to comfort her, the argument of a moment ago forgotten.

'It was her screams that woke us up,' said Mr Eldon quietly. 'Screaming the place down, she was. I had to break down the door to her room.'

'She'd locked it?' asked the Doctor curiously.

'No,' Mr Eldon shook his head. 'It was barricaded. A chair wedged under the door handle.'

'I didn't do that!' wailed Kerry.

'We know you didn't, love.' Mrs Eldon hugged her daughter to her chest.

'We found her lying in the middle of the floor,' continued Mr Eldon. 'She was shaking, convulsing, like she was having a fit, and covered in …. slime of some kind.'

'Slime?' The Doctor and Ace looked at each other in surprise.

Mr Elson nodded. 'Horrible stuff it was, thick, sticky slime. It was all over her, in her hair, her nose, her eyes … We thought it was suffocating her so we wiped off as much of it as we could with her bedsheets and then Tracy helped me get her into the shower.' He rubbed his hands together at the memory. 'Still can't seem to get rid of the smell of it.'

'Ectoplasmic material …' The Doctor leaned across the table excitedly. 'Did you keep the bedsheets?'

Mr Eldon shook his head.

'We burnt the lot, said Mrs Eldon defiantly. 'Even the slightest whiff of the stuff was enough to set Kerry off again. I never want to smell the filthy stuff again.'

'That's a shame, said the Doctor sadly. 'I'd really have liked to have got a proper look at some of that slime …'

CHAPTER ELEVEN

On the other side of Perivale, the Range Rover carrying Graham, Yaz and Ryan pulled up in the street outside the block of flats where Chantelle lived. Inside the car, the three of them were still arguing. It was an argument that had been going on since they'd left Kirkwood Farm.

'I'm just saying that making explosives in a secret location isn't exactly normal,' said Yaz.

'But she's the CEO of a world-renowned charity!' argued Graham. 'Do you really think that she'd be doing that if she's some kind of terrorist?'

'I don't know!' Yaz was getting exasperated. 'It just gives me cause for concern, all right?'

'Look, she's a friend of the Doctor's,' pointed out Ryan, opening the passenger door and clambering out into the street. 'Do you really think that she'd be hanging out with someone dodgy?'

'She hangs out with you, doesn't she?' said Yaz, climbing out after him.

'Hey!'

'Come on, you two.' Graham glared at them. 'Pack it in. We can argue until the cows come home. Personally I like the girl.

The Doc seems to like her too, so that's good enough for me. Now, shall we get on with looking for these hoodies?'

Graham set off up the stairs to the first floor where Chantelle's flat was. With a despairing roll of his eyes, Ryan followed him. Yaz stood for a moment. Why was she so wound up about Ace? She tried to tell herself it was just anti-terror training, instinct or natural caution. But it was more, she knew.

The thought kept occurring: *Maybe I'm not the first Yaz, but just another Ace: young, adventurous, ready to run and fight through time and space.*

But Dorothy McShane was proof that you couldn't run and fight for ever. 'Ace' had left the Doctor and the TARDIS under a cloud of some kind, and whatever had happened between them went deep. Deeper than Yaz would've liked.

Oh God, she thought, *am I actually jealous?*

She dragged herself back to the present, looking up at the flats. She'd been called to plenty of similar developments up in Sheffield in her time. Blocks like these always seemed to attract trouble, and it was always the same – a tiny minority making life miserable for the majority. Her gut feeling was that Graham was probably right, that this was going to turn out to be nothing but bored kids rather than alien abductors, but the only way to prove that was to investigate.

Glad to have something to do, Yaz mounted the concrete stairs. From the first floor she could hear Ryan's voice. He seemed to be happy about something.

She emerged onto the narrow walkway to see Ryan and Graham talking to a slim, blonde woman from one of the flats.

'Yaz, it's Chantelle!' said Ryan pointing at her excitedly.

'Yeah, Ryan, I know. It's who we've come to meet, remember?'

'No, I mean it's *the* Chantelle!' Ryan was grinning from ear to ear. 'From *Checkout Girls vs Sea Monsters* and *Alien Bikers!*'

Yaz sighed. 'Those particular classics must have passed me by.'

'Well you must have seen her in *EastEnders* a few years back?' Graham seemed almost as star-struck. 'She was the temporary barmaid in the Vic.'

'Look, who the hell are you lot?' said Chantelle grumpily. 'If this is just about getting signed photos ...'

'The Doctor sent us,' said Graham.

'The Doctor?' Chantelle went very pale. 'Oh no ...'

'And Ace,' chipped in Ryan.

'Ace?' Chantelle raised a perfectly manicured eyebrow. 'She's calling herself Ace again, not Dorothy?'

'Yeah. Well, maybe.' Yaz frowned. 'Is that important?'

'Not really.' Chantelle shook her head. 'If she wants to start using her old nickname again that's her business, but if any of you start calling me Squeak—'

'Look, we understand that you might have seen something unusual,' Yaz interrupted, suddenly suspicious that the Doctor might have sent them off on a wild goose chase just to get them out of the way. 'Is that right, or are we wasting our time here?'

'I saw something, yeah.' Chantelle glared at her, obviously unhappy about being cut off. 'In the alleyway over there.' She nodded towards the dark pathway running behind the flats.

'Aliens?' asked Ryan. 'You actually saw them?'

'I saw something—'

'Not just kids?' Yaz interrupted again. 'Hardly unusual for kids to be causing trouble on an estate like this ...'

'No, definitely not kids,' said Chantelle icily. 'I've never seen anything like this before.'

'Can you show us?' asked Graham.

Chantelle stared at the three of them for a moment, then nodded. 'OK. You'd better come in while I get a coat.' She stepped back inside her flat, followed eagerly by Ryan.

As Yaz approached the door, Graham stopped her. 'What's going on, Yaz?'

'What do you mean?'

'I mean you, coming on all Gene Hunt, all of a sudden. Ace and this girl are on *our* side you know?'

'I know.'

'Well, then. It's not like we didn't know that the Doctor had a past ...'

Graham followed Ryan into Chantelle's flat. Yaz stepped in too, feeling troubled. Ace's past was their future. How did you go back to a normal life after everything that travelling with the Doctor exposed you to? Why would anyone ever leave the Doctor? Was it by choice? Was it because they had fallen out? Was it the Doctor's decision? Was it Ace's ...?

Dorothy McShane, businesswoman and charity worker had at one point been Ace, travelling companion to the Doctor – travelling through space and time, fighting monsters, putting the universe to rights, just like she and Ryan and Graham were doing. And then it had all stopped.

With a pang of guilt, Yaz realised that however odd a feeling it was for her to discover that the Doctor had old friends, it must be so much worse for Ace to realise that she had new ones.

Making a promise to herself to talk to Ace about the explosives in her workshop, rather than just making judgements about them, Yaz followed the others into the flat.

She didn't have to be a policewoman or a fan to work out what profession Chantelle had ended up in. Framed covers from dozens of different fashion magazines lined the walls, Chantelle's face staring out from every one of them. Graham seemed entranced by a picture on the cover of an American edition of *Vogue*, Ryan on the other hand was more interested in the cast and crew signatures on the framed *Alien Bikers!* poster that hung at the far end of the hallway.

As Chantelle emerged from the living room pulling on a voluminous puffer jacket, Yaz gave her an apologetic smile.

'Look, sorry, I came on a bit strong there. Old police habits die hard ...'

Chantelle gave her an understanding nod. 'That's OK. If you're hanging around with the Doctor then I can only imagine what sort of stuff you're putting up with.'

Ryan raised an eyebrow. 'You know about the Doctor?'

'Met him when I was little.' She paused. 'I just hope he can sort all this weirdness out ...'

'Um, he's a she now,' said Yaz.

Chantelle stared at her for a moment, then laughed. 'And I thought there was nothing left that could surprise me. Come on, I'll show you where our friendly neighbourhood aliens were hanging out.'

The four of them left the flat and made their way round to the alleyway where Chantelle had seen the mysterious figures.

'They appeared over there,' said Chantelle, pointing at the streetlight at the far side of the recycling area. 'One minute nothing, the next, there they were.'

'Right,' Yaz nodded. 'Then I guess this is where we start.'

Graham was sceptical. 'Surely the chances of them coming back to exactly the same area two nights running are pretty remote?'

No sooner had the words left his lips than there was the sound of something moving from the far side of the yard.

'I can see something hiding in the bushes behind the bins,' whispered Ryan.

'You know,' Chantelle backed up a step. 'I'm really in no hurry to have a second encounter ...'

Yaz quickly took in their surroundings. 'Ryan, if you circle round to the left and Graham, you head right, then we should be able cut off any chance it has of escaping down the alleyway.'

'And me?' asked Chantelle dubiously.

'Stay here. Stop it getting out this way.'

'What are you going to be doing?'

'I'll just go straight at it. With luck, one of us will be able to catch it. Now move. Quickly!'

Leaving Chantelle at the entrance to the recycling area, Yaz, Graham and Ryan started to spread out, using the various bins and skips as cover. As soon as she was happy that the other two had cut off any escape route, Yaz edged forward, trying to see if she could get a better look at whatever was hiding in the shadows.

As she approached, there was another scuffle from the bushes and an angry voice hissed at her. 'Go away! You'll scare them off!'

Yaz stopped, surprised. Whatever it was it certainly didn't sound like an alien. 'Who are you? What are you doing hiding down there?'

'*Go away!*'

Ryan and Graham had realised that something was up now, and had abandoned all attempts at stealth.

'That doesn't sound like an alien to me,' said Ryan striding over. 'It's just a tramp or something.'

'Come on out,' snapped Graham. 'Stop wasting our time.'

An angry, red-faced figure emerged from the bushes.

'I don't believe it,' Chantelle groaned. 'Kim Fortune. Again ...'

'I was just on the verge of capturing one of the creatures on film!' yelled Kim, waving a camera in Yaz's face. 'Three flippin' hours I've been waiting behind that skip.'

'You need to find yourself a better hobby, mate,' said Ryan with a snigger.

Kim glared at him. 'They're here, I tell you.'

'Yeah, right.'

Yaz sighed. 'We're not going to get anywhere like this.' She was about to suggest that they started looking in another part of the alleyway when there was a sudden explosion of movement and a small figure burst from behind one of the skips. Realising its escape route was blocked, it turned and hissed angrily, bright eyes blazing from beneath its dark hood.

'I don't believe it!' gasped Graham.

'That's one of them!' yelled Kim. 'Don't let it get away.'

The creature darted towards the entrance to the alleyway but Kim was determined not to let his scoop escape and lunged forward, catching the creature off balance. The two of them crashed to the wet tarmac.

'I've got it,' screamed Kim, the creature twisting madly in his grasp. 'Help me!'

Before the others could do anything, the creature gave an ear-splitting screech of rage and turned to face its captor, its mouth wide. A torrent of evil-smelling slime burst from its lips, splattering into Kim's face. He jerked back, screaming in horror, releasing his grasp on the creature and desperately trying to rub the thick liquid from his eyes.

'Urgh!' Graham recoiled in disgust. 'That's revolting!'

'Graham, help me!' yelled Yaz running forward to help clear the slime from Kim's nose and mouth.

The creature hissed angrily at them, slime dripping from its chin, then it turned and fled along the alleyway.

Ryan raced after it. 'I'll get it!'

'Ryan! No!' Graham cried out after him, but it was too late. The creature and Ryan had vanished into the blackness.

'Yaz.' Graham looked at her pleadingly. 'I'll deal with this. Get after him.'

Yaz scrambled to her feet. 'Chantelle, help Graham with Kim. Get that stuff off him.'

Without waiting for an answer, she hared off along the alleyway after Ryan. From the darkness ahead she could hear the creature screeching and angry shouts from Ryan.

'Oh, no you don't!'

In houses all along the alleyway lights were coming on in upstairs windows as people tried to see what the commotion was. Ahead she could see the cause of that commotion. The creature was trying to scramble to safety over a high, wooden fence. Ryan was hanging on to one of its legs.

As Yaz approached, he turned and flashed her a breathless, triumphant smile. 'I caught it!'

Before Yaz could reply there was the sound of splintering wood and the fence collapsed. Yaz caught a last fleeting glimpse of Ryan, his expression turning to one of shocked surprise before he and the diminutive alien vanished from view in an avalanche of fence panels.

'Ryan!'

Yaz dashed forward, skidding to a halt at the hole that had been created in the fence. Ryan and the hooded figure were tumbling wildly down a steep embankment. At the bottom of the slope Yaz could see the gleam of metal rails glinting under the streetlights. They were falling onto the tube tracks.

With no way of arresting his fall, Ryan crashed down hard onto the tracks. Yaz held her breath, praying that he realised the danger that he was in and kept his arms and legs clear from the live rail. Miraculously, both he and his quarry seemed to have avoided making contact.

Yaz scrambled through the gap in the fence, looking for a safe way to climb down and help him. As she did so there was the distant blare of a whistle and, to her horror, Yaz caught a glimpse of the bright lights of a tube train hurtling along the track towards the prone bodies of Ryan and the alien.

'Ryan!' she screamed. 'Get off the tracks!'

All thoughts for her own safety gone, she raced down the slope, half running, half falling. Below her she could see Ryan trying to get to his feet, but the train was so very, very fast ...

Yaz closed her eyes. There was the shriek of brakes, a horrible, high-pitched, keening scream and a sudden, deafening crack. Then there was silence. The air was filled with the horrible smell of charred flesh.

Terrified of what sight might greet her, Yaz opened her eyes. Ryan was standing to one side of the tracks, his hands shaking.

Relief washing over her, Yaz hurried over to him. 'Ryan, thank God! Are you OK?'

Ryan just nodded, traumatised by his narrow escape. He was staring at something on the tracks. Yaz followed his gaze, bile rising in her throat.

Whereas Ryan had escaped by the narrowest of margins the hooded figure hadn't been so lucky. The wheels of the tube train had virtually cut it in half and what was left was definitely not human ... The lower half was wearing jeans, sure, but there was a long rope of a tail hanging out from the back of the waistband – and the top half looked far more like some kind of giant, misshapen rat.

Yaz and Ryan looked at each other. 'I think we'd better call the Doctor,' said Ryan quietly.

CHAPTER TWELVE

A little over an hour later, everyone was back at Ace's laboratory at Kirkwood Farm. The tube-track accident meant that Perivale was now swarming with police and London Transport officials and so Ace had decided that the safest thing was for everyone to relocate until things calmed down a bit. The last thing they wanted at this stage was the police or some other organisation getting involved. With no obvious casualty, the authorities would hopefully come to the conclusion that it was just trespassers on the track – a common enough occurrence – and things would quickly return to normal.

There *had* been a casualty, of course, and that casualty was currently laid out on a laboratory bench being examined by the Doctor. Ace was busying herself analysing the slime that had been scraped from Kim Fortune, pointing out, when the Doctor had looked surprised, that chemistry *was* the one thing that she'd actually taken an interest in at school.

Kim himself was perched on a stool on the far side of the laboratory wearing a disposable paper boiler suit. His clothes had been saturated in the slime and Ace had had to bundle them into a hazardous waste container to stop them stinking out the workshop. She couldn't imagine how unpleasant the drive from London must have been for the others – nor how Sanaul would react to the mess inside the Range Rover.

Kim was staring around the workshop like a kid who had just been let loose in Santa's toy workshop. Letting him into her batcave was a gamble, but Ace had figured it was less of a gamble than leaving him on his own back in Perivale, especially if the authorities were crawling over everything. For the sake of security, however, she had insisted that he'd been blindfolded on the journey here. He'd resisted that, of course, complaining that he was perfectly trustworthy, but apparently when Graham had given him the alternative option of being locked into the Range Rover boot for the journey he'd quickly agreed to the blindfold.

Graham was still fussing over Ryan. The lad had had a lucky escape by the sound of it; another second and there might have been two bodies to deal with. Ryan was making light of it, of course, embarrassed by the attention that his granddad was paying to him. A lot of that bravado seemed to be for Chantelle's benefit; he was obviously smitten.

For her part, Chantelle didn't seem to be too bothered by Ryan's clumsy attempts at flirting. Far from it. In fact she seem to have taken a bit of a shine to him too. Ace smiled to herself. Given her track record – and although he was way too young for her – she could probably do a lot worse.

Yaz was with the Doctor, watching the autopsy intently. Ace wanted to like the girl, she really did, but Yaz wasn't making it easy. She seemed suspicious of everything. The two of them needed to sit down and have a proper talk at some point.

Ace sighed. There was too much else to concentrate on to worry about that right now. She turned her attention back to the readout on the benchtop spectrometer. She'd run several tests on the unpleasant slime on the assumption that it was venom of some kind, but the results were indicating something different.

She opened the centrifuge and lifted out one of the test tubes, holding it up to her nose. Despite the fact that over an hour had gone by, the mucus was still as pungent as before.

'Professor?'

'Hmm?' The Doctor didn't look up from her work.

'I don't think this is a venom at all.'

'Oh?'

'I think it's some kind of hormonal scent marker.'

That got the Doctor's attention. 'Really?' Putting down her scalpel she joined Ace at the spectroscope, slipping on a pair of wire-rimmed spectacles and peering intently at the readout. 'You're right. Pheromones, volatile hydrocarbons ... It does seem to be some kind of tracking marker.'

'So the abducted girls were tagged for collection?' Yaz had joined them too. 'Could that ship be a collection device of some kind?'

Ace was impressed; Yaz really didn't miss anything. 'All right.' Ace nodded at the alien body on the bench. 'So we know that *it* is using its saliva as some kind of marker. Any idea what *it* is yet?'

The Doctor nodded. 'It's a Ratt. It looks so messed up because we caught it mid transformation.'

'Transformation?' Ace frowned. 'It's a shapeshifter?'

'More of a therianthrope. Like Ogrons or Quarks, they're used by various nasty races as hench-aliens for hire. They don't have advanced shapeshifting ability, but it can certainly hop between humanoid and animal form. It was obviously trying to transform back into its animal state when the train hit it. Messy.'

'So all those rat sightings ...'

'Oh, that's gross.' Chantelle had overheard them. 'Are you saying that all of those rats we've been getting around the estate might be aliens?'

'What is it they say? You're never more than six feet from a rat?' Graham gave a low whistle. 'That's a lot of aliens ...'

'And that's just in London,' Ryan said. 'Think of all the other cities of the world with rat problems.'

'And abductions?' Kim had appeared between Ryan and Chantelle. 'I've seen figures that show unexplained disappearances in big cities all around the globe.'

Before the discussion could go any further, there was a loud rap on the door. Everyone turned to look at Ace.

'You get visitors in your secret lab?' The Doctor raised a quizzical eyebrow.

Ace grinned at her. There was only one person it could possibly be. She hurried over to the door and unlocked it.

Will Buckland was standing there holding the silver box containing the Squidget.

'Hello, Will. How's my car?'

Will grinned and kissed her on the cheek. 'Glad to see that you've got your priorities right. Your car is fine. No concern that I got back to Earth OK?'

'Why should I have?' asked Ace. 'Aren't you "the most qualified astronaut that ever lived"?'

'I think that was the *Time* headline, yes ...'

'Well then ...' Ace ushered him into the workshop, closing the door behind him. 'You know everyone, I think?'

'Yeah,' Will looked around the room. 'Quite the party.' His smile faded as he spotted Kim Fortune. 'Although I'm surprised that some people made the guest list.'

'Don't worry about him,' said Ace, relieving Will of the box. 'He's not going to give us any trouble.'

'Especially now my show's been canned,' Kim said miserably. 'After just a pilot. The channel hated it ...'

'Maybe bigger problems to deal with, right now, eh?' Ace interrupted.

'Oh, sure,' said Kim, 'it suits you, doesn't it, the truth going unsaid—'

'Kim, you want truth, try shutting up and you might see it.' Ace placed the box on top of one of the workbenches and unclipped the top. Immediately there was a happy-sounding burble from the Squidget.

'What on earth?' Graham looked up in alarm.

'Oh! Brilliant!' The Doctor hurried over and peered into the box.

'Ugh!' Chantelle wrinkled her nose in disgust as Ace lifted the Squidget out. 'What is it?'

'It's Ace's Squidget! A biomechanical multi-function universal interface,' cooed the Doctor, waggling a finger delightedly at the Squidget. 'And he's a beauty! Can I hold him?'

'Sure,' said Ace letting the Doctor take the wriggling grub from her. 'Watch out for slime on your coat.'

'He seems happy to be home,' said Will watching the Doctor fuss over the alien device. 'We didn't get so much as a squeak out of him once I'd landed back at Devesham ...'

'Really?' Ace did her best to sound innocent. 'I guess that he must have been tired after a trip to the Moon and back.'

Realising that he wasn't going to get any more out of her, Will turned his attention to the rest of the workshop. His eyes widened as he caught sight of the deformed alien corpse in the laboratory. 'You've been busy.' He peered at the corpse with interest. 'So are those the things that built the ship?'

The Doctor shook her head 'No, I don't think so. The technology on board that spaceship was incredibly sophisticated, Ratts aren't capable of building something like that.' She gave a sigh of frustration. 'I wish we had more info about it ...'

'Well, I might be able to help with that.' Will reached into his jacket pocket and removed a sheaf of paper. 'I thought that there was something about our mysterious alien ship that seemed familiar. Sam did a bit of digging into the Space Defence Centre records and found this ...'

He handed the piece of paper to the Doctor who quickly scanned its contents.

'It's been here before,' she said, quietly. 'Over 30 years ago.'

'Thirty years?' Ace felt her stomach lurch.

Will nodded. 'It appeared out of nowhere in an identical orbit around the Moon, and then vanished just as suddenly, leaving a weird energy signature that has been baffling scientists ever since.'

'Ace ...' The Doctor glanced over at Ace, her expression serious. 'I think you'd better have a look at this.'

Heart pounding, Ace took the paper from her, already knowing what she was going to see. She glanced at the date on the top of the memo.

14 September 1987.

'That's the day before I was taken from Earth.' She stared at the Doctor in disbelief. 'It's all connected. The station up there, the abducted girls, the time-storm that took me to Iceworld. *Everything* is connected.'

'Hang on,' Yaz had been listening to every word. 'Are you saying that you know where the abductees have been taken? This Iceworld place?'

'Sounds like a supermarket chain,' chipped in Ryan.

The Doctor shook her head. 'Iceworld was just where Ace was taken to. The ship ... the *collector* ... is some kind of booster relay. Maybe ... once the target has been scent marked by the creatures, it can lock onto them and beam them to their final destination. Given the size and power of the collector, the final destination could be anywhere in the universe.'

'Then let's find it.' Ace's shock was quickly turning to anger. She had initially believed that what had happened to her had been an accident, some freak trick that the universe had played on her. Whisked from her bedroom and dumped on an alien planet light years from home, forced to fend for herself, forced into demeaning jobs to earn enough to buy food to eat and have somewhere to sleep. Then she had met the Doctor and learnt that she had been the pawn of some ancient evil entity – one of the Wolves of Fenric. Now to discover that she might have just been one of hundreds …

She screwed up the paper angrily. 'There's only one sure way of finding out where those people have been taken, isn't there?'

The Doctor glanced across at the eviscerated corpse and nodded. 'Yeah …'

'Oh no …' Graham gave a groan of despair. 'I know what you're going to do. You're going to set bait.'

'It's the only way.' Ace looked at Yaz and Ryan. 'But no one is going to force you two to do this if you don't want to.' She looked pointedly at the Doctor. 'No one gets talked into anything.'

The Doctor opened her mouth to protest, and then thought better of it.

'I'm up for it,' said Ryan defiantly.

'Yes.' Yaz nodded. 'Me too.'

'OK then.' The Doctor placed the Squidget back into its box. 'I've got some homing tags in the TARDIS. I'll go and get them …'

As the Doctor vanished inside the TARDIS, Graham turned angrily to Ace. 'Now wait a minute. Why does it have to be these two? Why not you, or me or the Doctor or your astronaut pal?'

'Wrong demographic,' Ace explained matter-of-factly. 'Yaz and Ryan are closest in age to the other abductees. We'll mark them with some of the mucus from the shapeshifter, take them to different locations and wait for them to be abducted. The Doctor can track them and then we can follow on in the TARDIS, rescue the abductees and deal with whoever is behind all this.'

'Wait …' Ryan suddenly looked uncomfortable. 'You're going to smear me with some of that gunk? Gunk that came out of that rat-thing's *mouth*?'

'C'mon Ryan.' Yaz grinned at him impishly. 'That aftershave you used to use smelled worse than that.'

Ryan glared at her, aware that Chantelle was watching him in amusement. 'That stuff was a present from my gran!'

The Doctor re-emerged from the TARDIS clutching a couple of complex-looking devices resembling diver's wristwatches built into a red tubular casing. 'Here we go.'

Ace took one of them from her and turned it over in her hands admiringly. 'Neat. Are they going to have the range?'

The Doctor nodded vigorously. 'Ought to ...'

Ace tossed the tracking device to Ryan to who caught it clumsily, almost dropping it. 'OK, we'll try two locations and see if we get lucky. Ryan, you go with Chantelle back to Perivale. Yaz, you can come with me. We'll head back to my place. Will, you should get back to the Space Defence Centre. We need eyes on the ground back here.'

Graham sighed. 'Looks like you're stuck with me again, Doc. What do we do?'

'The dream team!' The Doctor grinned. 'We go back to the station and get ready to track Yaz and Ryan. That station collects matter transmitted from Earth and boosts it onwards through the unknown. We need to know where the abductees are going.'

'What about me?' piped up Kim Fortune. 'You're not going to leave me here, are you?'

Ace looked at him, pathetic in his disposable overalls. The last few hours had certainly taken away the man's bravado but there was no way she was going to leave him alone here.

'You need to go home, Kim. Go home and say nothing about any of this. You can go with Chantelle and Ryan.'

'But surely—'

'Surely, nothing!' Ace retorted, recent revelations making her tone harsher than she intended. 'You talk to *anyone* about this and you could ruin *everything*. We've probably got one shot at getting those girls back: you do anything to jeopardise that ...'

She left the threat hanging. She was in no mood to have to deal with any nonsense from Kim Fortune at the moment.

'It'll be all right, Kim,' Yaz said more softly, putting a hand on his shoulders. 'You could use some rest ...'

Ace almost snorted. Let the girl soft-soap him! She hadn't been hounded by the man for interviews time and again. Shrugging into another disposable paper suit she helped the Doctor wrap up the dissected body of the Ratt and moved it into one of the laboratory freezers. Yet another alien loose end for her to tidy up once this was over. At least she knew the name of this particular breed.

Once the body was packed away she decanted some of the slime from the creature into a couple of plastic containers. Stuffing one of them into a canvas holdall she was about to turn and call Ryan over for the other one when she found Yaz standing there.

Ace held out the bottle. 'Can you give this to Ryan?'

Yaz took it, obviously wanting to say something.

Ace was starting to tire of this. 'Do we have a problem?'

'Are you certain that your friend's the best person to pair with Ryan?' Yaz looked over to where Chantelle was standing. 'She seems like a bit of an ...'

'Airhead?' It was obvious to Ace where this was going. 'Let me ask you something. Do you trust Ryan?'

'Yes, of course.'

'I mean really trust him. With your life.'

'Yes!'

'Well, I trust Chantelle, OK? And that's all you need to know. This works both ways, Yaz. You know nothing about me or my friends, I get that, but I know nothing about you lot either. You're with the Doctor, so that's good enough for me. I would hope it would be good enough for you too.'

Before Yaz could respond, Ace turned and opened one of the tall fridges, lifting out one of the boxes of Nitro-90. She removed several small spheres and slipped them into pocket-sized containers that she had designed specially to transport the explosives safely. Ignoring the look Yaz was giving her, she slid the containers into her bag. She didn't care what Yaz thought of her. This was her choice, her responsibility, her insurance in case things went pear-shaped. She had her own ways of making sure everyone was kept safe.

She turned back to Yaz. 'I'll have a quick word with Ryan and Chantelle, OK? Check we all know just what we're doing.'

'Right,' Yaz said. 'Um … thanks.'

'I do responsible pretty well these days.' Ace smiled, swinging the bag up onto her shoulder. 'Let's get this done.'

Chapter Thirteen

Ace had found the drive from Oxfordshire back to central London a long and awkward one, and she guessed Yaz felt the same. Any attempts at casual conversation had been half-hearted, and had quickly petered out. In the end both of them had given up, the silence just building the tension between them.

By the time Ace pulled up in the basement of the Charitable Earth building, they hadn't spoken a word to each other for nearly an hour. Hoisting the holdall onto her shoulder, she led the way over to the lift and pressed the button for the 18th floor. As the lift sped its way towards the top floor, she decided that it was time to sort this problem out once and for all.

The doors opened and they stepped out into the penthouse apartment. Sorin was sitting directly in front of the lift staring at them balefully. Ace knew that there was no way that Sanaul wouldn't have been checking in on him whilst she had been away, but she also knew that the cat would act as though he'd been utterly abandoned and would treat her accordingly for the next couple of hours at the very least – probably days. Scratching him behind the ears, she placed the bag on the floor and extracted the bottle of mucus and a tracking device. Sorin sniffed at them both suspiciously, then turned tail and stalked off into the shadows.

Yaz had crossed to the full-length windows and was staring out at the city. 'Nice view.' Try as she might, she couldn't hide the fact that she was impressed.

That, thought Ace, was a good sign; someone who appreciated a good view couldn't be all bad.

'It's even better from the roof.' Ace crossed to a door in the far wall and unlocked it, handing the bottle and the tracker to Yaz. 'Don't open the bottle in the apartment. I'll be up in a minute.'

Yaz hesitated for a moment then nodded and made her way up the narrow stairs.

Ace watched her go, then stepped back into the apartment, picked up the holdall and made her way up to her bedroom.

Dumping the holdall on the bed, she stared at her reflection in the mirror. God, she looked tired. She had forgotten what life with the Doctor was like. No wonder her travelling companions were getting younger – they had to be, just to keep up with her. She figured that Graham had to be permanently knackered. The thought of him made her smile.

She picked up a small, spherical pendant on a chain from the bedside table, removed one of the marbles from her holdall, snapped open the pendant and slipped the Nitro ball inside. Then she closed the pendant up again and hung it around her neck.

As she crossed to the door, a dark shape in the corner of the room caught her eye. Her old jacket. For all her complaints, being around the Doctor made you feel … young again.

On impulse she lifted the jacket from its hook and slipped it on. It had been 30 years since she had last worn it and it felt like yesterday. She was suddenly aware that putting it on meant something.

It was time to put old demons to bed.

*

Graham stood in the monitor room of the alien transit station, tapping his toe against a gristly fold in the floor. It made a quiet, obscene squelching noise that was horrible but somehow compulsive.

The place was a pit, and he hated it. Alien ships that were plastic and metal could be cold and creepy but at least Graham understood something of what held them together. They were just your space equivalent of buses, only with star bells and warp whistles and galactic go-faster stripes. Even the TARDIS, for all its glowing crystal immensity, was packed with tech. The station, though, felt all wrong. Standing there, Graham felt like a bug in the middle of a burnt-black steak that had been chewed up and spat out, and you didn't know when sharp teeth might bite down again.

He looked at the blue block of the TARDIS, savoured its paintwork, windows and solid straight lines, a sane refuge in this damp cavern of a craft. Wires and cables snaked out of the open doors to a console on a stand, the size and shape of a portable barbecue. The Doctor stood hunched over it; the Squidget was perched on top of a clunky old computer monitor, its thin tentacles connecting it to the weirdly rippling walls of the spacecraft.

'How's it going now, Doc?' Graham asked.

'Won't be long,' she responded. 'Good boy. Clever boy!'

'Eh? What did I do?'

'I'm talking to Squidget!' The Doctor flashed Graham a look like he was crazy. 'He's managing to link this ship's operating systems to my little porta-console here so I can trace the homing tags in real time. No mean feat.'

'Is that why you're using that ancient TV as a readout?' asked Graham. 'So the tech's as basic a link for that thing as possible?'

'Good boy!' the Doctor cried. 'Clever boy!'

'Blimey, get a room, you two.'

'I was talking to you, Graham!' the Doctor protested. 'You're spot on. This monitor's my way of making little Squidget's job simpler. Oh, you're a pet. What a clever boy.'

Graham smiled to himself. 'All right, you don't have to overdo it.'

'I'm talking to Squidget!' said the Doctor.

With a sigh, Graham wandered back into the TARDIS. The control room hummed and glowed, clean and warm and quiet. Too quiet. He missed Ryan and Yaz, their voices and banter, filling up the space.

He walked up to the two-way comms link and flicked the switch. "Ere, Will. You reading me? Over.'

The voice of Will Buckland crackled from the speaker. '*Space Defence Centre receiving you, Graham, go ahead. Though we don't normally respond to "'Ere". Everything all right? Over.*'

'Risking Yaz and Ryan's lives is not all right,' Graham said flatly. No reply came, so he added, 'Over.'

'*I don't like it either. Untrained civilians taking such a lead in this? It's madness. Over.*'

'Yaz and Ryan are more trained in weird space stuff than anyone else on the planet,' Graham retorted. 'Except maybe your ex-ladyfriend. Over.'

'*And she breaks every rule going. Did you want something in particular, Graham? Over.*'

A bit of company, if I'm honest, thought Graham. 'Just checking you're still keeping an eye on us,' he said. 'Did the Chinese manage to get their rocket off the ground?'

'*Not as far as we can tell. They're not saying anything publicly, but it looks like technical problems.*'

'Well, if it launches, the Doc'll need to know about it. Over.'

'*She will,*' Will confirmed. '*But for the moment planet Earth is sleeping soundly. I'm starting to think I might never sleep again, however. Out.*'

'Out,' Graham echoed, and headed for the doors as if it had been a command.

The Doctor was gazing at her screen, which was aglow with green numbers on a black background. In the centre, like a sweeping second hand on a clock, a needle described a circle in a steady radar sweep. Constellations of tiny yellow dots littered the background.

'We're good to go,' the Doctor announced. 'So long as the homing tags are working, when Ryan and Yaz get spacenapped I can follow them anywhere.'

'And they *are* working, right?' Graham said anxiously.

The Doctor hit a button on the console, and two white blobs stood out in a field of static. 'Yes! We're all good.'

'What if they fall off or conk out?'

'Not a chance. These tags are conflict-grade life-beacons used by the Hondopel Peace Corps in search and rescue expeditions across the battlespaces of the Andromeda galaxy.'

Graham raised his eyebrows. 'You mean, they're basically army surplus?'

'I mean they can only be deactivated by the wearer inputting the proper code.' The Doctor gave him a reassuring smile. 'To remove one by force is considered a war crime. You don't mess with the Hondopels.'

'But won't these Honda-things come looking for him?'

'I tweaked the signal so it's sending out on unofficial frequencies,' she said smugly.

'OK, but you know how clumsy Ryan can be,' Graham persisted. 'What if the beacon gets damaged?'

'They're designed to withstand practically anything. Laser blasts, radiation, cellular disruption, alien mucus ... even your bog-standard explosion—'

A noise like thunder rumbled through the twisted fleshy walls. Both the Doctor and Graham were thrown to the sticky floor as a savage blast shook the station.

Graham groaned, rolling onto his back. 'Explosion, you say?'

'I wish I hadn't.' The Doctor was back on her feet, quick as a cat. 'Speak of an explosion and an explosion appears! That's the old saying, isn't it—?'

Another giant impact flung her forward, face-first into the side of the TARDIS. Graham felt the floor flex beneath him and then buck him to his knees as the aftershocks tore through the infrastructure. 'It's "Speak of the devil",' Graham shouted.

'It'd better not be him again,' the Doctor muttered.

A horrible hooting noise ripped through the room. Graham clutched his ears, not sure if this was some sort of siren or the station itself screaming in pain.

'Get on to Will, see what's happening,' the Doctor shouted over the din, fingers flickering over her console. 'I'll see if Squidgy here can pull up an external feed …'

'Gotcha, Doc.' Graham scrambled up, dived back through the TARDIS doors and threw himself onto the communicator. 'Will, what the hell! We've been hit twice. Thought you had eyes on us, mate? Over!'

'*Nothing's been launched from down here, Graham.*' Will's calm voice carried over the speakers. '*Whatever's hit you, it came from space. Nothing's showing on radar. Other scans running now. Over.*'

Graham waited tensely, cold sweat inching down his back.

'*Mass anomaly detected together with two huge radiation spikes. Looks like some kind of spacecraft just opened fire on you and it's closing fast.*'

'Over,' Graham breathed, in unison with Will. The wailing noise from outside suddenly stopped, leaving only the sickly background hum of the station systems, edged now by a catching, skittering note. He turned and ran back outside.

The Doctor stood in front of the screen, sonic screwdriver raised in one hand. 'That's better!' she said brightly. 'Now we can hear ourselves think.'

'Doc,' Graham said, 'Will reckons it's aliens attacking us!'

'Wish I hadn't heard *that*. P'raps I should turn on the alarm again.' Her fingers buzzed over the console's buttons. 'What've we got, then, some kind of invisibility screen, shielding them from us …?' She waved the sonic like she was warding off a wasp.

The station shook again with a muffled clang that rang like a bell chime underwater.

Graham was pleased to have kept his footing. 'That blast wasn't as bad as the others,' he said hopefully.

'That's because it wasn't a blast.' The Doctor bit her lip. 'It was them docking.'

'You mean they're coming aboard?' Graham stared aghast. 'Who are they? What are they after?'

'Questions, questions. Let's start with the easy one. Who are they?' The Doctor made an adjustment to the sonic and buzzed it at the screen, which was showing nothing but stars in space. 'If I can just disrupt their cloaking thingie we should get a proper look at them ...'

Space on the screen rippled and suddenly a shining spacecraft was revealed, looming close. It was a large spherical design with ornate latticework, spinning through space.

'Oh no ...' said the Doctor quietly. 'It's an Astingir ship.'

Graham was none the wiser, but didn't like the tone her voice had taken. 'Is that, like, a space adjective?'

'The Astingir are a persecuted race. They became reluctant warriors.'

'Reluctant? They just gave us both barrels!'

'They gave this *station* both barrels,' the Doctor corrected him, 'not us.' She looked rapt, thinking hard. 'Of course, this must be *Wraith* technology.'

'Must be what now?' Graham was struggling to keep up.

'The Wraiths! A vicious, space-going race with a penchant for attacking interstellar empires that had grown too big to be effectively governed, inefficient, past their prime. They swept through the Astingir system, destroyed and subjugated its people.'

'But the Astingir retaliated, yeah?' Graham gestured to the screen. 'Or else how are they attacking us now?'

'They won the war, in the end,' the Doctor agreed. 'But that wasn't enough for all of them. I know that some dedicated their continued existence to erasing all trace of the Wraiths from the universe.'

'Well, just tell them we're nothing to do with these Wraith things,' said Graham.

'I'm not sure they'll believe us.' The Doctor looked oddly guilty and turned quickly to the screen, crossing her fingers and almost hopping with barely repressed energy. 'Come on, Yaz! Come on, Ryan! Get yourself safely kidnapped and I'll be straight after you …'

'Well. Perhaps these Astingir things don't even know that we're here,' Graham suggested.

'*Attention!*' came a deep husky voice, amplified and echoing through the station. '*You are advised that this structure has been confiscated pending demolition and is now property of the Astingir Sovereignty. Your presence here, and preliminary DNA scan, marks you as alien collaborators with the Wraith species. Your surrender is required.*'

Graham sighed. 'They know we're here.'

'*The punishment for collaboration …*' The voice faltered, as if reading from a script: '*… under Article 17 of the Reconstruction Accord, is incarceration, trial and life imprisonment. If you fail to surrender, you will be executed.*' The speaker gave a throaty rumble, almost a whinny. '*Prepare to be boarded.*'

'Well, that's just marvellous.' Graham looked at her helplessly. 'What do we do now?'

'They're a very intelligent race. They suffered very badly through the war. It's left them … unfriendly to outsiders.' The Doctor's mind was racing. 'Thing is, the Wraiths are all gone, trapped forever where no one can get at them. That's why it never even occurred to me that this station would be Wraith in design. Who could gain access to Wraith technology …?'

Graham shrugged. 'Surely if the tech was left behind, just abandoned, then anyone could've taken it.'

'Not without a genetic data stamp to gain full access to the systems.'

'Well maybe they've got an even better squidgy wotsit than Ace has.' Graham pointed to the quivering interface. 'Doc, whoever took this thing, we're the ones who're gonna carry the can. What do we *do*?'

'*I* will go and have a chinwag with their boarding party,' the Doctor declared. 'You stay here and watch those controls. The tags will start transmitting the moment Ryan and Yaz leave Earth. When the red light there comes on, it means they're on the move and you need to pull down on this lever to capture the transmat signature, that's the thing we'll need to follow.' She tapped a chrome handle set into the console. 'Ah, I do love me a lever. So. Got it?'

Graham ran over the procedure in his head once more, and nodded. 'Got it.'

'First, though – got a hanky anywhere, Graham, and something to tie it to? I'm gonna need a white flag ...'

Chapter Fourteen

Ace made her way back downstairs, grabbed two glasses from the rack in the kitchen and a bottle from the fridge and then joined Yaz up on the roof.

She found her on one of the long rattan couches that were dotted around the edge of the roof terrace, staring over the parapet at the glistening Thames far below. It was cold, her breath forming clouds around her head; Ace was glad for the jacket on a practical level, feeling it snug around her. She set the two glasses down on the table beside her and unscrewed the cap of the bottle.

Yaz frowned. 'I don't drink alcohol.'

'Good thing this is fizzy grape juice, then.' Ace poured two glasses, handed one to Yaz and then sat down next to her. 'Cheers.'

The two of them clinked glasses, the frown still not leaving Yaz's face. Ace leaned back in her seat, sipping at her drink. 'We've not got off to the best of starts, have we?'

'I guess not.'

'Well, that's a shame, because I think we have a lot in common.'

'Hardly!' Yaz gave a snort of amusement. 'You're a multimillionaire, I'm ...'

'What? What are you exactly? Beyond being someone who travels with the Doctor, that is?'

'I'm a police officer,' said Yaz proudly.

'Really?' Ace raised an eyebrow.

Yaz bristled. 'A *probationary* police officer, but all the same ...'

'All right, don't get so defensive. I spent a lot of time around of police officers when I was younger, that's all.'

'Why doesn't that surprise me?'

Ace ignored the jibe. 'I just wish they'd been a bit more like you.'

'Oh. Why?'

'Because they might have understood ...'

'Understood what?'

'What I was feeling.' Ace took a deep breath. 'I was 13. I had a friend a lot like you ... She died. Burnt to death in a racist arson attack on the flat where she was sleeping.'

'Oh ...' Yaz's face softened. 'I'm sorry. Did they get the people who did it? I mean, you didn't ...' She tailed off.

Ace gave a barking laugh. 'You think I went all "vengeance is mine" on them? Hunted them down and killed them? You really don't think much of me, do you? No. The police caught them. The three of them spent a year in a young offenders institute and that was it.' She stared out into the night for a time. 'I took out my anger on a derelict Victorian manor house.'

'You blew it up?'

'I wish.' Ace took a sip of her drink. 'No, I burnt it down. Got charged with arson.'

'OK, I get the reasons, but why are you messing with explosives now? I mean, you run a charity, that's not a front, is it?'

Ace frowned. 'Course it isn't!'

'So why are you making your own Improvised Explosive Devices?' Yaz put down her glass, staring at Ace with a confused look. 'I mean, in normal circumstances that would class you as a terrorist ...'

'But circumstances are anything but normal with us, aren't they? We hang around with the Doctor, we know how dangerous the world is. I just like to make sure I have some insurance, for when it's needed.'

'Even so ...' Yaz obviously wasn't convinced.

'You actually sound like the Doctor.' Ace gave her a mirthless smile. 'Look, I was 16 when I joined the Doctor. "No Nitro-9, Ace," he told me. Sixteen ... and he leaves me to fight off a squad of Cybermen with nothing but a handful of gold coins and a catapult. But when he was in danger, he was the first to use my homemade explosives.'

'No way,' said Yaz.

'The Doctor is more than happy to use weapons of mass destruction when it suits him ...' She corrected herself: 'Her. She just likes the moral high ground of getting someone else to carry them on her behalf.'

Yaz shook her head. 'I don't believe that. She despises violence ...'

'Until it's necessary!' Ace leaned forward. 'Has she ever told you about some of the things she's done? She tricked the Cybermen into destroying their entire space fleet; hundreds of spacecraft, thousands of Cybermen, wiped out. She destroyed the Daleks' home planet Skaro using a weapon she helped to design, just to stop them using it themselves. An entire planet and everyone on it!'

'An entire planet?' Yaz sounded less certain now. 'I thought that destroying one Dalek using a microwave was pretty bad ...'

'Ha! So what was that you were saying about improvised devices? And I bet she wasn't the one who had the microwave ...'

'No.' Yaz shook her head sadly. 'It was Ryan's dad.'

'You see!' cried Ace. 'It's always the same. I didn't see it at first, but gradually ...'

'Is that why you left?' asked Yaz.

Ace nodded. 'We were escaping from a tricky situation. The Doctor used me. People died.'

'People?'

'Well, aliens. They looked sort of like horses … but they were still people.' She closed her eyes, remembering the horror of the moment.

'Dorothy …'

The sound of a woman's voice calling her name made her start. She looked around in surprise, trying to locate the source of the voice.

Yaz looked at her curiously. 'Are you all right?'

'Didn't you hear that?'

'Hear what?'

Before Ace could reply, the call came again, echoing from the stairwell, distant, but urgent. 'Dorothy …'

Ace got up from her seat and began to make her way towards the door. The voice called her name again, sharper now, angrier.

'Dorothy! Answer me!'

Dorothy stopped dead, the blood draining from her face. The voice was unmistakable. The same disapproving tone she remembered from her childhood. It was the voice of her mother.

'Are you OK?' Yaz was getting concerned now.

Dorothy just stared at her. What could she say? That she thought that her mother was here? Her estranged mother.

Her *dead* estranged mother.

Shock turning to anger, Dorothy turned and strode towards the voice. If someone was playing games with her then they were going to regret it.

Now her senses were being overwhelmed by the smell of nitric acid and the past exploded into her head. It was as if she was back in her bedroom again, perfecting her homemade explosive in the improvised laboratory she had set up.

'Are you stinking the house out again with those horrible chemicals of yours?'

Her eyes began to stream, but Dorothy couldn't tell if it was because of the nitric acid or because of the sheer strength of the moment. With a cry of despair she ran forward, fists clenched, all the resentment of childhood that she had thought had been successfully buried surging to the surface once more.

'Who are you?' she yelled. 'Why are you doing this?'

Then something the Doctor had said in the batcave came back to her: 'Time Dilation Syndrome.' Graham might have switched off the cloaking shields in the present but the effect had tumbled through to the past.

What was being switched on now that was bringing her own personal past back to haunt her?

The Doctor strode down the station's sinewy corridors, sonic in one hand and white flag – a slightly used hanky tied to an old car aerial – in the other. Everything depended, she knew, on how deeply the Astingir had scanned the station. If they already knew who she was, no words would make a difference.

She was dead.

Before long she reached the cavernous space that formed the Functional Abyss – the charged space at the station's core. The Doctor felt the hairs on the back of her neck stand up at the potential of the place: soon, enough subatomic particles would be crunched to bore a quantum portal through local space-time. Whatever was collected from the Earth below would arrive here and the transmat signal, boosted a quintillion-fold, would shoot it across the stars to wherever it was expected.

If the Astingir had come here, the Doctor reasoned, then perhaps they knew the destination of the transmat and were following the trail backwards. If they could be persuaded to part with that info, it could save a lot of faffing about. They could pool their resources, find whoever was responsible for the abductions from Earth and rescue those who'd been taken. The Astingir would make good allies.

Unless, again, they knew who she was.

The Doctor thought of Ace and sighed. *I should never have let you go, that day*, she thought. She closed her eyes.

A sudden thick stench of burning flesh caught in her nostrils, stinging her from her reverie. A huge chunk of burnt-toffee bone fell smoking from the wall beside her. On the other side she glimpsed two golden hooves glowing white with energy; a clatter, and a dark, equine head pushed through the smoke. The eyes were dark and gleaming, the mane plaited with thin strips of white metal, which denoted rank as well as giving armoured protection.

'Greetings … Legate, is it?' The Doctor beamed and waved her white flag. 'Nice to meet you, I'm the Doctor.'

The equine creature in the golden armour moved back and was lost from her sight. The rest of the wall quivered and shook and finally collapsed. The Legate stood in the doorway; behind her, two more Astingir were rearing up as if ready to trample anyone in their path.

The creatures looked like centaurs, only horsier: each possessed the four legs and body of a stallion, with an armoured humanoid torso rising where the neck should have been. The arms and hands were like those of a weightlifter, and that horse-like head sat between the shoulders. Each of the Astingir held an ornate metal spear in both hands; like the creatures themselves, beautiful but deadly.

'So!' the Doctor said cheerily. 'Basically, I'd like to surrender, while maintaining the charges against me and my pal are wrong. See, you don't fully understand the situation – not your fault; I don't even understand it myself, and if *I* don't understand it yet, well, who can? I'm on the case and I promise to share the moment I know what's going on. We can sit down – well, stand about – and chew the hay, sort things out … Deal?'

The Legate, still gripping her spear in her hands, raised a gold-shod hoof as if in greeting, or salute. The Doctor's hopes rose and she grinned and waved. But then she heard the hum of electronics, the flash of lights transmitting data in the intricate armour over the Legate's haunches. The spear lit a sudden blood-red.

'Scan confirms intruder's identity,' the Legate said brusquely. 'Centaurions: kill it.'

'Bye, then!' The Doctor turned and ran. The Astingir roared as they reared up and clattered after her in pursuit.

And in the heart of the Functional Abyss, flickers of energy began to dance.

CHAPTER FIFTEEN

In the penthouse apartment downstairs the door to Ace's office swung open and Sanaul peered into the darkness. 'Miss Dorothy?'

Getting no reply, he was about to turn on the lights when a dark shape caught his attention. Sorin was sitting on the other side of the room staring at the air-conditioning grille in the wall, his tail flicking to and fro.

'Sorin?'

The cat ignored him, not even an ear twitching in his direction. Sanaul frowned. Sorin usually came running whenever he appeared, demanding food and attention. For him to be ignored so completely was unusual to say the least. Sanaul crossed to where the cat was sitting, crouching down to see what had captured the cat's attention.

'What have you found there?'

The cat suddenly made a noise that was part growl, part hiss, his ears flattening against his head. Sanaul looked at him in surprise; Sorin was such a good-natured cat that he rarely ever hissed, let alone made a sound like that. Sanaul reached out to try and calm him when a sudden noise from inside the air-conditioning grille made him freeze.

It sounded like claws on metal.

Lots of claws.

Before Sanaul could think about what to do next, the grille practically exploded off the wall, and a tide of dark furry bodies tumbled into the room. With a yowl of sheer terror, Sorin turned and fled. Sanaul recoiled in disgust as the rats swarmed around his feet. His disgust turned to terror as, one by one, the rats started to snap and contort, transforming into hunched, demonic-looking figures.

As they reached out for him with dirty, clawed hands, Sanaul screamed.

The terrified cry from downstairs seemed to bring Ace out of her nightmare.

'Sanaul?'

Ace raced for the stairs, leaping down them two at a time. Yaz hared after her.

The sight that met them at the bottom was like a vision of hell.

The rat-creatures were everywhere, chattering to each other in low sibilant voices, their pungent smell filling the apartment. Yaz could see a man crouched in a corner, his suit torn and, his olive skin streaked with blood from dozens of cuts. One of the Ratts was holding Ace's cat by the scruff of the neck.

Ace gave a scream of rage, pushed to the very limit of her control.

'How *dare* you!'

The Ratts turned in unison to stare at her. The one holding Sorin gave a hiss of pleasure and released the terrified cat, who fled out through an open door into what appeared to be an office.

Ace was practically shaking with anger. 'You think that you can come into my house and do this to the ones I love?' she screamed. 'You think that I'm just going to stand by to let you *do that*?'

Wiping furious tears from her eyes, Ace grasped the silver pendant that hung around her neck and tugged, snapping the thin silver chain.

'Sanaul!' she yelled. 'Duck and cover. Three-second fuse!'

The man's eyes widened with shock.

Yaz realised what Ace was about to do. She stared incredulously. 'You're not serious?'

'Shut up and get your head down!' yelled Ace, hurling the silver sphere into the morass of rat creatures and pushing Yaz back onto the balcony.

Three seconds later there was the 'crump' of an explosion that shook the stairwell. No sooner had the sound faded than Ace was back on her feet, launching herself into the clouds of smoke that now billowed through the shattered glass doors.

Ears still ringing from the blast, Yaz staggered after her. The apartment looked like a war zone, broken glass and plaster covering everything. A huge hole had been blown in the floor where the tiny explosive device had landed, and well over half of the Ratts had seemingly fallen through to the floor below. The others were staggering around, dazed and coughing.

Ace was on the far side of the room, helping the injured man to his feet. 'Get out of here, Sanaul, get yourself to hospital and phone Will, tell him what's happened here.' She pushed him towards the door to the office. 'And check that Sorin's OK.'

'But Miss Dorothy, you can't stay in here with those … those things …'

'Oh, I think I can deal with them.'

Ace strode across the room and extracted a silver baseball bat with a black handle from a smashed glass case on the wall. Hefting the bat in her hands, Ace turned to the recovering rat creatures and gave a grin that bordered on the insane.

'Right, you lot. Wanna try that with someone who'll fight back?'

The Ratts hissed angrily and started to advance on her.

'Ace, no!' yelled Yaz. 'There's too many of them!'

'You just get some of that slime on you! And make sure you've still got your tracker!'

With a roar, Ace waded into the sea of rat creatures, swinging the baseball bat like a broadsword. Wet, hooded bodies flew through the air as the bat made contact and the air was filled with white sparks and screeches of pain and anger.

Yaz shook her head in disbelief. The woman was clearly crazy. As she watched the battle unfold, it was obvious that it was becoming one-sided. Whilst anger, adrenalin and the element of surprise had initially given Ace the upper hand, there were still dozens of the rat creatures to contend with.

As Yaz watched, they began to back Ace into a corner, working as a pack to cut off any chance she had of escape. Abruptly one of the creatures turned and stared at her, as if noticing her for the first time. With a jolt of fear, Yaz checked that her homing beacon was secure, pressed up against her collarbone, and then scrabbled in the pocket of her jacket for the bottle of mucus, snapping open the cap and smearing the vile slime over her wrist and neck.

The effect on the Ratt was instantaneous. Immediately its pupils dilated, the rodent-like nose twitching wildly as the stench enveloped her. With a hiss it scampered forward, and Yaz had to stifle a cry of revulsion as it came up close, peering up at her with gleaming, eager eyes.

As the creature opened its mouth, its wet lips quivering, Yaz screwed her eyes closed, bracing herself, but the spray of mucus didn't come.

'Oh, no, I don't think so …' The Ratt's voice was high and whining.

Yaz opened her eyes. The creature was grimacing at her in distaste.

'Not suitable,' it spat. 'Smell's wrong. Not suitable at all.'

It turned, its thick tail lashing out at her legs and sending her sprawling. She watched as it scampered across the room to rejoin the pack. The creatures had completely overpowered Ace, beating her almost unconscious as she clutched the bat to her body, pinned to the floor.

The Ratt that had dismissed Yaz pushed through the tangle of bodies and loomed over Ace's prone body, its nose twitching excitedly.

'Ahhh ...' Its eyes closed in an expression of delight.

With a wet coughing sound it unleashed a wad of mucus over Ace's face, making her retch. She tried to twist away from the stream of thick matter that splattered from the creature's mouth, but the pack had her held securely.

The creature wiped its lips, then turned to stare at Yaz with an evil gleam in its eyes. 'Such a *generous* donation this one makes.'

Yaz watched as a sickly green glow started to envelop Ace's prone body, spreading rapidly to encompass the surrounding rat creatures.

'No!' Yaz fumbled with the homing beacon at her neck, but it was too late. There was a sudden flare of light, and when it had faded Ace and the rat creatures had gone.

Yaz got to her feet, making her way carefully around the ragged hole that had been blown in the apartment floor. A cold wind was blowing in through the shattered windows, and in the distance Yaz could hear the undulating sound of sirens getting closer and closer.

She pulled her phone from her pocket and dialled the Doctor's number in the TARDIS.

'Doctor? Graham?'

Graham's eyes were glued to the screen, which was again showing the radar sweep of the Doctor's monitoring system. He was listening out for any sounds of approach, or suggestion of danger. The temperature seemed to have risen, and the smell in the air was changing, becoming sourer; damage done by the Astingir's forced entry, he guessed. Little shivers and shudders seemed to run through the floor and walls, whispers and groans sounded in the floor. *It's your imagination,* he told himself; and then told himself firmly to believe that.

'Doctor! Graham?'

The voice carried from the TARDIS.

It was Yaz.

'Yaz?' Graham dithered for a moment – he was meant to watch for the red light at all costs, but now Yaz was calling in, something had happened. If he went to her, and Ryan was taken, and he wasn't there to throw the lever ...

'*Come on, Doctor.*' Yaz sounded distressed, urgent. '*Pick up, please!*'

Graham turned and charged inside the TARDIS, hit the phone link. 'Yaz, love, it's me,' he blurted. 'You all right? What's happening?'

'*They didn't take me!*' Yaz cried. '*I was covered in that slime but they still didn't take me.*'

'Who?'

'*The Ratts, they attacked us—*'

'Yaz, are you safe?'

'*I'm fine. Listen, Graham, they left me behind and took Ace!*'

'Ace?' Graham felt his heart plunge down to his socks. 'But she—'

'*She's not wearing a tag,*' Yaz snapped. '*I know!*'

The change in the atmosphere, the noises from the flesh of the station: now Graham understood their meaning. *They beamed Ace up and pushed her on, and I was as much use as a chocolate teapot.*

'Where's the Doctor?' said Yaz. 'She's got to be able to find Ace somehow.'

'She's ...' Graham swallowed hard; there was no point scaring Yaz further. 'She's out just now, checking something. There's still Ryan, though, right, with his tag on? Wherever Ace has gone, he'll be going there, right? Stands to reason.'

'*I've just been attacked by a dozen giant rats in hairy skin hijabs, Graham, nothing stands to reason.*'

'We'll still be able to find her,' he insisted. 'Have you tried calling Ryan?'

'Yeah. He didn't pick up.'

Graham swore under his breath. 'I'd better keep watching the controls for him, he could be buzzed up any minute, yeah? Moment the Doctor's back here, I'll get her to call you. Stay safe. You got a cup of tea?'

'No.'

'Do it! Get a cuppa. Priority.'

'Right.' He could hear the smile steal reluctantly into Yaz's voice now. *'Take care of each other up there.'*

'Always.'

Graham's heart was heavy as he turned and went back outside. The screen remained black-and-green and serene. 'Come on, Ryan,' he muttered. 'And come on, Doctor …'

CHAPTER SIXTEEN

Chantelle stepped through the door of her flat, and gave a deep sigh. Home. All she wanted to do was kick off her shoes, pour herself a glass of wine and unwind, but things never went that easily when Dorothy McShane was involved.

'OK. Make yourself at home, it might be a long evening.'

Ryan came eagerly into the flat, obviously delighted at the prospect of spending the evening with her. If it had just been Ryan then she might have been happier about it too ... But Kim Fortune was still standing there, looking pathetic.

'What about me?'

'Just go home,' she pleaded.

'I can't go on the tube dressed like this.' Kim pulled at the paper boiler suit. 'Your friend took all my clothes!'

'Well, what do you want me to do about it?' snapped Chantelle, her patience rapidly running out.

'You could at least let me use your shower,' said Kim forlornly. 'I was covered in that stuff, remember?'

Chantelle was about to tell him to get lost, when she realised how miserable he looked and thought better of it. He *had* been covered in slime, and they'd been in such a rush to get out of

Perivale that they hadn't really had the chance to clean it off him properly. 'OK,' she nodded, standing aside to let him into the flat.

'Thank you.' Kim hurried past her gratefully.

'Bathroom's at the end of the corridor on the left,' said Chantelle, locking the front door and latching the security chain. 'And I'm pretty sure I've got some clean clothes that might fit you.'

'Really?' Kim looked at her in surprise.

'Yeah. My last boyfriend was always leaving his stuff here but, given that I dumped him last month, you can do me a favour and take some of it.'

She paused. That wasn't strictly true. It was Craig who had left her, not the other way round, but she still wanted shot of everything. 'I'll leave it outside the bathroom door for you.'

Kim smiled at her, but Chantelle was having none of it. 'Touch any of my stuff in there and I'll throw you into the street naked, understood?'

Kim's smile faded and he just nodded and hurried off down the corridor.

Chantelle shook her head. Dorothy owed her big time for this one. Shrugging off her coat and dumping it next to the hall table, she made her way to her bedroom. Throwing open the wardrobe doors, she picked out trousers and a shirt for Kim and threw them onto the bed. It had been a relatively warm December so Craig hadn't left any jumpers here, but she had plenty that Kim could borrow.

She considered picking out one of her pink cashmere sweaters embroidered with unicorns for him to wear home ... then realised that she was neglecting her other guest. She glanced in the mirror and grimaced. She was in no state to receive company. Grabbing a scrunchy from the dresser, she tied her hair back into a bun and put on some fresh lipstick. Satisfied that she had made some effort to make herself presentable, she scooped up the clothes from the bed, dropped them on the floor outside the bathroom and went to join Ryan in the front room.

'Kim still here?' asked Ryan as she entered the room.

'He needed to clean up before he went home.' Chantelle slumped down into an armchair. 'Given what he's had to put up with, I figured that was the least I could do.'

'Oh …'

There was an awkward pause.

'Would you like a drink?'

Ryan gave a huge sigh. 'I could murder a cuppa.'

Chantelle laughed. 'You sound just like your granddad.'

Ryan looked embarrassed. It made Chantelle like him even more.

'It's just you and him?' she asked.

'Yeah.' Ryan nodded. 'Since my gran died …'

'Oh … Sorry.' Chantelle could have kicked herself for asking such a stupid question. To her relief, Ryan was smart enough to sense her unease.

'It's OK. It can be dangerous, hanging with the Doctor. Reckon you've seen some of that yourself …'

'Yeah.' Chantelle nodded. 'Enough to scare me witless when I was a kid.'

'But you know she always tries to make it right, yeah?'

'So Dorothy used to tell me.'

Ryan frowned. 'You don't believe her?'

'I think the Doctor screwed her up. She's not said as much, but I can tell. It broke her somehow. Life with him …'

'What about you?'

'Me?' Chantelle looked at him in surprise. 'I'm fine.'

'Really?'

'Why wouldn't I be?'

'I dunno.' Ryan shrugged. 'You've got this crazy jet-setting life, but you seem sad somehow. Like none of it really matters to you.'

'Of course it matters.' Chantelle felt herself bristle. 'I'm rich, I'm famous.'

Ryan just looked at her.

'Oh, OK …' Chantelle sighed. 'You're right. I'm sick of it. Sick of what it almost turned me into, sick of the never-ending parade of weirdoes that come crawling after me …'

'I hope you don't include me in that?'

'You're better than most.' Chantelle grinned. 'But you still hang around with the Doctor, so that makes you a bit weird.'

'Fair enough,' Ryan said. 'Talking of weird – oh, my days! I still can't believe that the Doctor used to be a he. What was he like?'

Chantelle shrugged. 'Not much to look at, really. Little bloke in a straw hat wearing a stupid jumper.'

'Well, the clothes sense hasn't changed much!' Ryan gave a guffaw. 'Perhaps you could give her some fashion tips …'

Ryan's amusement was infectious, and Chantelle found herself chuckling too. The stress of the day had taken its toll, and soon the two of them were helpless with laughter.

'I think we need that drink,' she said wiping tears from her eyes, 'and something a bit stronger than tea.'

'Whatever you say,' said Ryan, his smile brilliant. 'I'm going to need it if I've got to splash some of this stuff on me too.' He pulled the bottle of mucus from his pocket.

'Oh, God. Do we have to? It'll stink the place up!'

'Well, you must have some air freshener or something?'

'I've got better than that. My mum bought me some scented candles!'

Chantelle clambered from her seat and pulled half a dozen candles down from a shelf, lighting each one in turn. Soon the flat was full of the scent of Madagascan Vanilla.

'Right, that should help disguise the smell.'

'I wouldn't be so sure about that,' said Ryan, his nose wrinkling as he removed the top from the bottle. 'This stuff's pretty strong.'

'Here. Let me help you.' She took the bottle and dipped in her finger. 'Lovely. Just pretend it's massage oil.'

'You saying you wanna give me a massage?'

'Don't be cheeky.' She leaned forward and rubbed some onto his cheeks in slow, circular motions. 'How's that?'

Ryan looked at her steadily. 'Not so bad.'

Chantelle was just leaning forward in her chair to apply more of the slime, when a sudden loud scratching noise made her freeze.

'Did you hear that?'

Ryan nodded. 'D'you think it's starting already?'

There was a loud 'crack' from the hallway, followed by a terrified scream.

'Kim?'

The two of them scrambled from their seats and rushed out into the corridor.

Kim was standing half-dressed outside the bathroom, staring in horror at a small hooded figure that was advancing towards him.

'Who the hell are you?' yelled Chantelle. 'And what are you doing in my flat?' The figure turned and snarled at her, its face fierce and animal-like. As it did so, a rat scurried over Chantelle's feet, making her cry out in surprise. Ryan snatched an umbrella from the stand near the door and lifted it ready to strike, when the rat suddenly swelled and cracked.

Chantelle and Ryan watched in horror as, with a series of violent explosive snaps, the rat started to transform, expanding in an impossible distorted manner until a second hunched figure stood in the corridor before them.

This time Chantelle could see it in close detail and she stepped back in revulsion as she realised that what she had taken for a hooded top was, in fact, the creature's skin, pulled in thick, wet folds over its head.

Ryan recoiled too at the sight. 'That's disgusting.'

Kim seemed unable to take his eyes from the creature. 'It's real. It's alive. Undeniable proof that *they* walk among us.'

He celebrated his triumph by collapsing in a dead faint.

Ignoring Chantelle and Ryan, the first Ratt scurried over to its recently transformed fellow.

'The boss isn't happy! We are behind quota!'

'It's not our fault!' came the whining reply. 'The abduction of the Kerry-thing was interrupted.' It kicked out at Kim's unconscious body. 'What about this? Is *this* suitable?'

'Oh yes,' the first creature nodded. 'This one is ideal material.' It turned, staring directly at Chantelle and Ryan. 'But two further donations would be most welcome.'

Ryan hefted the umbrella. 'What the hell do you mean, donations?'

Chantelle gave a gasp of horror as the creatures began to advance along the corridor towards them.

As the Doctor ran, she felt the power rising through the ship like a charge through a battery. The flesh-stuff of the ship was quivering, alive with energy.

She quickened her pace. Behind her, she could hear the clop and clatter of the Astingir centaurions galloping after her. 'It's a two-horse race,' she breathed. She knew they would run her down long before she reached Graham.

Skidding to a halt, she jabbed her blackened car aerial into the sticky substance of the wall beside her. Then she pressed the sonic against it and buzzed hard.

The wall shuddered and groaned as a gristly creeper – a power cable – was drawn out through the thick morass. With no cutting tools, the Doctor bit into the creeper and pulled on it hard. Thick amber oil spurted out from the creeper at high pressure, throwing the Doctor back, spluttering, as the two horse-creatures rounded the corner.

'Centaurions, stop!' she yelled.

Ignoring her, the Astingir kept coming but as they splashed into the tide of slick oil their hooves slid from under them. One fell, dropping its spear as it landed hard. The other centaurion stumbled over the hindquarters of its fellow and smashed its head against the wall with a roar.

The Doctor turned and ran on.

'Graham!'

'Doctor?' Graham heard her shouts echo down the dark access corridor and her footfalls as she approached.

'I felt the ship power up. Who was it, Ryan or Yaz? Did you mark the trail, did you—?'

'It was Ace! They took Ace!' Graham yelled back. 'Get in here!'

'Ace?' Wide-eyed, clothes stained with stinking brown goo, the Doctor skidded back inside. 'They can't have taken her! She—'

'Doesn't have a tag, yeah, so she didn't show on this thing, did she?' He kicked the console. 'Yaz told me, she said they were attacked by those rat-things.'

'She's safe?'

'I think so—'

'Was she wearing the pheromone slime?'

Graham nodded. 'Said it made no difference!'

'I don't understand.' The Doctor suddenly tensed, looked behind her. 'But! First things first. We're about to be charged by a pair of very angry – and now quite slippery – centaur warriors.'

'Of course we are!' Graham groaned.

'We need to hold them off long enough to trail Ryan when he gets taken.' She concentrated hard. 'But how?'

'What about the TARDIS force field?' Graham said. 'If you could sort of project it out here …?'

'Yes! Extrude the force field. Brilliant.' Abruptly she dashed off into the TARDIS. 'Keep watching the console!'

'What if they *don't* take Ryan?' Graham called after her. 'Didn't work with Yaz, did it? Maybe that gunky stuff's not even important ...?'

But even as he spoke, he felt the same tension coiling through the floor beneath him, a waft of that same vile smell. Graham felt his heart pound to a halt as the red light snapped on. He reached for the lever, slammed it home.

The walls exploded around him as a gigantic tremor tore through the station, flinging Graham to the ground in a shower of filth and ichor. Squidget convulsed, its tentacles writhing. The lights dipped and the floor lurched beneath him. The howling alarm started up again, a shriek of pain.

Pain and, this time, despair.

CHAPTER SEVENTEEN

'Doc?' Graham shouted. 'What the hell was that?'

The Doctor staggered out of the TARDIS, white-faced. 'The Astingir! They've set off charges in the Functional Abyss.'

'They've stuffed up the workings?' Graham looked up at her from his hands and knees. 'But Ryan just came through! Red light came on, I pulled the lever—'

'Oh no, Squidget's down!' The Doctor picked up the quivering interface and cradled it as she studied the blank screen. 'Massive power surge, it's shorted him out – along with the whole console.'

'Where's Ryan?' cried Graham. 'How do we find him?'

'Oh, my days …!'

At the sound of the familiar voice, both Graham and the Doctor turned to find Ryan, wedged in a split in the middle of the wall behind them, like human Polyfilla. With a disgusting squelch, he was pushed forward as if the fabric of the ship itself was spitting him out. His face and clothes were drenched with slime.

'Ryan!' The Doctor dropped Squidget and ran to him with Graham. They took hold of an arm each and pulled hard. Ryan fell to his sticky knees. 'You must've been collected just as the

159

Functional Abyss cut out,' cried the Doctor triumphantly. 'There was no power to boost you onwards!'

'So Ace has been time-stormed away, but Ryan and Yaz haven't,' Graham muttered.

'Ace?' Ryan shook his head weakly. 'Not her as well. They've already got Chantelle and Kim …'

The Doctor looked appalled. 'They took Chantelle and Kim?'

'Easy, son.' Graham put a hand to Ryan's sticky head to soothe him. Ryan closed his eyes. 'That's it, sleep. You're all right now.'

'Why take *them*?' The Doctor was frowning. 'And take them *where*?' She jumped up and crossed to the console. 'I'll do a broad-range scan, perhaps I'll find some trace of a trail while it's fresh—whoops!'

She had tripped over Squidget, which was still convulsing on the floor. As she fell, a blast of energy lanced over her head from behind her and sparked into the console. It exploded in a burst of smoke and flames.

'Doc!' Graham pointed a finger at the shadowy shapes at the end of the corridor. 'Them horse-things are here! What about the TARDIS force field?'

The Doctor slapped a hand to her forehead. 'Got distracted, didn't I!'

As she scrambled to her feet, a dark, fleshy barrier dropped down like a guillotine from the ceiling, sealing them off from the approaching Astingir.

'Fire door,' the Doctor announced, jumping back up. 'Thank heavens for that.' She whipped off her coat and used it to beat out the flames on the console. 'No time for force fields, we'd better evacuate. Graham, get Ryan into the TARDIS.'

Graham already had an arm under Ryan's neck and shoulders. 'What about you?'

'I've got to fix this thing!' she cried, buzzing the sonic desperately at the charred and smouldering console. 'That broad-range scan, it's our last chance to—'

The fire door blew open. Huge chunks of fibrous matter dirtied the air. One struck the Doctor on the back of the head, and hurled her into the console. They both went down with a crash and clatter.

'Doctor!' Graham shouted, appalled. But already, equine heads and glowing red spears were pushing through the shattered doors.

Two sets of dark alien eyes fixed on Graham and Ryan. One of the creatures pushed through, heavy and powerful, its armour gleaming in the low-level lighting. It glared down at the Doctor and pressed a button on the girdle around its humanoid waist.

'Cardiovascular activity ceased. Life signs extinguished.' It cantered round to where Graham knelt, speechless, clutching Ryan's unconscious form like a child with a teddy. The centaur thing loomed over him.

'You are property of the Astingir,' it said, and nodded its long head to its fellow. 'We will take them to the War Chariot.'

The Doctor woke with a cry and found the station around her was screaming too. The hot air smelled of smoke and waste and decay. She put a hand to her chest, felt the skittering heartbeats; it was a long time since she'd shut down her cardiovascular system. Shock of the impact perhaps, or just instinct – knowing who it was who'd blasted through the fire door.

'Still got it,' she muttered, getting woozily to her feet, wincing at the feel of the bump on the back of her head.

What she didn't still have was Graham and Ryan. Besides her and the TARDIS, the room was empty.

'No,' the Doctor muttered, staring around. 'Oh, no …' She shrugged on her soot-smeared coat, climbed through the split and oozing fire door and staggered off down the corridor. The station lurched to one side, and she fell against the wall. A vile brown fluid was dribbling down from the ceiling. Particles in the air sparked and spat around her like hot fat, in a light show that was both beautiful and frightening.

She kept stumbling along the corridor. 'Ryan!' she yelled, 'Graham!' and the dying ship seemed to groan back at her. The floor beneath her suddenly gave way and she clutched at the rotting walls to stop herself falling through to the floor beneath.

'This is hopeless.' Clawing her way back up, she had to close her eyes as dizziness swept across her. Then she heard a voice calling to her, distorted through the bowed corridor, back the way she'd come. A man's voice. 'Graham?' she yelled. 'Ryan, is that you …?'

But it wasn't. As she staggered back to the collection point, the Doctor realised the voice was coming from the TARDIS. It was Will.

' … *for God's sake, somebody come in, please, over.*' A pause, the crackle of static. '*Look, if you need a rescue mission it's no good, that station will be gone before I can get to you, over.*'

'Rescue's too late already …' The Doctor started working the TARDIS controls, scanning for traces of life on board. There were none. Flicking on the microphone she leaned forward. 'Space Defence Centre? This is the Doctor.'

'*Thank God. What the hell's been happening? Over.*'

'That alien ship, what happened to it? Over.'

'*Ship has gone, Doctor, repeat, it's gone. Once it had blown the hell out of that station, it took off fast.*'

The Doctor's hearts were sinking. 'And took Ryan and Graham with it,' she said miserably.

Will's voice sounded strained as he continued. '*Everyone's going crazy down here. Alien space stations, alien spaceships … when's it going to be all … Over.*'

'You tell me, Will. What did you mean, the station will be gone? Over.'

'*That ship's blown it out of lunar orbit. In 12 hours the whole thing will burn up in Earth's atmosphere.*' Will paused. '*Did you get a fix on Ryan*

162

and Yaz when they were taken? I mean, they were taken, right? I can't get hold of Dorothy to confirm. Over.'

The Doctor sighed heavily, pressed transmit. 'No fix, repeat, no fix. And ... Dorothy's been taken too. Over.'

There was silence for what felt like a whole minute. *'Taken?'* Will's voice sounded quite fragile but hardened fast. *'Repeat, Dorothy taken? Taken where? Over.'*

'Transported. Beamed across space. I don't know where.' Now the Doctor was glad for the primitive two-way radio that didn't allow for interruptions until transmissions were ended. 'But I promise you, I'll find her, Will. I'm coming back down, now, and I'll make contact as soon as I'm able. We're going to figure this out, and I'm not even going to say "Over", because it's not, OK? It's not ... over.' The Doctor took a deep and shaky breath. 'Ryan, Graham, Ace, Chantelle, Kim ... Wherever you are, I'll find you. I swear, I'll find you.'

She turned and strode outside, picked up Squidget and tucked it under her arm. Then she pushed the ruined console back into her ship, and closed the doors behind her.

A few seconds later, with a strangled groan, the TARDIS disappeared from the dying station.

Interlude

1990

Ace pelted through the warped landscape, her boots thudding over ground the colour of burnt sugar, sticking close to the cover of crumbling arches and rocky ruins. Her head still spun and sparked with the visions she'd seen, and her skin crawled with the touch of the Wraiths. Behind her she could hear sounds of pursuit as Astingir troops took their trail, but beyond that crash and clatter she sensed the shadow-men she'd seen in the Anvil following too, looming out at her from the ruined doorways, rising from the blackened stone to press fingers against her flesh.

'Keep running, Ace!' The Doctor puffed as he ran along beside her, one hand holding his hat on his head, the other clutching his umbrella. 'If we're caught here, we'll be killed.'

She felt a thrill at his words, as ever. The Dalí-esque world of ruins about them was just another arena in which to risk their lives for the good of things: a clear, straightforward flight from the dark to the light. And yet a part of her, still shifted sideways by the Anvil, was wondering, *What happens when I get too old to run any longer? The Doctor will go on forever, but what about me?*

Again, the image of Earth in the far future, drowning in a chemical slime; again, the burning drive to fight that future, whatever it took.

'Wait, Ace!' the Doctor shouted as they ran through a tall doorway into a vast, distorted cathedral. He looked up at the roof, which was still partially intact, supported by struts rising from a long, blackened beam that ran horizontally overhead. With fresh purpose, he led Ace over the cracked glass floor to the far wall. 'Rest a moment,' he told her.

'Why?' Ace asked him. 'I thought you said these Aston thingies would execute us.'

'They will. This world isn't just Death Row for the Wraiths, but for anyone who dares to visit. There are thousands of proximity sensors in orbit to warn the Astingir of approaching craft, but the TARDIS has always phased through those with ease.' He frowned. 'At least I thought she had.'

Ace rolled her eyes. 'If they've picked up the TARDIS coming and going, that would explain why they've stuck sensors at ground level too. They want to know what you've been up to here ...'

'Excellent reasoning.' The Doctor's smile shied far from his eyes. 'Well, in any case, we can't outrun the Astingir. We need to use our heads.'

'Mine is splitting,' Ace said. 'Feels like someone stirred my brains with a rusty spike.'

'Yes, I'm sorry,' the Doctor muttered, his attention once more on the beam above them. 'I didn't appreciate quite how much the Wraiths' touch would hurt you ...'

Ace looked at him. 'What?'

The Doctor closed his eyes, didn't respond.

'What do you mean, you didn't appreciate how much it would hurt?' Her eyes hardened, a flicker of fear in her guts. 'Professor, back at the Anvil when you pulled me clear ... you weren't worried that I'd been touched by those things, were you? You were worried that maybe I *hadn't* been ...'

Again, no answer.

A sudden rise of anger pushed out her accusation: 'Weren't you? Why did we really come here today, Professor?'

'This is not the time, Ace!' snapped the Doctor his arms flailing wildly as they always did when he was agitated. 'Look!'

Across the caramelised expanse of the ruined cathedral, Ace saw the first of the Astingir squad burst through the arch. The armoured beast looked like the mutant offspring of a centaur and a horse: a humanoid torso reared up from the powerful white stallion body, but the horse-like head crowning the broad shoulders was no bigger than a man's. Ox horns speared out from behind the ears, and in its muscular arms it gripped a futuristic bow and arrow that shone with eerie light. It looked both beautiful and horrible as it trotted in a tight circle, perhaps suspicious now its quarries were in sight.

As more Astingir pushed through the doorway, Ace could see what the Doctor had meant about not outrunning them. Their legs looked so powerful, muscles rippling under gleaming metal armour and ash-white hide.

'You will surrender,' called the first, in a deep, throaty voice.

'Will we?' Ace took a step towards them, her anger making her reckless.

'No,' hissed the Doctor. 'Sit down.'

'What?'

'Do it!' The Doctor turned to the Astingir, raised his hat and gave them his daftest smile. 'Good afternoon, gentlemen— I mean, gentlehorses. Tell me ... why the long faces?'

The Astingir stared, but Ace stared even harder.

'Seriously, Professor?'

'Funny. That one normally brings the house down.' The Doctor plonked his hat back on his head and shrugged. 'I can see I'll need a little extra help ...' In a sudden blur of movement, he stepped on Ace's shoulder and used it as a springboard as he leaped into the air, umbrella raised handle first like a grappling hook. The curved edge of the question mark caught on the brittle beam above as the Doctor swung and tugged.

As one, the Astingir raised their gleaming bows and loosed laser arrows that sputtered and seared through the air about the Doctor, barely missing him.

'Professor!' Ace staggered up, as the beam finally broke under the Doctor's weight and he fell down into Ace's arms in a shower of carbon fibres. The two of them fell to the floor as more laser arrows snapped and whooshed all around, punching holes in the melted rock.

A deep creaking noise came from the high rafters. With the long beam now broken, the integrity of the roof it had supported for so long was threatened. Already the Astingir were being showered by falling debris as cracks opened in the roof and half-melted buttresses began to crumble.

'Out of here!' roared the Doctor, and Ace scrambled along-side him as he made for a nearby doorway. With noise enough to crack the planet wide apart the entire cathedral came crumbling down behind them, the tremors throwing them to the ground.

'There!' The Doctor got up and brushed his hands together with satisfaction. 'No time for a lie down, Ace. That will only hold them back for a while.'

Hold them … Again, Ace felt the spectral touch of the Wraiths clawing through her flesh and bone to mark the soul inside. 'Professor … they held *me*. I can still feel the touch of them. Burning. Like a brand.'

'I'm so sorry, Ace.' The Doctor offered his hand to help her up. 'I didn't think—'

Ace ignored the hand. 'Tell me why you brought me here, Professor. It wasn't just to check up on things, was it?'

'Time to leave.' He glanced anxiously behind him. 'Once we're back in the TARDIS, I'll—'

'Tell me!'

'Because there's no such thing as an ultimate weapon, Ace. Or an ultimate prison, for that matter.' The Doctor looked pained, now, wringing his hands. 'One day the Wraiths may find a way out of this trans-temporal hell they've been caught in. You think they won't want revenge, that they won't wage war on the cosmos again?' Again, more forlornly, he reached out to her. 'On that day someone who can interact with them would make a useful ... emissary.'

Ace met his eyes, got up by herself. 'And now they've touched me, I can do that? Interact?'

'You must believe me, if I could've done it myself, I would have. But I've crossed the time fields in the TARDIS too often, I'd slip through their fingers.'

Those long, sharp fingers, scratching her ... Ace felt a kind of icy calm damming up her darker feelings. 'So you needed someone rougher round the edges. Someone who has form dragging others between worlds, the way I did between Earth and the Cheetah planet ...' She got up. 'Someone whose first trip through time and space was the hard way, through a time-storm ...'

'Ace, it was only a precaution. You know we must be ready for evil to strike at any time—'

'It's *you* who strikes! And always at me.' Ace turned and stalked away. 'I can't believe I let this happen again. Let you keep me in the dark and—'

Another crash cut short her temper. The Astingir had galloped round the ruins and a broken spire came toppling down as they passed. Pointed ears flattened to their equine heads at the sight of their prey, they charged forward and raised their golden bows and arrows.

'Run!' The Doctor shooed Ace like a chicken. 'Higher ground, the more rubble the better, it'll slow them down.'

Ace nodded. That at least made sense; the Astingir were faster than Cheetah people, mount and warrior in one, but the human form was better for climbing. She made for a large boulder blocking the path ahead. A laser shaft went shimmering past her head and half the stone blew apart, peppering her with shrapnel. She and the Doctor scrambled over it, and had scarcely reached the other side before the rest of it was cracked in two by a volley of blazing arrows.

'They'll just clear the path and ride on through,' Ace puffed.

'Keep going,' the Doctor told her. 'They'll run out of arrows in the end.'

Ace did keep going, of course she did, it wasn't in her nature to stop. But as she and the Doctor kept up their sweat-soaked sprint through the burnished ruins, she glimpsed movement to the side, and then movement up ahead, and heard galloping hoof beats like the soundtrack of her heart. This had been the Astingir's world once; they knew the landscape and were fanning out, overtaking and outflanking the fugitives. Wearing them out. Driving them toward territory better suited for the showdown.

'They're playing with us,' Ace realised.

The Doctor gave her a mournful look. 'I don't suppose they get much chance for a chase here.'

Ace kept going, looking all about for somewhere to hide. There were deep fissures in the ground here and there, but the sides were smooth, with no ledges to climb down out of the creatures' reach. There were buildings with doors wide open, offering shade and shadows for hiding places, but the horse creatures could simply play them at their own game, loose off a couple of arrows and crush them in moments.

The Doctor led the way up a steep, smooth slope, leaning on his umbrella for balance, poking handholds for Ace with the metal point to help her climb. They heaved themselves onto a ruin of stained-black concrete, wide, crumbling walls but no roof. The cracked stumps of pillars rising around them like fingers on a closing fist. Again, Ace shuddered at the touch of the Wraiths inside her. Her head felt itchy, sweat was pouring down her face.

With a groan, a wall toppled and fell inward to reveal all eight Astingir cantering through the thick clouds of dust like sinister spectres, dark eyes fixed on their prey, bows and arrows raised.

Ace looked at the Doctor. 'Back the way we came?'

'Away from the TARDIS? No use.' The Doctor shook his head. 'You wouldn't be carrying ...?'

'Nitro-9.' She nodded, fumbling in her backpack for a canister.

'Remain still.' One of the horse creatures was leading the others slowly forward. 'You are trespassing on our world. You have defiled a Site of Mass Contrition.'

The Doctor raised his hat again. 'For which I imagine you'll want to take us prisoner and place us on trial?'

'The punishment, under Article 26 of the Pan-Conflict Termination Treaty, is immediate execution.' The leading Astingir turned to his squad. 'Firing party ...'

'Wait!' Ace shouted. 'We didn't know ...'

Didn't know ... Again, the voices of the Wraiths, echoing through her own thoughts. She screwed her eyes tight shut and cracked open the can. It hissed angrily, the timer fuse counting down.

'Take aim.' The Astingir carefully aimed their bows, the air shimmering about them with the heat of the coming blasts.

Ace threw the Nitro-9 into the middle ground between them; perhaps the explosion would catch the horse creatures off-guard. They could escape under cover of the smoke, at least be harder to hit ...

As the Astingir leader bellowed, 'Fire!' the Nitro-9 ignited. It was a good blast, and Ace's heart danced like the flames that erupted from inside, smiling as the black smoke came roiling out. She turned to the Doctor and grabbed his arm. 'Come on, then ...!'

But he shushed her as tremors came shaking through the ground. Awful, whinnying screams came from the Astingir, fading as the vibrations increased.

'What's happening?' Ace shouted over the thrum and rumble.

The Doctor had already turned to run again, making for a dark mouth in the wall nearby. They passed through it and up a rubble-strewn slope. Reaching the crest, Ace could see the TARDIS nestling blue and solid in the broken, half-baked landscape.

As she looked back, she saw what she'd done. The Nitro-9 had blown an enormous chasm in the desiccated floor, and the foundations had collapsed beneath. The blackness left behind was that of an abyss. All trace of the horse creatures had vanished save for a single golden bow lying at the edge of the split.

'The Astingir,' Ace whispered.

The Doctor was mopping his face with his paisley cravat. 'The floor gave way under them.'

'Then ... they're dead?'

'You couldn't have known,' the Doctor told her quietly. 'And they would have killed us. You had to do it.'

'I always have to, don't I?' Ace said. 'It's why you keep me around.'

They made their way up the blasted hillside in silence, until the crumbling city lay far behind them and they reached the cool, bright safety of the TARDIS. Ace leaned against the console and felt herself trembling, and not only from her exertions. It was one thing to blow a Cyber patrol to smithereens, or to beat the hell out of a Dalek. But the Astingir were living beings, strong and wild and fast, and only there at all because the Doctor had forced them to be, manipulating them just like he manipulated everyone. Manipulating her.

And I killed them. All of them.

She watched him brush the dust and detritus from his hands and clothes, unaware of the dirt piling on the floor about him. She felt so tired. And they burned in her mind again, the visions hammered hard from the Anvil. The snatches of so many other lives away from here ... the fragments of futures she could embrace or avoid. Build or destroy.

Or fight for.

The Doctor rolled his hat up his arm so that it landed neatly on his head. 'Well, Ace! Where to next?'

'Professor ...' Ace looked down at the floor, and swallowed hard. 'Professor, this is the day we say goodbye.'

PART THREE
2020 AND BEYOND ...

CHAPTER EIGHTEEN

'Things are bad,' the Doctor announced. 'I won't sugar-coat it –
even though sugar is something I heartily approve of under usual
circumstances. Things are very bad.'

'You don't have to tell me,' Yaz said. 'Believe it or not, I noticed.'

She gestured round the disaster area that was Ace's penthouse
home. The police box, standing blue and bold beside the window,
was about the only thing in the whole place still intact. The split
torn in the floor gave a view down onto the ruined offices below.

'Poor Sanaul,' said Yaz. 'I hope he's going to be OK. He was
more injured than he was letting on.'

'Intensive care is the best place for him,' the Doctor said.

'Those rat-things made such a mess of him.'

'But he's gonna be cared for. Intensively. Plus Sorin will be
waiting for him when he's out.' The Doctor glanced over at the
TARDIS. 'Poor little Squidget needs some care too. I've got him
hooked up to a recharge cradle, but he could use a proper over-
haul.'

'I know how "he" feels,' said Yaz. It was so good to have the
Doctor back, but Yaz had been expecting her to come whizzing
back here to collect her and then zoom off to Ryan and Graham's

rescue. Instead she had parked herself heavily in a slashed leather office chair, looking properly deflated.

'I won't lie, Yaz, things are—'

'Bad, I know.' Yaz breathed out heavily. 'These horse monster things kidnap Ryan and Graham while you're out cold, and even though Ryan's wearing an indestructible homing tag you said you could follow anywhere ... there's not a sign.'

The Doctor caught her note of disapproval gloomily. 'I promise, Yaz, I could've made it work. If you'd only been time-stormed away, it would've been a cinch!' She sighed. 'I wasn't banking on the Astingir coming along. Their War Chariots have quantum warp engines, they can slip through the tiniest wormholes in space-time and cover vast distances in minutes. Searching the whole of the universe for one tiny signal ...' She shook her head wearily. 'It's going to take time.'

'Meanwhile, I was never taken in the first place, so my tag is totally useless, a bunch of those Ratts kidnapped Ace instead of me, and a load more stole Chantelle and Kim away God knows where.' Yaz put her face in her hands. 'It's a total mess.'

'An absolute and *utter* total mess,' the Doctor agreed. 'Things are very bad. Very, very bad—'

'Don't start that again.' Yaz leaned forward urgently in her seat. 'Doctor, what are we going to do? Search the whole universe till we find them?'

'If that's what it takes,' the Doctor said firmly. Then she seemed to crumple, shook her head sadly. 'Why did these creatures take Ace at all? It shouldn't have happened.'

'It should've been me,' Yaz said.

'It shouldn't have been any of you,' the Doctor said. 'I should've found another way ...'

'Don't,' Yaz said softly. 'It's *them* you'll find. Ryan and Chantelle and Kim ... and Ace, too.'

'Ace.' The Doctor looked suddenly heartbroken. 'You know how much I can gabble on, Yaz. You know how good I am at talking. I once talked a Dalek to death. An actual Dalek! And Ace was with me then, right here in London, 60-odd years ago … Good God, all the talking I've done. But, you know, trying to talk to Ace … where were the words?' She shook her head, baffled. 'I'm pretty good at uncovering things. I've discovered the rarest things in the strangest places, clear across the cosmos. But the right words to say to that woman? Nope. Never. She was sat beside me in the car and I still couldn't find them.'

Yaz felt a twinge of jealousy at the strength of the Doctor's sorrow, but it didn't stop her sympathetic smile. 'It isn't too late,' she said firmly. 'You'd have been proud of her, you know. Helping to protect me, fighting off those things with just a baseball bat …'

'Baseball bat?' The Doctor stared suddenly into space, like someone in a cheesy film having a flashback. 'She used a bat? What did it look like?'

'Silver,' said Yaz. 'Had a—'

'Black handle?' The Doctor jumped up. 'Then she used it! She used the bat! The *more-than-a-bat*.'

'Doctor, what are you on about?'

'That bat – it was affected at a subatomic level by an incredibly advanced piece of technology.' She was pacing the room. 'Boosted its percussive powers, made it into a kind of super-bat. I managed to break it, of course, you know me, always breaking stuff. But I had it fixed up, good as new, and I gave it back to her …' The Doctor stopped walking. 'On the day she left.'

'Well, she used the hell out of it. Saw off a ton of those Ratt things.'

'Yes! And she was still holding it when she disappeared?'

'I'm pretty sure, yeah.'

'Brilliant! Perfect!' The Doctor was beaming. 'Don't you see? The bat's bristling with distinctive alien energies. I might be able to pick up its trail and lock down the location of Ace, and Chantelle and Kim and all those poor souls who've been going missing from the streets …!'

'What about Ryan and Graham?'

'I'm gonna find them too. I'm already scanning.' The Doctor frowned. 'I wish I knew why.'

'Why you're scanning for Ryan and Graham?'

'Why the Astingir took them prisoner. They're not a bloodthirsty species – unless they suspect they're dealing with friends of the Wraiths.'

'At least you know where those horse-things will be making for,' Yaz reminded her. 'Same as us: whoever, or whatever, is behind all this.'

'And if we can only follow the trail and find them first, we can be ready for the Astingir,' said the Doctor. 'And get Graham and Ryan back.'

'So how do we do that?' Yaz asked.

'It's gonna be tricky!' The Doctor smiled slowly. 'But where there's a Will ...'

There were several apartments built into the Space Defence Centre where, during the long, tense days of Moon-shots or probe launchings or closest approaches, exhausted staff members could crash at the end of a shift without leaving the premises. As Director, Will Buckland had the biggest and best of these apartments, but it was still little better than student accommodation, and cramped further after his installing of a small double bed. He could never stay contained in a single, would wake with a shock from hitting the carpet face first.

It was 4am now, but Will wasn't in bed. He was staring out of the window, at the woods around Devesham, and the dim stars beyond. His team would be coming off the night shift soon; Will knew that they were whispering about him, questioning his judgement and decisions, unwilling to accept he couldn't divulge the nature of the party left on board the station in orbit. They knew he was talking to someone in the auxiliary comms room, the feed shut down to all other personnel. Still he could hear their whispers: the talk of ESA and NASA enquiries, possible shut-down, of his being unfit for command.

But only one voice had stayed in his head. The Doctor's voice, telling him that Dorothy had been taken. That she was some-where out there in the infinite.

He heard a rumpling of sheets, glanced behind. Sam was sitting up in bed, wearing his shirt, rubbing her eyes. 'Any word?' she said.

'Nothing,' Will replied, and turned back to the window.

'I'm so sorry.' Sam shifted, and her tone was cajoling. 'Why don't you come back to bed? You've been awake for 30 hours straight, you're still recovering from that mad trip up to—'

'I'm fine,' Will snapped.

'You'll think more clearly if you only—'

'Don't.' He turned and looked at Sam. 'Please, don't.'

'What are you even doing, Will?' Sam's voice had hardened. 'Think you can spot Dorothy out there with the naked eye?'

Will didn't rise to it. 'I'm just thinking.'

'I hope you're thinking what the hell you're going to say to the NASA delegation when they call tomorrow.' Sam's anger was simmering. 'I tried to cover for you, told them that you had the observations under control, that the radiation signatures given out by the station were only superficially similar to those taken from the UFO in 1987 ...'

'Superficially?' Now Will turned to look at her, frowning. 'I checked the figures myself – thought that the energy patterns from the two were more or less the same?'

'Not when you let a computer study the *real* values over the relative.' Sam's stern gaze was let down both by her elfin features and by wisps of bed hair. 'The *patterns* of the signatures were more or less the same. But the energy spike in '87 was larger by a factor of about ten.'

'Ten times larger?' Will breathed. 'So the one up there is only a minnow by comparison.'

The information felt significant, but Sam was right; his brain was just too tired to make much headway.

Then his mobile rang, the tone cutting through the pre-dawn quiet. Sam looked at him, expectant. 'It's the Doctor,' he said. As Sam groaned, he picked up.

'*Wavelengths, Will!*' the Doctor boomed in his ear. '*I need to study the radiation signatures from the collector ... reckon it'll help us find Ace! Sorry, Dorothy. Although, that is ace news, isn't it?*'

'You really think you can find her?' Will almost laughed out loud.

'*I hope so! So! Radiation signatures ...?*'

'You're in luck,' Will said. 'Sam just did the maths. We'll get right on to rolling out a data summary.'

Sam rolled over and buried her head in the pillow.

CHAPTER NINETEEN

Will had arranged to rendezvous with the Doctor at Dorothy's batcave. Sam had agreed it was sensible for him to drop off the radar while the official investigation into his conduct was launched, at least until this business was over.

Well, 'agreed' was possibly too strong a word. She had shouted angrily that he was acting like an irresponsible teenager and that his career was finished whatever he did now, so why not go ahead and disappear like his old flame had done and leave her to hold everything together at the Space Defence Centre like she always did.

So that was exactly what he'd done, once she'd helped him compile the data on the radiation wave signatures of all the extra-terrestrial craft to have come visiting, and held him close and kissed him goodbye and flung him out of the centre in the sleepy light of dawn.

Will had the windows open and the stereo blasting as he drove, keeping carefully to just a little over the speed limit. He couldn't afford to be stopped, or risk a crash. He couldn't be delayed, not now.

The Doctor and Yaz were already there by the time he'd arrived. They'd found what looked like an industrial steel sink ringed with pipes and cables: a regeneration cradle, the Doctor called it, something to put the juice back into the metal squid-thing, depleted after misadventures on the space station he chose not to ask much about.

Details didn't matter. Finding Dorothy did.

Will showed the Doctor the summaries on his tablet.

'So the station that came in 1987 gave a boost ten times greater than those in 2020?' The Doctor frowned. 'Funny. You'd think they'd have the same capacity … Come on.'

She hurried into the police box in the corner of the laboratory. Yaz turned and beckoned to him. 'Come on in.'

Will did as he was told. He'd glimpsed the interior up on the station, he'd watched five people walk inside the thing, but the impossibility of the space inside it still went against everything he'd been taught.

The Doctor started flicking controls on the TARDIS console, and a vista of deep-field space glowed into life on the 360-degree scanner that shrouded the crystalline rafters – the gaseous smudges and spirals of galaxies were scattered all around, little bigger than stars, and just as numerous.

'Is that the whole universe?' Yaz whispered with a thrill.

'A tiny portion of it,' the Doctor answered.

'The observable universe is made up of maybe two trillion galaxies,' Will added.

'And we're not just looking from Earth. With these 4D charts we're looking out from galactic zero.' Glowing frames appeared over certain areas as the Doctor worked, enlarging the galaxies mapped within those borders, zooming in to inspect key areas than vanishing as she moved onto the next starscape. 'We know that Ace was time-stormed away to Svartos. That's in the Ninth Galaxy. Well, I say Ninth but it depends where you're counting from: it's the Seven-Billion-

and-Third Galaxy if you're standing on Hastus Major.' She was circling the console, stabbing here and there with her fingers like a heron poking waters for fish.

A dark-shrouded planet crowned with a colossal crystal citadel came into view.

'Svartos,' the Doctor announced, scrutinising the controls. 'In 1987, Svartos would've been … round about here. And, yep, there's a good strong space-trail showing.'

Yaz watched as a glittering line snaked across the virtual sky, as if Earth and Svartos were just two points on some enormously complicated join-the-dots.

'So what?' said Will. 'Dorothy's not on Svartos now, is she?'

'No,' the Doctor agreed, 'but checking the various radiation signatures tells us this: that last night, Ace, Chantelle and Kim and the others were time-stormed somewhere else, at far lower power.'

'In which case, they should be ten times closer than Svartos is,' Yaz reasoned. 'That's good, isn't it? You have the energy trace from Ace's bat, and we have an area to search!'

'Trouble is, the TARDIS *has* searched that area,' the Doctor informed her. 'And the bat's not there.'

Yaz felt her shoulders sag. 'Are you certain?'

'Watch. Another broad-range scan …' The Doctor yanked on a glowing lever and a criss-cross grid swept over the holographic universe above them. 'Yeah. Certain. No trace from the bat, and no trace of time-storm trails converging.'

'But if those time-storm trails are less prominent,' Yaz argued, 'they'll just be harder to spot.'

'Yes! Way, way harder to spot,' the Doctor said. 'And why do you think that might be the case, eh?'

Will looked at Yaz, who shrugged blankly. 'We don't have time to play guessing games, Doctor.'

The Doctor took the hint. 'Time-storming Ace to Svartos in 1987 was a one-off trip – Fenric, or whoever his agent was, didn't need to cover his tracks. But now, in 2020, they're time-storming a *lot* of people and they don't want anyone to know …'

'So they turn down the power?' Yaz concluded.

'Right.'

'But that doesn't make sense. Ace's magic bat would still be showing, and you said there's no trace of them anywhere within range.'

Will looked ashen. 'They've been obliterated.'

'Well, that would make no sense at all, would it?' The Doctor snorted. 'Why go to the trouble of finding them and snatching them off-world just to obliterate them?'

'Then, if they're not anywhere within range … they must be *out* of range.' With a thrill of dread, Yaz suddenly understood where the Doctor was leading them. '*Boosted* out of range? To another collector station, that boosts them on again?'

The Doctor grinned, nodded excitedly. 'Perhaps a whole chain of thousands of collectors working in relay! Or just a few, flitting in and out through wormholes, each passing the others, further and further out on a random course. Boosting the low-level signal on and on through time and space …'

'The same way satellites boost phone signals around the planet,' said Will, 'only on an intergalactic scale?'

'Or the same way spoof servers can re-route internet traffic, completely obscuring the actual destination. Because ultimately, it's the destination we need to know.'

Abruptly, the Doctor stormed outside. Yaz and Will swapped a glance and followed her.

'Can't you just scan for the bat?' said Yaz. 'I know it's like look-ing for a needle in a haystack …'

'More like looking for a sub-atomic needle in a hundred thou-sand million, billion haystacks,' the Doctor told her. 'The universe is a very big place.' She had crossed to where Squidget was lying in the regeneration cradle, and studied the readout. 'Question is, how much do the Astingir know about where to look? They're dedicated to destroying all Wraith technology. I doubt their War Chariot randomly picked on that collector orbiting the Moon – it's simply the first in the chain.'

'Unless they followed it backwards,' said Will grimly.

Yaz started in alarm. 'If they did, that could mean there are no collectors left to boost Ace and the others onward!'

'Meaning they could all be lost,' Will realised. 'Scattered in time and space ...'

'Never say die! We need to know the locations of the other stations in the chain.' The Doctor powered down the cradle. 'With the proper spatio-temporal coordinates, we can focus the search, speed up our rescue operation.'

Will raised his eyebrows. 'And just how do we find the exact spatio-temporal coordinates?'

The Doctor pointed up. 'Our local collector. Its job was to boost the victims on to the next station in the sequence – it has to know where that next station is. Best-case scenario, the entire forwarding pattern might be preserved in the computer systems.'

'Worst case, just the next collector in the sequence,' said Yaz. 'But from there we can find the location of the next ...'

The Doctor sucked in a breath in sudden horror. 'Which I bet is exactly what the Astingir have already done! We have to catch them up ...' She reached into the cradle and heaved out Squidget. A silver eye opened indignantly and its tentacles coiled as if having a stretch. 'Come on, fella,' she said, 'we've got a job to do.'

'But the collector has been knocked out of orbit, remember?' Will said. 'It's heading for break-up and burn-up in our atmosphere in ...' He checked his watch. 'In less than four hours. Conditions on board will be impossible.'

'Impossible?' The Doctor kicked open the TARDIS doors and waved Yaz inside. 'Will, I was marooned once for six months in an Obverse Sunset west of the Silver Devastation. Impossible conditions are a doddle. It's the *improbable* ones you need to watch out for ...'

She dashed in with Squidget and the doors closed behind her.

'Wait!' Will ran after her. But the grating wheeze of the TARDIS engines had already kicked in. A wind blew up from nowhere and the police box disappeared into it.

He stared at the empty space where it had stood.

Then, slowly, Will Buckland sank to his knees, closed his eyes, and lowered his head in a silent prayer.

CHAPTER TWENTY

Ace opened her eyes but the blackness wouldn't leave them. Her head felt hot, her body aching. The air smelled like fumes and burned in her lungs. *Where am I? Why can't I see?* Her heart began to race faster and flashes of horror jumped through her memory. *The thick smack of her baseball bat on a rodent's skull. Teeth and claws thrust up in her face. Something sickeningly slimy regurgitated over her flesh. The penthouse, her home, trashed and bloodstained and littered with bodies …*

Now there was nothing but the hot, sour air and prickling pins and needles in her limbs as she knelt up blindly. Ace rubbed her eyes but, although she felt the pressure, as she blinked still she could see nothing but blackness: as if she were still travelling through a void smeared faintly with stars. She remembered in flashes the intense feeling of flight, of leaving her body, of plunging helplessly through bright nothingness, just the same as when she'd been blown away from her bedroom and found herself in Iceworld. Taken, snatched and set down on the other side of the galaxy; only she'd been young then, her body hadn't ached like this, she'd not been so afraid because she hadn't known all there was to be afraid of.

Ace tried to take a deep breath but choked on the sickly, sulphurous heat of it. She fell forward and cut one hand on something sharp. A stone, or glass even, or …

The realisation struck her cold:

I'm back in the nightmare.

Now Ace was afraid that her eyesight would actually return. She didn't want the proof of it, didn't want to see the lurid landscape that she knew, with sick certainty, must surround her now: that vast, glittering desert, sand blowing over raw crystal and razor-sharp rocks. *If you've travelled faster than light,* she thought, *maybe your eyes are still in the dark?* It was a child's reasoning but that was just how she felt: like a frightened child, lost far from home.

'Let me wake up,' Ace whispered. 'Please, God, let me wake up now.'

As if in response, her vision sparked back into a blur of colour. Yes, there it was, the wasteland that had held her in her sleep for so long, and that now held her for real. 'Yaz?' Ace called uncertainly, but she knew already that she was alone. What had happened to Yaz, slimed up and tagged and ready to go?

'Your new golden girl's messed up, Professor,' Ace breathed. 'Looks like we're going old school.'

Three suns sat like cigarette burns in the filthy tarpaulin of the sky. Ace looked down at the stony, dusty ground, feeling sick. As her eyes remembered how to focus, she knew what she would see on the horizon.

It sat there like some giant spider in the distance, a crumbling alien castle of dark pumice. Even from here she could hear the grind of the engines inside and taste the smog belching from those vast, broken chimneys.

With relief, she saw she was still holding her baseball bat. The metal was stained with blackened red, and turned her stomach.

'I didn't start this fight,' she reminded herself.

Leaning on the bat, Ace stood up shakily. She could hear distant cries, moans, shouting. She wasn't alone here. There would be hordes of others, taken and trapped just like her, and Ace knew that she had to find them. She had to find the reason why she was here. In her dreams she'd been shown a premonition, but now she was a prisoner of her subconscious no longer. *I can act*, Ace told herself. *Change things.*

She brushed off her black bomber jacket, looked down at her badges, took strength from them. To how many alien worlds had she dragged her *Blue Peter* badges! Sometimes she'd imagined herself filming a Special Report from one of those far-off planets, relating the problems facing the inhabitants – or the casual visitor.

'This one's simple,' Ace murmured. 'Come here, and you're royally stuffed.'

She hummed the *Blue Peter* theme tune to herself as she forced herself to walk like she meant it toward the sinister edifice on the horizon, striding up the sandy rise with all its sharp edges, gripping the bat like she was ready to strike something hard.

Night was falling fast, the sickly glow of the three sinking stars fading to reveal an alien night of dust clouds and nebulae. As she reached the top of the sharp, sandy slope, Ace saw scores more people moving towards the weathered fort, moving alone or in straggling groups. Young people, young … *things*, humanoid but with very different features, limbs or hues to their skin.

Her bruised spine tingled. The scene was straight from her dream.

She sensed they were walking to the building, like her, because there was nowhere else to go. She remembered her sensory hallucinations before, hearing her mother's voice, smelling her old bedroom … the time-dilation effect had maybe pulled past events into her present. Perhaps her recurring nightmares had been the echo of future events – or rather, of events right now – thrown back through her consciousness in the same basic way.

I'm a long way out, Ace reckoned. *Further than I've ever come before.*

But where had her fellow travellers come from? Ace squinted through the gathering dusk, hoping to find potential allies, some race she recognised from her TARDIS travels.

Amid the legions trudging across the sands she saw two people who made her jaw drop in astonishment.

'Chantelle?' Ace shouted, stumbling forward. 'Kim! What the hell ...?'

For a moment she doubted her senses. But no: she didn't know how, but it was them. She was sure of it.

Ace quickened her step, wincing as the sharp rocks bit at her feet even through the soles of her boots. Then she heard a sound like twigs snapping close by and a waft of musk and decay.

A single word sliced through her brain: *Ratts.*

She turned, gripped the bat tighter. But a tail like a python whipped out and knocked her feet from under her. She landed on her back, gasped as the ground gouged at her through her jacket. Next second, a Ratt was straddling her, its hideous face pushing out from the hood of matted fur and flesh. Ace slammed the base of the bat handle into the side of its head, knocked it clear and rolled over onto it, using its hairy body as a springboard. She came up in time to confront another Ratt, and belted it under the jaws so hard it hurtled backwards in a clumsy somersault.

Now the first Ratt was scrambling up. Ace turned on him, panting, got ready to bring the bat down on it. Too late she saw a spike of glass and metal in its claws, and the arc of energy that crackled from its tip. Her body went into spasm like she'd been tasered, the bat tumbling from numb fingers. The power shut off and Ace was about to drop, helpless – when a third Ratt scurried up and caught her by the throat before she could fall.

'Get ... off me,' she hissed, as the claws tightened on her neck. Desperately she looked over to where Kim and Chantelle were continuing their ragged stagger across the plain. Neither of them had heard her; they couldn't even know that she was there. No one else had turned at the sounds of the struggle either. Was everyone under some kind of mind control?

The Ratt's tangled whiskers twitched as it pushed its horrible snout towards her. 'You're not going to processing like everyone else,' he hissed. 'The big boss wants to see you.'

The first Ratt was back on its misshapen feet. 'Sensed something different in you.'

'Something the *same*,' the third corrected.

'Big boss?' Ace managed to croak through the choking talons, her throat burning. But she knew already, the big boss was the thing she'd glimpsed at the end of every nightmare. The face in the sky.

She felt its image forming above her, a constellation growing three-dimensional features. Four burning red eyes in a demonic face that was more wrinkles than features. Ears like gigantic bat wings unfolded from the bald, clay-grey head. The thing had a skeleton's nose, two pits drilled above the awful mouth, a huge smiling sickle of a mouth with protruding teeth. All the terror of her nightmares bore down on her as the Ratt held her body in its choking grip.

Then the face in the sky spoke in a deep, sibilant whisper, like distant thunder. 'Bring her to me. I would know this one again.'

'Again?' Ace whispered.

'Personal invite. Ain't that nice?' said the Ratt, dragging her over the sand.

'No!' Ace shouted helplessly. She made one last desperate lunge for her baseball bat in the sand, but it was too late. She was being taken away from Chantelle and Kim, away from the huge smoking factory that everyone else was making for. 'No, I won't go.'

The Ratt smiled. 'If Halogi-Kari wants to know you, darlin', you're gonna be known.'

There was a hole in the dusty desert, as if the ground had grown a mouth.

It closed around the Ratt and Ace, who found herself dragged on into the hot, spiteful darkness.

CHAPTER TWENTY-ONE

'Could've been worse,' Graham said ruefully, leaning against a featureless wall. 'Could've had us mucking out the stables.'

'Stable would be nice and cosy,' Ryan said. 'Though this whole "War Chariot" spaceship thing smells like horse anyway.'

'True enough. You'd think they'd give us straw and a saddle-bag or something.' Graham paused. 'You know, I rode a horse once.'

'Wow.' Ryan scoffed. 'You should tell them. They'll be well impressed.'

The centaur creatures had fitted them both with metal collars and led them in chains through the shuddering space station into their golden warcraft. It wasn't much of a guided tour; pushed through the corridors and into a cold holding area, a cell with nothing in it but a contraption built into the wall that might've been a toilet and a trough with water in it. Ryan was subdued and fiddling with what looked like a small silver torch. Still recovering from his ordeal with the Ratts and the time-storm, Graham supposed, as well as the major elephant in the room.

Elephants, horses and rats, Graham reflected. This was a right menagerie.

'It's gonna be all right,' he said, trying to sound confident. 'The TARDIS'll be along in a minute. Rescue wagon knocking at our door.'

'You said the Doctor got hit, though.'

'She's been through worse. You know her. Tough as anything.' Graham nodded, hoped he was doing a good job of seeming self-assured. He sat stiffly on the floor. 'You'd think they'd give us a chair.'

'You ever see a horse sit on a chair?'

'Don't they ever have guests? I know we're prisoners but we must have some rights?'

'Nothing but wrongs, I reckon. Still. Feeling sorry for ourselves won't help.'

'It's you I really feel sorry for,' Graham said. 'You look rubbish, mate.'

'Thanks a lot!' said Ryan, but he was smiling as he turned his gaze back to his torch. 'Ace gave me this in the batcave before me and Chantelle left.'

'Hope they're OK,' said Graham.

Ryan nodded. 'We need to find them.'

'First we need to be found ourselves. You're wearing your tag, though, aren't you? Bleeping away every second, a big distress call. Couldn't ask for more, right?'

'Apart from the straw and the saddlebags,' Ryan said, and they both smiled. Then Ryan grew serious. 'Listen, Granddad. Ace told me that—'

He quickly shut up and shoved the torch back in his pocket as an invisible door in the wall cranked open. Two of the centaur-things pushed into the cell, dominating the space. Graham felt uneasy just looking at them; they looked so familiar in some ways, but so wrong. It was the little heads that did it, he decided: heads resembling a horse's but the size of a human's. Both the creatures were ashen white in colour, with manes as black as their eyes, plaited with strips of metal. One wore golden armour, the other silver.

The golden one flared her nostrils. Graham saw the white hairs around her eyes; she'd been around a bit, this one. 'I am Legate Aquillon, Charioteer-General in the service of Operation Deep Avenge.' She tossed her head towards her fellow. 'This is Centaurion Masst.'

Graham cleared his throat, stepped forward. 'I'm Former Bus-Driver Graham O'Brien, and this is, um, Teen Loiterer Ryan Sinclair.'

Ryan flashed him a look, mouthed, 'Seriously?'

'We've done nothing wrong, ma'am,' Graham insisted. 'This boy was kidnapped from Earth. I was on that space station cos we were trying to rescue him. Me and the Doctor.'

'The Doctor is an enemy of our race,' said Aquillon. 'A known war criminal with the power to change appearance: an ally of the Wraiths and murderer of our kind.'

'No way,' said Graham. 'Wrong person.'

'DNA scan proved her culpability.' Aquillon swept her fierce gaze onto Graham. 'If you are in her service, you will be executed.'

Ryan swallowed hard. 'We're not in anyone's service. We're not military, nothing like that, and neither's the Doctor.'

'You are her associate, then.' Aquillon pushed her head closer to Ryan, eyes shining. 'Her spy.'

Ryan met the dark depths of her gaze. 'Her friend.'

'The Doctor's not an ally of these Wraith things!' Graham protested.

'Permission to use the think-scan on them, Legate?' Masst tried to come between Aquillon and Ryan. 'If our prisoners are telling the truth ...'

Aquillon snorted. 'Are the think-scans even still functional after all this time?'

'One is.' Masst sounded defensive. 'I've cannibalised parts from the others to sustain it. They'll give us the answers we want—'

'Nothing lasts, does it, Centaurion?' Aquillon's voice was low and husky. 'Better we learn to get answers for ourselves.' She pulled down hard on the chain around Ryan's neck, and Ryan fell to his knees with a gasp. 'I repeat: you are an associate of a known war criminal, Ryan Sinclair!' The rasping voice was more insistent this time. 'You are her spy.'

'No!' Graham started forward, but Masst raised an ash-white hand. 'The Doctor was trying to save a whole bunch of kids who were kidnapped from planet Earth by these alien rat-things.'

Aquillon ignored him. 'She was assisting allies of the Wraiths.'

'She was not!' Ryan said. 'Reckon it's you who needs the think-scan—'

'Prisoners will *not* be insolent.' Aquillon kicked Ryan in the chest with a front hoof. Ryan was thrown back against the wall, lost his balance and collapsed into the water trough with a clatter. Water went everywhere. The Legate clopped closer, raising her hoof again.

'What d'you think you're doing?' Graham shouted.

Thank God, it seemed Centaurion Masst agreed; he quickly placed himself in front of the dazed Ryan, squaring up to his own CO.

'Is this who we are now, Legate Aquillon?' Masst said quietly. 'The Astingir, trampling lesser races underhoof because it pleases us to?'

You could almost see the steam hissing from Aquillon's nostrils. 'The boy is—'

'The boy is still a boy,' Masst said quietly. 'And we are old, and we are tired.'

Aquillon snorted. 'Stand aside, Centaurion.'

'I say again, is this who the Astingir are?'

The Legate glared at her subordinate, but Ryan could see the anger dimming in her eyes. 'We have chosen who we are.' Aquillon's voice was quieter now, restraint asserted. 'We stand vigilant and vengeful until our end.'

'Until our end,' Masst echoed, as if this was something learned by rote. 'Yes. So we have pledged.'

Graham watched and waited anxiously.

Then Masst moved away and gestured to Graham. 'Assist the boy.'

'I'm all right.' Ryan tried to rise, staggered forward. He didn't notice his shirt gaping at the neck, enough to show a flash of the red metal device attached to his collarbone.

'Wait.' Aquillon pushed forward again, her white-hide fingers tearing at Ryan's shirt. 'What technology is this?'

Masst sniffed, as if he could tell the tech by scent alone. Perhaps he could. 'It is not of local origin,' he announced.

'It's not, but I am,' Ryan insisted. 'I'm from Earth. So is Graham. You need to put us back.' He looked at Masst, hoping for more mercy, but the Centaurion was waving a wand with a bulbous gold eye that clicked and whirred, scanning him, perhaps. 'Please, just put us back on Earth. What can we do to you? Nothing!'

'This technology does not come from Earth.' Masst's black eyes narrowed, and he flattened his ears to his skull. 'It is a military-grade life-beacon used by the Peace Corps on Hondopel.'

'So!' Aquillon reared up in anger. 'All this time our prisoners have been summoning help?'

'It is emitting a test signal, not a distress call,' Masst clarified.

'Yeah, she didn't want them Hoodoo Pels to break off their own Search and Rescue missions to go after Ryan,' said Graham. 'It was just so the Doctor had something to follow, so she could find where everyone was being sent on to by that station place. If she was working with the Wraiths she'd already know where they were going, wouldn't she?'

Ryan nodded quickly. 'Stands to reason, yeah?'

Aquillon wasn't listening. She removed a tool from her belt and pressed it to the beacon. Ryan yelled out in pain; the beacon hissed and smoked and he clutched at it, trying to pull it clear.

Graham helped him, burning his fingers but eventually prising it off. It clattered to the floor.

Graham stared at Aquillon, sickened. 'What the hell do you think you're doing?'

The Legate raised a hoof over the beacon. 'It must be destroyed.'

'Under Article Six of our own Interstellar Peace Accord, we are forbidden to interfere in other conflicts,' said Masst urgently. 'And it is enshrined across that sector of space that to destroy a Peace Corps beacon is tantamount to a declaration of war against the Hondopel. To do so risks bringing a dozen races into a defensive alliance against us.'

'The analyser confirms that the signal is not a distress call, merely testing,' said Aquillon. 'Our actions will be excused.'

'Perhaps ... But can the Astingir afford to fight another war?'

'Can *you* afford to defy me again, Centaurion?' Aquillon ground the beacon into scrap beneath her hoof then seized Ryan by his metal collar and shoved him over to Masst. 'We must know who was listening to that signal ... who may be coming for them right now.'

'Only the Doctor was listening out for that signal,' hissed Ryan, 'and you killed her!'

The Legate ignored him. 'Time is of the essence, Masst. Get answers.'

Masst bowed his head and turned, leading Ryan struggling from the cell. Graham tried to follow – but Aquillon brushed him aside with her flank. The Astingir exited the room and the cell door slid back down.

'Oi!' Graham banged on the door, terrified. 'Centaurion Masst – don't hurt him! Think-scan him or whatever you have to do, you'll see we're on the same side ... please!'

There was no response. Nothing. Graham pressed his clammy forehead against the door, thinking about the way the horse-creatures had argued in front of their prisoners. Not exactly a well-disciplined military force. More like soldiers who'd been on duty so long and so hard they were at breaking point.

And that made Graham more afraid.

Ryan tried to stay calm as Centaurion Masst herded him through the War Chariot's dim corridors. The ship had seen better days; not all the lights in the golden ceiling were working, there were dents and scrapes in the tarnished walls and the floors had been worn uneven by the endless hooves that trod it. They passed two more Astingir troops, wearing dark, netted under-armour, tattered and torn; Ryan supposed they were off duty ... and that the nearest military outfitters had to be a few star systems away.

He was pushed into a square room with what looked like intricate brass Victorian plumbing – hissing pipes, valves and dials with quivering needles – over three of the walls. Something like a brass lampshade built into the ceiling pointed at the fourth wall, which was bare and white.

'What is this place?' Ryan asked.

'The think-scanner,' said Masst, and the plumbing seemed to hiss a little more spitefully.

'Is it gonna hurt?'

'It shouldn't do, if you don't resist.' Masst held one of the pipes and it glowed, as the hissing grew to gurgles. 'I will ask you questions, and the machine—'

'Scans what I'm thinking?'

'That is correct.' Masst studied him. 'You are familiar with the technique?'

'Well, this ain't my first rodeo, you know?' Ryan bit his lip. 'Um, no offence, sorry. I've never been to a rodeo.'

Masst was unmoved. 'Stand back against the wall, please.'

'I really haven't! Scan me and you'll see. I've never even ridden a horse.'

'What is a horse?' Masst enquired.

'Er – doesn't matter.' Ryan started towards the wall, then hesitated. 'Look, is my granddad gonna be all right with your ... Legate, was it?'

'We are not animals.'

Ryan would've given a wry glance to camera if he could've. 'Yeah, well. See, I ... I'm just a boy,' he said, wide-eyed, remembering what had got Masst rattled last time. 'I'm scared, I don't know what's going on ...'

But the centaurion wasn't buying it this time. 'If you are innocent as you claim, you have nothing to fear.' He gestured to the wall. 'Proceed.'

Ryan did as he was told and stood against the wall. He had a sudden flashback to being eight years old, his nan pushing a ruler down over his hair to mark his height with a pencil. Then, with a chill, he realised the image in his mind was flickering in front of him, a little blurred and in muted colours like a filter was placed over the image.

He felt his insides squeeze at the sight of his happily smiling nan. But then the image hissed away like steam.

'Everything on this damned ship is so damned old,' Masst muttered. 'Should've been impounded decades ago.'

'Why wasn't it?' asked Ryan. 'If chasing after these Wraith things is so important, why are you travelling around in a worn-out old ship?'

'I am conducting the enquiry.' Masst was holding the pipework, and gasped when a gout of steam scalded his hand. Nan's image returned fuzzily. Ryan gazed at it and wished she were still alive. Wished she were with him now.

Masst noticed his attention. 'She is ... family?'

'She was,' Ryan corrected him. 'She's dead now.'

'I have lost family too,' Masst said, lowering his head. 'My life-partner. My child.'

'The Wraiths?'

'No. An accident. A meaningless travel accident.' Masst trod forlornly around the chamber. 'When it happened, I was on patrol, destroying a Wraith weapons cache on an outer world, two hundred light years away. I was denied leave to return for my family's burial.'

'Rough.' Ryan felt some actual sympathy. 'Aquillon's orders?'

'We are pledged to defile, to destroy, to desecrate all trace of Wraith civilisation.'

'We? The Astingir army, you mean?'

Masst didn't answer at once. Just as he did open his mouth, the image of Nan broke up in smoke, and the pipes in all three walls began to throb with energy. The bubbling sound seemed to bring Masst round from his introspection.

'The interrogation will commence,' he said. 'Ryan Sinclair, you claim you were abducted from your whole world. By the Doctor?'

'No!' Images of the Doctor fixing the signal device to his body formed from thick vapour. 'Anywhere she goes, I go willingly.' He paused. 'I ... *went*, willingly.'

'Then what form did your abduction take?'

The image blurred and now showed the Ratts pressing in around him and Chantelle. He felt a deep pang of disquiet for where she might be now, and a rush of purple washed through the image.

Masst studied the dials and meters in the pipework. 'You wish ... that you were with that person.'

'I wish we were all safe. That the Doctor was all right, and those Ratt things were gone.' He looked at Masst again. 'What are they, then? Got form have they, working for the Wraiths?'

'We are not familiar with such an alliance,' Masst admitted.

'But you reckon the Doctor's teamed up with them? You need to get your facts straight.' Ryan looked at Masst. 'She wouldn't have been trying to help the Wraiths, she'd have been trying to stop them. What did she do that made her public enemy number one to you lot, anyway?'

'She defiled a Site of Mass Contrition, a clear offence under Article 26 of the Pan-Conflict Termination—'

'So she's no good at following the rules!'

'She attempted to breach the barriers that surround the Quantum Anvil, within which we have trapped the Wraiths. She encouraged the extermination of a Defence Herd while attempting to evade capture ...' Masst stopped talking, black eyes widening and he twisted one of the valves. With a roar of steam and a brighter glow from the brass lightshade, the holograph image plucked from Ryan's mind froze. 'With her.'

'Huh? That's Ace,' said Ryan, baffled. 'Dorothy's all right. Old friend of the Doctor.'

'Aquillon was right. Our mission has not yet run its course.' Masst strode through the image and pushed his scowling face up close to Ryan's. 'You say you are innocent, that the Doctor was innocent. And yet this woman – the Doctor's friend – was the one who acted for her, reached out to the Wraiths, killed our people.'

Ryan saw the hate in Masst's eyes and it scared him. 'Mate, you've got to believe me, I only met her a couple of days ago! How was I to know?'

Masst wasn't listening. 'The Legate must be told,' he said. 'The Herdworld must be told! Our vigilance will be remembered, our actions rewarded. And, yes.' He placed a hand menacingly on Ryan's shoulder. 'Our vengeance must be shared.'

CHAPTER TWENTY-TWO

Ace felt feeling return to her limbs slowly, in vicious fits and starts, as the Ratts dragged her through the tunnel that ran beneath the desert. It was cold, the sweat drenching her back that of one waking from a nightmare. Glowing stones were set into the roof at regular intervals, just enough light to make the shadows ahead look more frightening still.

Finally the Ratts stopped beside a door made from beaten iron, adorned with finely crafted figures, squat and powerful; Ace thought at first they were embracing, passionately intertwined. But, no, they were fighting, killing, tearing each other apart. Was it the dim flicker of the light that made the figures seem to dance and tremble, and sent iron blood surging from the open wounds?

The door swung open, soundlessly, and before Ace could react she was pushed through it into a vast chamber hollowed from solid rock. Perfumed smoke filled the air, cloying and conspiring with the shadows to confuse her senses. The door slammed closed behind her, the echo like a fist battering her ears. She felt a deep, instinctual fear, a sense that some past nightmare, buried for so long, was now running her close.

It seemed she was alone, for now, anyway; no doubt the thing that had brought her here wanted to increase her apprehension. Ace forced herself to stay calm, to do what she'd always used to do alongside the Doctor – assess the space, check for best-option exits and for anything she could use for a weapon. She badly wanted to cough on the smothering incense but was damned if she'd give anyone the satisfaction of knowing they'd got to her.

Looking about, it was like being in some kind of alien castle. Two dozen scarlet pennants – strips of rich, heavy fabric, three metres wide – hung down from a roof lost in shadow until they almost brushed the polished stone floor. An ornate throne that looked to have been carved from some colossal ivory tusk reared up into the space from the middle of a wide, circular dais edged with a sinister sculpture – carved, gleaming figures frozen in the midst of writhing agony, twisted, broken, screaming.

Exits? She couldn't see any. Weapons? None. What little furniture there had been extruded from the space. But perhaps she could climb the pennants, perhaps there was a gallery hidden above, somewhere she could escape to …

Steady, she told herself. How the hell are you going to climb up there? You're not 18 any more. You're a middle-aged woman.

Some fleeting movement on the pennant beside her, scuttling like a spider, made Ace cry out and back away. A short, squat, crumpled figure, clothed only in thick flaps of elephantine skin the colour of faded bruises, dropped down to the floor in front of her, panting like a dog. Two stubby arms and legs hung down from the trunk like melted wax. A devilish face pushed out from between two thick folds of skin, pudgy and grey-eyed watching her with malicious interest.

'Yes. Yes, it *is* you,' said the figure, in a voice that was unexpectedly high and singsong. 'Forgive my late arrival to you, Child of Earth. I was checking my records. Checking, yes.'

Ace said nothing. She supposed that without the TARDIS here translating, the creature must be trying to speak English. She was about to respond with some choice Anglo-Saxon for it to chew on when finally she coughed, her throat parched dry from the ordeal in the desert and now the scented smoke. The figure watched her whoop and heave, then chuckled and turned from her. It crossed to the dais and paused, as vestigial hands and feet pushed out from thick rolls of flab at the end of its limbs. Then it climbed over the sculpted bodies, caressing them almost sensually as it went. Ace could see three horns, curved like a goat's, protruding from the back of its head, and smaller ones tracing the line of its spine. Finally it climbed onto the throne in the giant tusk.

'Who are you?' Ace said at last.

The creature stared at her with unblinking, malevolent eyes. 'I am Halogi-Kari.'

Ace folded her arms. 'Not feeling so good myself.'

'My name is Halogi-Kari. Bringer of time and distance.'

'Not enough distance if you ask me.' Ace shrugged. 'Keeping that seat warm for the big boss, are you?'

'You misunderstand, perhaps.' Halogi-Kari tittered. 'You are in my sanctuary, Child of Earth. Here, there is no authority higher than me.'

'Nothing over three-foot-two, you mean? Got it.' Ace swallowed, more dust than saliva it seemed. 'Why am I here, then?'

'Your ... difference was detected.' Halogi-Kari clasped his three-fingered hands together and looked upward. There was a low chime, a creak – and another roll of heavy fabric unravelled down from the ceiling, landing just beside Ace. She couldn't help but jump, and the thing on the throne cackled earthily.

Then, with a chill, Ace saw herself in the thick fabric panel: herself as a 16-year-old, screaming in her bedroom for help as a yellow glow engulfed her. Help that could never arrive; already the time-storm was taking her away to Svartos.

The pennant billowed towards her and as Ace put out her hand instinctively, she felt a shock of vivid memory – like the time-storm was snatching her again right now, its fire sparking through her bones, making her lightning that struck hard across the void. She cried out, fell backwards to the polished stone.

Halogi-Kari giggled again. 'Bringer of time. Bringer of distance.'

'It was *you* who took me?' Ace breathed.

'The personal touch. At Fenric's command.'

Ace sneered at him across the chamber. 'Just another of Fenric's Wolves.'

'Ah. Alas, once I lived as a wolf, yes. These days, I've been starting to think I am sheep only. Yes, only a sheep. But *you*, Child of Earth, you remind me of the days I was a wolf. I sensed something in you, you know. And I have excellent records. Impeccable records of everyone I've taken through the years. See …'

The hanging fabrics began to shift and stir like waking ghosts. Ace saw faces form in the stitch work, some human, some not, but all with one thing in common: they were silently screaming, shaking, terrified. Hundreds, thousands maybe, begging for mercy, their fear taken, like a souvenir, to create this monster's tally of suffering.

'Stop it, you sicko,' Ace hissed, then glared at him and yelled, 'Stop it!'

The screaming shades faded and the fabric shifts swayed to a stop.

'You see, Child of Earth, with all these faces, only one did I ever see twice.' Halogi-Kari leaned forward on his ivory perch. 'Your face. I took you once from that world. And then you are back?' He laughed again. 'To take you again I would've thought impossible. Yes, impossible!'

'Not the first time I've been called impossible.' Ace glowered at him. 'What are you, sicko – some sort of kidnap-fixer? Someone

210

gives you a target and you time-storm them away and put them down again wherever you're told?'

The creature considered. 'In my glory days, yes. That is fair to say. But then, you see, things stopped. You know that this is true, I think.'

'You don't know me,' Ace promised him.

Halogi-Kari just smiled and lowered his voice to a teasing whisper that chilled her blood. 'I know what you are,' he said. 'And I feel that you will be of great value to me.'

'Go to hell.' Ace bunched her fists, determined not to show him how rattled she was. 'I mean it, sicko. Suppose you just drop the shadowy master-criminal rubbish and tell me why I'm here?'

'Criminal? I? No, no, no.' Halogi-Kari hopped off his carved ivory throne, and the impact set his thick flaps of skin quivering. 'I am most careful when it comes to breaking laws. I must be! I cannot risk a further sentence from the Shadow Proclamation.'

'The who?'

'Space Police. Upholders of Galactic Law.' The creature's little mouth made each word sound like a knife strike. 'They learned of my activities and deemed them illegal.'

'And, what – they got you doing time?' She smirked. 'Shame they didn't throw away the key.'

'Be assured, I was confined for a long time. A long, long time.' He walked across the dais towards her. 'This is why I operate the way I do.'

Ace stiffened at his approach. 'What, you mean, using your rat monsters to front the operation?'

'The Ratts are my paid employees. My work is legal, Child of Earth. I operate under the guise of charity.'

'Charity?'

'You understand this word, I think.'

'Yeah. You could say so.' Ace stared at him, her anger rising. 'You've been abducting homeless kids, poverty survivors, dragging them halfway across the universe to chuck them in a foot-shredding desert and you call that *charity*?'

'I do.' His feet shrank into his veined, lumpy limbs and he jumped down from the dais with a smile. 'After all, what is charity but giving away that which is unwanted – or unneeded – to somebody else ...?'

'You twisted scumbag.' Ace felt the urge to throttle this monster with her bare hands. She started forward, but staggered almost at once. Her head was spinning, and she overbalanced. It hit her at last: why he'd been going on like this, biding his time ... *God, Professor, how slow have I become?* 'This smoke in the air,' she whispered. 'It's ... not incense, is it? It's ... some sort of drug.'

'You are more compliant now, I think, Dorothy. Yes?' Halogi-Kari gave an excited little jump in the air and scuttled towards Ace, black eyes shining, a clawed hand bulging from beneath the fleshy stump of his right arm to make a beckoning gesture. 'Now I can show you what is to come.'

CHAPTER TWENTY-THREE

'Less than 23 minutes till the whole place goes up!' cried the Doctor, as the TARDIS set them back down, a touch reluctantly, perhaps, aboard the collector. 'Let's hope it won't take long to get the space-time coordinates for the next station in the sequence. Let's hope there aren't too many more in the sequence after that. Let's hope we find everyone quickly. Is that too much to hope for?' She tossed Squidget over her shoulder and a big grin at Yaz. 'Nah! Come on.'

Yaz stepped out of the cool of the crystalline control room into a charred, fetid space where fluid sizzled on the blackened walls. It was like arriving on the inside of a rotisserie chicken with the heat on high, while someone blasted the flesh with a taser for good measure. The background hum and murmur of strange power had been replaced by piteous sounds like groans and mewlings and drunken shrieks.

'So which bit are we in?' Yaz said.

'I was aiming for the data store, but it's hard to say. This place is a long way gone,' the Doctor said sadly. 'Breakdown of core systems means the superstructure's just rotting away ...'

'There'll be nothing left to break up in the atmosphere at this rate.' Yaz almost fell over as the station lurched and a deep, belching roar shook the floor. 'How is your gadget going to get any good intel out of this wreck?'

'Remember when we first arrived and Graham accidentally disconnected the cloaking circuit?' The Doctor strode out into the heaving corridor, waving Squidget in front of the wall to her left like a big silver slug. 'That command sent a temporal shiver through the whole station.'

'Yeah, time dilation, you said. The cloaking thing turned off in the past.' Yaz's head hurt. 'I still don't get how that's possible.'

'Time Dilation Syndrome is common to crafts like this that crunch subatomic particles to open up a split in the space-time continuum.' The Doctor watched as Squidget began twitching, sniffing the wall like a hound. 'You know, the Wraiths used these stations in a concentrated formation to push whole fleets into the heart of enemy territory for surprise attacks.'

'Very nice. But how does the time dilation help us?' Yaz paused. 'Wait a moment. You think you can return the whole station to 24 hours ago, when it was still working properly?'

'That's right! Not all of it, and not for long. But maybe just a little section.' The Doctor pulled a face. 'Course, ultimately it'll mean the station blows to bits way faster, but you can't have everything.'

Yaz felt sick. 'Blows up with us still on board?'

'Not ideally.' Suddenly Squidget lunged forward and buried its nose in the wall with a wet squelch. A clean, clear 'BEEP' quickly followed.

'Yes!' the Doctor cheered. 'He's found the main interface. He's connected.'

The next moment Yaz felt the hairs on her neck rise and a dizzying headache as the walls around her lost their burnt stickiness and became that familiar – and disquieting – shining, sticky brown. 'Oh, God … it worked!'

'Now, keep going, Squidge!' the Doctor told the metal animal, which seemed to be chugging at the wall as if swallowing whatever was inside. 'You've got to get into the data store and download the transference log ...'

'How long do we have?' Yaz asked.

'Oh. Ages. Probably.' The Doctor's smile was looking more strained than usual. 'I was wondering how whoever or whatever inherited this collector station got full access to the Wraiths' systems access codes. They'd have taken them to their graves ...'

Squidget gave a warning burble.

'Let's not think about graves right now.' Yaz began to fiddle with her hands. She felt useless, surplus to requirements. *But I can still think*, she told herself. 'Doctor, you said what the Wraiths used this place for. But the new owner is settling for sending some random people clear across the universe. Why?' Yaz shook her head. 'What's so special about them?'

'What's so special about anyone? Ask the people that love them.' The Doctor frowned. 'Although, I don't suppose that a lot of those people felt that anyone *did* love them; that's what made them easy pickings.'

'Only they're not that easy, are they?' Yaz countered. 'The new owners here could've sent them through space in one big hit, like they did with Ace in '87. Instead they're using their stations like runners passing the baton in the longest relay race in the universe.'

'That's true. You'd think they'd pick a planet closer. So presumably, they can't.' The Doctor gasped suddenly. 'Yeah, think about it. What if you're under scrutiny from someone really big and powerful – so you have to move cautiously. No drawing attention to yourself. No big energy emissions that risk ructions in local space-time. You play safe and sneak what you need on a trail that's next to impossible to follow for all but the most determined detectives, halfway across the universe ...'

Squidget chirruped loudly, and Yaz jumped. 'Has he done it?'

'He's done it.' The Doctor looked up as the station shuddered again, and a deeper, louder groan rose up from around them. 'He's *really* done it. Squidge has triggered a ray phase shift!' She waved the sonic around Squidget, studied it, and then bit her lip. 'There's gonna be fireworks. Ace, get back to the TARDIS.'

'Ace?' Yaz felt herself frost over. 'You want fireworks, call me by her name again—'

'Yaz! Go!' The Doctor was wide-eyed with horror. 'We've got 30 seconds till break-up.'

'What?' Yaz grabbed the Doctor's arm. 'Come on.'

'No!' The Doctor shook her free. 'I have to find the next station in the sequence. Still got 22 seconds. Go!'

'I'm not leaving you out here,' Yaz insisted.

'I need you to!' the Doctor told her, squeezing Squidget tighter. 'Go into the TARDIS and throw the big green lever on the panel furthest from the doors.'

'What'll that do?'

'Something really important. Something vital. Go!'

Yaz scowled as she turned and ran back to the police box in the now-regenerated data store. But the walls were starting to blur, the shake in the floor was building like a wave. How many seconds were left to them now – 13? Fewer?

Diving into the TARDIS, Yaz ran to the far side of the console just as she'd been told.

There was no green lever.

'No way,' Yaz breathed.

Anguished, terrified, she ran back to the TARDIS doors – and cannoned straight into the Doctor rushing back inside. Both of them went down in a tangle of arms and legs while Squidget was thrown up in the air.

'Only three seconds left!' the Doctor yelled. 'The doors are still …'

As she spoke, the doors slammed shut.

'Closed,' said Yaz in a daze. 'By themselves.'

'No. By him!' The Doctor pointed to where Squidget lay in the console, its metal proboscis dipping into the crystal console like a butterfly's tongue into nectar.

And then the collector blew up.

Yaz yelled as the TARDIS was ejected violently from its landing point, a wave of pressure rattling her teeth. She was sent rolling over and over, crashing against the side of the console as the familiar ferocious gnashing of the ship's engines filled the air about them.

Then everything was calm.

'The collector has collapsed in on itself.' The Doctor knelt up and smiled awkwardly. 'That was a bit close.'

'You tricked me,' said Yaz.

'No, I didn't,' the Doctor answered softly. 'I told you coming in here would do something really important, something vital, and I meant it – it would keep you safe.'

'You know me, I don't need keeping safe,' Yaz protested. 'And I suppose the TARDIS was pre-set to take me back to Earth, wasn't it?'

'Well, yeah. Emergency protocol.'

'And I'd never see you again.'

'No, you would've! Cos, the emergency protocol comes with a really cool hologram generator …' The Doctor seemed to appreciate that this was cutting little ice, and got up and dusted herself down. 'Anyway, the important thing is, we got the coordinates!'

Yaz nodded. 'So we can go after Ace.'

'And Chantelle, and Kim, and all the rest,' said the Doctor. 'Remember the Astingir will be heading there too with Graham and Ryan.'

'You don't know that,' said Yaz. 'Look, these Astingir must have a chain of command, someone they report to. We have to go to them, tell them to let our friends go.'

'We won't get far. See, I'm a war criminal in their eyes, Yaz,' the Doctor said sadly. 'I hate what the Wraiths did to them as much as they do, but they can't see that Ace and I were only trying to *help* them, to stand a chance of stopping the Wraiths if they ever found a way to get free—'

'They can't see because you never gave them a chance to,' Yaz snapped. 'You did it all in secret! Didn't let anyone in on what you were up to. Not even Ace knew, did she? And look at the mess we're all in now.'

The Doctor blinked, stung.

'Ace told me how you lied to her.' Yaz wiped crossly at a tear that was trying to jump down her cheek. 'How you thought you knew what was best for her and you did it without telling her, and you did it over and over again.'

'Yaz, it wasn't like that ...'

'Or maybe it was. I'm sure you had reasons for doing it – the less she knew the better, the greater good and all that, but ... it was still your choice.' Yaz crossed to her, a sad smile on her face. 'Maybe you need to own that choice a bit more, Doctor ... you know? If you want to find the right things to say to the likes of us.'

The Doctor put her hands in her coat pockets and looked down at the floor. 'Yaz. I'm sorry that I manipulated you into going back to the TARDIS. I was afraid you would die, because you're brave and you're loyal and you're willing to risk your life for others, and it would be my fault. But I also know that you are *you* – Yasmin Khan, who's brilliant – and you don't need me to make choices for you.' She looked up and smiled a little. 'Not even if it would mean you got to see an unexpectedly cool holographic message delivery service.'

'Those,' said Yaz, taking the Doctor's hand, 'were good words.'

The Doctor's smile slowly spread across her face. 'Yeah?'

Squidget chimed, jolting them back to the moment. The overhead scanner display showed more space and stars, and a dotted line was pitter-pattering across the darkness.

'That's it, he's found it,' the Doctor murmured. 'The next collector station in the chain. Three hundred years in the future, somewhere in Galaxy Four. Or, if you're standing on Hastus Major, Galaxy Six Billion, Twenty-Two Million—'

'It's there,' Yaz interrupted. 'Thank God. And if we go there, we can find the location of the *next* station …'

The Doctor punched in the coordinates, Squidget gave a ring of approval, and again they were shifting at speed through time and space.

Chapter Twenty-Four

Some ten years ago now, Chantelle had been sent business class to New Zealand on a calendar shoot in the Coromandel. She'd just broken up with yet another idiot, taken too many pills for heartache and jet lag and woken on the first day of the shoot feeling like death. She'd posed on a beach with steam blowing across dramatically from the fresh-dug hot water pools welling up from the sand. Some of the pools had been merely tepid, others scalding hot; the sand itself had been too hot to walk on in places.

Chantelle remembered how she'd barked at a runner on the shoot to get her a bowl of cold seawater to soothe her feet, tearing into the poor kid when the best he could find was a old bucket, sending him out to find something better. He'd come back with a grimy washing-up basin taken from the only nearby café and she'd ordered him fired.

His look of hurt and disbelief as the director was forced to send him away … It had haunted Chantelle so many times since.

And she could almost feel that runner's eyes boring into her now as she trudged across the blazing sands of this godforsaken place, her exposed skin dry and burnt tight, feet stinging, shoes red-black with congealed blood. Oh, God, for a single drop of cold water now. For any relief or comfort. Anything.

The sinister building they'd been walking towards for so long was looming ahead of them. Kim's hand brushed against hers as they staggered along together. She took it without thinking, without looking up; she couldn't bear looking at the other weird creatures scuffling along in their ragged, limping scrum. She pretended for a couple of moments that he was that boy she'd dismissed so curtly: *I'm sorry*, she wanted to say. *See, I've never known when I'm well off, and now ...*

A handful of Ratts were clustered around the building, pushing the new arrivals towards little booths cut into the pumice walls.

'Why didn't they bring us straight here?' Chantelle said quietly. 'Why make us walk all the way over when it's so hard?'

'I was wondering that too,' Kim said. 'I guess to ram it home that we can't run away and there's nowhere to go, even if we could. They probably want to crush all the hope from us. Makes us, you know, easier to handle.'

'Right,' Chantelle sighed. 'Because we know we're as good as dead.'

'They can't have gone to all this trouble just to kill us,' Kim reasoned.

Now she glowered at him. 'You think they're throwing us a cocktail party?'

A Ratt bore down on them and shoved them towards one of the little nooks in the wall. Inside, one of the twisted rodent-like creatures sat, shielded by shadow from the relentless suns, with a pile of what looked to be plexiglass sheets. With filthy, long-nailed hands he shoved one at Chantelle.

'Pass,' he hissed with stinking breath. 'Look and blink.'

She looked at him, blank and fearful. 'Excuse me?'

He rolled his yellow eyes. 'This is your pass to the shelter. Hold it up to your eyes and blink once to confirm you came willingly and accept all terms and conditions of entry.'

Automatically, Chantelle lifted it towards her face.

Kim batted down her hand. 'No, wait. We didn't come willingly.'

'You did,' the Ratt argued. 'You came from over there. No one made you.'

Kim pointed around angrily. 'We didn't come to this planet willingly, did we!'

'We'll die if we don't get inside,' Chantelle told Kim.

'What are the terms and conditions of entry?' Kim persisted.

'No one ever cares about them,' she protested. 'And I need to get out of this sun.'

'I always read the T&Cs,' Kim said.

'Big surprise.'

'We need to know the terms and conditions,' he told the Ratt.

The Ratt leaned back on his seat and grunted. 'Troublemaker here.'

Immediately a further Ratt came up; Chantelle recognised it as the creature who'd spat on them and taken them here, and she took a faltering step back – as the Ratt slammed down the tip of its broad tail on the back of Kim's neck like a cosh. Kim fell down hard in the dust and cried out as his hands and knees were cut open.

The Ratt in the booth peered out, blinking in the sunlight. 'The terms and conditions simply confirm you are freely making a charitable donation to our organisation.'

Chantelle helped the bleeding Kim to his feet. 'Donating what?'

'Yourselves,' said the Ratt.

The other stuck its snout in Kim's face. 'You know how it is where you come from,' it said. 'You know them bags of unwanted stuff you leave at the end of the drive for charities to come round and collect?'

Kim nodded dumbly.

'Well, basically, you are a bag of unwanted stuff. Aren't you?' The Ratt showed off its filthy teeth. 'And we have collected you for processing and brought you to our plant here.'

Chantelle stared. 'We're not charity donations!'

'The homeless people, the runaways,' Kim said quietly. 'I interviewed some of them. They all said they felt worthless, discarded, given up on by their families. When you're younger, especially, you feel all that stuff so sharply ...'

'Those kids weren't bagged up and left at the end of the garden, were they!'

'Metaphorically, maybe,' Kim said.

'But we're not homeless. I'm successful.' She glared at the Ratt in the booth. 'I'm a celebrity. I've got fans, for God's sake!'

The Ratt behind her held up a small metal gadget that blew up a holographic bubble. It was her from last night, being spied on. *'I'm sick of it. Sick of what it almost turned me into, sick of the never-ending parade of weirdoes that come crawling after me ...'*

'They've been spying on us,' Kim realised.

'We know trouble when it comes sniffing around our business, don't we,' said the Ratt. 'And we know a loophole in the law when we see one, too.'

'It's clever.' Kim actually half-smiled. 'I lost my TV show dream, my mum's been threatening to throw me out ... We believe no one wants us, no one would miss us – and so these things reckon they can just take us away.'

'Maybe Ryan had abandonment issues too, as well as that gunk on his face?' Chantelle sighed. 'I don't know. When I said what I said I was just feeling down. I *am* gonna be missed, course I am. Why d'you think I've stayed in a grotty flat on my old estate my whole life? Because I care about people, and they care about me.'

'You Earth-things!' the Ratt chortled. 'You say one thing, do another, change your minds the next day ... Do you really think anyone can be bothered to understand you?' He put his gadget back in his jacket pocket. 'We have your brain scan and an audio confirmation confirming a state of feeling discarded, unwanted, unloved. In a technicality of galactic law, that entitles us to remove any unwanted dross from any Level 5 world as an act of charity, and put you to better use here. See, here you're needed. Ain't that nice?' The Ratt held out one of the plastic sheets to Kim. 'Your consent is just a formality.'

Chantelle looked bleakly at Kim. 'He's basically saying they look at Earth like it's a charity shop, found us on the shelf and took us off the planet's hands.'

'That's about it. Must be the same for all these other ones too.' Kim took the sheet and stared down at it in his hands. 'And now we have to confirm they can do what they like with us, or we'll be left out to die.'

Chantelle blinked back a tear and looked at her reflection in the plastic sheet. She saw how haggard she looked, her peeling face, hair a disaster, clothes filthy. *Oh, God, I really am a charity case,* she thought, and as she blinked, the plastic changed colour to bright green.

'Accepted,' said the Ratt in the booth. A heavy wooden door cracked open in the outer wall. 'In you go.'

Without another word, Chantelle took stumbling steps towards it.

The cool darkness inside was like a sweet caress. The stone was worn smooth at her feet. She stood trembling, eyes closed, grateful for the sudden respite.

The door slammed shut behind her and something sinuous wrapped around her waist and clamped tight. Screaming, Chantelle was dragged away into the thick shadows.

Step after step, step after step …

Ace found herself following Halogi-Kari through the carved marble passageways of his palace like she'd been put in some sort of voodoo trance. She could think for herself, but felt detached from her own body. Any thought of running out or attacking the scabby little bilge-bag died before it could power her limbs to action, flitting out of conscious reach. It was like trying to focus on the blind spot that heralded one of her migraines coming on; she just couldn't do it.

Halogi-Kari had been telling her how he needed thousands of 'units' – flesh and blood people, the homeless and the dispossessed.

'Why did you come back to the Earth all these years later to take those poor kids?' Ace asked. In her mind the words were charged with anger, but they came out quite conversationally.

Halogi-Kari was equally equable in his reply. 'The territory was already scouted from the time I collected you. I knew how many I could take from the cities of Earth before sending them onwards through the chain of Wraith Stations, each of them so far from my stronghold here on Peerie Canto that the Shadow Proclamation would never suspect my involvement.'

'Wraith …?' Ace felt a scratch of dread along her spine. 'The stations were made by the Wraiths? How did *you* get them, then?'

'I helped to design them. The Wraiths employed me to time-storm their forces into their victims' territories.' Halogi-Kari stopped his murderous waddle, turned and fixed Ace with those unblinking black eyes. 'Such a reputation I had! No wonder Fenric came to me.' He laughed, a sickening sound that soon died away in his flabby throat. 'When the Astingir brought down the Wraiths with their Quantum Anvil, the Shadow Proclamation learned of my involvement and sentenced me to one hundred years' imprisonment.' His smile became crafty. 'But while they authorised the Astingir to impound and destroy all Wraith warcraft, the transit stations escaped seizure. I had hidden them too well.' He nodded his head, and the veins seemed to curl inside his thick hide. 'Ohhhh, I could have put your world to the sword, you know. Yes. I could have time-stormed its military forces, enslaved its people and achieved my aims all in one go! How sweet that would have been.'

'But you didn't. Cos I'm betting one more brush with the Shadow Proclamation and you're …' She wanted to swear, but the drug she'd been fed must stop any and all aggression. 'You can't stand up to them, can you?'

'You think so?' He tittered again. 'The Proclamation think my wings are clipped. They send their officers on random inspections to be sure my businesses are legitimate. To them ... I am making amends as a patron of charity.'

Ace wanted to laugh in his face but it came out as a fond chuckle, and she bit her lip so hard her tongue tasted blood. 'Sounds like the Wraiths deserved to be reduced to nothing more than endless possibilities. But you ... *you*, Halogi-Kari, deserve one single outcome.'

'To die, you think?' He narrowed his dark eyes and smiled. 'Come, Dorothy. Everyone deserves a second chance, don't you think? At my charity, we believe it strongly. Yes, strongly.' He sniggered. 'Even the Wraiths deserve a second chance.'

Ace stared at him helplessly.

'Let me show you, my dear.' Halogi-Kari turned and waddled away once more. 'And I will show you how you can help me.'

CHAPTER TWENTY-FIVE

A low, tremulous clang carried through the Astingir ship, and Graham was on his feet in moments. He looked nervously at Ryan. 'Sounds like this old crate has landed.'

'At last,' Ryan said, and seemed relieved.

'How can this be good? Now the horsey-centaurs know we've hung out with Ace as well as the Doctor, they're never gonna listen to us, are they?' Graham sighed. 'That Aquillon, she's a right 'mare.'

'Mare. Is that a horse joke?'

'There's nothing funny about this. We're public enemies numbers one and two.'

'No point having a rep if you don't live up to it.' Ryan pulled the torch from his pocket. 'Now we've landed somewhere, and there might actually be somewhere to go, we can think about using this thing.'

'Eh? Use a torch?'

'Ace gave this to me, remember? There's something *inside.*' Ryan fumbled awkwardly with the top of the cylinder. 'You do it. Top bit unscrews.'

'What's inside?' Graham shook it.

'Don't!' Ryan held out his arms in a *stop-and-calm-the-hell-down!* gesture, as what looked to be a milky-white marble fell into Graham's palm. 'That's concentrated Nitro-90,' Ryan whispered. 'Magnetic. Force of impact sets it off on a three-second fuse. Little ball, big old blast.'

Graham felt the blood drain from his face as he stared down at the pellet in his hand. 'How big a blast?'

'I dunno. It's not like Ace sat me down with a PowerPoint presentation.'

'All right, so, what d'you reckon we should do?' Graham asked him. 'Blow our way out of here and leg it?'

'Maybe. See what's outside, at least.' Ryan tipped out a further three spheres. 'See, we've got four of these all together. Enough for a show of force, yeah?' He looked up at Graham. 'Once they see what we can do, we get them to throw down their weapons. Maybe we can reason with them – threaten to wreck something important if they don't take us back to Earth.'

'S'pose so.' Graham sighed. 'I don't like this, mate. Too dangerous. Stuff could go wrong, people could get hurt.'

'We'll get worse than hurt if we stay around here.' Ryan put two of the deadly marbles back in the little cylinder, holding the third in his palm. 'And if we go now we've got the element of surprise, haven't we?'

'I'll be surprised if this actually works without blowing us to bits,' said Graham, looking at the marble in his palm. He gave Ryan an encouraging smile. 'Still. No time like now, eh?'

The two of them backed away into a corner, as far from the door as they could get. Graham had an old tissue in his pocket and made slightly grotty earplugs to protect them both against the blast. Then he took a deep breath, and threw the Nitro-90 at the hidden door in the wall.

It struck the surface and bounced back at them.

Graham swore. 'The wall's proper gold. Gold's not magnetic!'

Ryan kicked wildly at the ball and caught it a glancing blow, just enough to send it skittering back towards the wall. Then he and Graham turned their backs – as the tiny explosive went off.

The noise was insane, the heat was instant and fierce, and Graham feared it had burned the clothes from his back and half his skin with it. The shockwave flattened him against the wall he was braced against, and an alarm began to howl. They turned through the smoke to find a gaping hole in the floor and wall, strange components within spitting sparks from the darkness.

'Come on!' Graham yelled, ducking down under the glittering, jagged remains of the doorway.

Ryan was right behind him, a Nitro-90 sphere in his fist, staring around. 'Where do we make for?'

'Why are there no signs in this thing!' Graham said despairingly.

An urgent clatter of hooves suggested company was on the way.

'Well, it was that way to the think-scanner –' Ryan pointed down the corridor – 'so let's try the other way.'

A blast of brilliant energy flashed over Graham's head and tore sparks from the wall behind him. 'Let's try it right now!' he shouted, leading the way along the high arched corridor.

Ryan yelled back over his shoulder: 'Stay back, we don't want to hurt anyone!' He threw down another marble. The blast seemed to follow almost at once, knocking both men off their feet.

Graham looked back dizzily and saw a massive hole had been ripped in the floor, and a section of the wall had caved in. Another alarm, higher pitched, added to the cacophony.

A centaurion loomed up through the smoke, raised its golden crossbow. Graham stared death in the long face.

Then a ceiling panel fell onto the centaurion's head, knocking it cold.

'Oh my days,' Ryan said, 'now they're really gonna be mad.'

The corridor led to a heavy-looking door with a thick glass window. It slid open as they approached – but led into a small circular chamber, bare but for the door in the opposite wall.

'Airlock,' Graham remembered. 'We came through here on the way in.' There was a two-button control panel. Graham tried both, and the door behind them slid shut, quickly followed by the one in front of them sliding open.

Both Graham and Ryan hurried through the door and into the dark, fetid room beyond.

'Oh, you've got to be kidding me,' Ryan groaned, taking in the weird organic feel. 'We're back on the station!'

'Maybe not. That one was properly messed up, it was shaking, screaming, going down.' Graham pulled on a sort of sticky vine growing from the wall, and another door opened onto a corridor pulsing with light. 'This looks all right. I think we're on board *another* station.'

'Like the first one.' Ryan pulled a face. 'Course, the Astingir go after any Wraith tech to destroy it, don't they. This place must be next on the list!'

There was the muffled noise of a laser blast behind them. A furious equine face appeared at the glass panel in the door leading back to the Astingir ship.

'Back off, Aquillon,' said Ryan, holding up the cylinder and attempting his toughest look. 'I've got Nitro-90 in here. Plenty of it.'

The Legate flattened her ears. 'You use the same weapons as your murderous friend.'

'We don't want to hurt anyone,' Ryan went on, 'but we don't want you to hurt us!'

'So if you come in here,' said Graham, 'Ryan's gonna blow up your whole airlock. Think about that. How you gonna get off your ship and on again then, eh?'

Suddenly Ryan fell back dizzily against the wall. 'Granddad...?'

'It's all right mate, I've got this,' hissed Graham, not taking his eyes from the horse-creature through the glass. 'So, Legate, just stay right where you are and we're golden. Well, you are, and your ship is ...'

'Granddad!' Ryan shouted.

This time Graham turned to him, in time to see Ryan shimmering like a reflection in water, slowing fading away. 'Oh, my God,' he breathed in horror. This collector was fully functional, of course – and doing its job, boosting an abducted human being onward to its next destination.

'Ryan, no!' he yelled. 'Don't leave me ...!'

But Ryan already had. The final thing to fade was the glint of alien light shining off Ace's metal torch.

Defenceless and alone, Graham turned back to Aquillon, who was watching him with ever-narrowing eyes.

'Um ...' Graham licked his dry lips, wiped clammy palms on his jacket. 'I've got plenty of those Nitro-90 things too, OK, Aquillon? Pockets full of them ... so, yeah, stay back or I'll ...'

With a snort of anger, the Astingir slammed her hand against the control and the door began to slide open.

Graham turned and ran for his life.

The pounding of hooves echoed around the dark, gristly corridors. Graham felt the blood pulse in his temples as he ran, each gasp for breath like a hook in his throat. He turned right through an open doorway into a corridor where the floor was smothered with vine-like cables, and began running like he'd done as a kid through the tyres in the school obstacle race, knees high, trying not to trip. Would it slow down the centaurs? He prayed it would.

There was a shaft leading off to his left and he threw himself into it. Perhaps they wouldn't realise he'd ducked off the main corridor and keep racing on. That was possible, wasn't it? Wasn't it?

The sound of hooves was coming closer. They were still after him. Could horses hunt? These weren't horses. They were aliens, and angry as hell.

Graham glanced back and saw a glint of golden armour. A laser bolt flashed past and blackened the wall beside him. Chest tight, legs beginning to cramp, he tried to go faster. There was a door to his right and he dodged through it. It gave onto some sort of wide-open space with six steaming, scaly cylinders – cooling towers, perhaps – rising up from the floor. A hiding place! Perhaps he could get inside one of them and …

The Astingir's energy blast hit the floor so close behind him it threw him onto his face. For a few seconds he was stunned, dizzy. He rolled onto his back and saw Legate Aquillon canter slowly into the chamber, Masst and another centaurion at her side.

'My enemy's friend is my enemy,' said Aquillon. 'For your many crimes, I condemn you to die.'

She raised her crossbow, the laser bolt beginning to form.

Graham closed his eyes, as they filled with tears, for Ryan, for Yaz, for the Doctor.

See you soon, Grace, love, he thought, as he heard the spit and sizzle as the bolt fired.

But it never hit him. Graham opened his eyes, in time to witness a second bolt bounce away as if deflected by the air itself.

'That idea you had, Graham,' came a familiar voice behind him. 'The one about extruding the TARDIS force field to protect us? That was proper genius, that was!'

Graham looked round and saw the Doctor beaming and Yaz rushing forward to help him up. He grabbed her in a happy embrace, squeezing her tight.

'Oh, you two!' he cried, clutching hold of the Doctor too.

'Where's Ryan?' Yaz asked, anxious.

'He vanished, just now. This stupid place boosted him on to wherever those Ratts wanted to take him.' Graham held the Doctor's eyes. 'Doc, I was so scared, I thought they'd killed you.'

'So did they, I'm glad to say.' The Doctor pulled gently away and took a step closer to the Astingir. There was steel behind her smile. 'Howdy, Legate. Thanks for dropping off my friend. I'm busy, you can go now.'

'I don't think so, Doctor.' Legate Aquillon's eyes had narrowed to dark slits. 'You are a most-wanted criminal by order of the Astingir Senate. Your execution—'

'I'm glad you mentioned "criminal",' the Doctor said. 'See, when you destroy a Hondopel distress beacon, even one transmitting on a civilian channel, people know, and people care. Turns out the Peace Corps track all their beacons automatically and they'd already traced it to your ship when you stopped it working. The TARDIS picked up a diplomatic protest to the Astingir Herdworld, and your government's response was interesting.'

Aquillon stared at the Doctor but said nothing. Only the hum and pulse of the force-field generator laced the oppressive silence.

'They condemned the action and put it down to a rogue legion with no official standing. A rogue legion on a genocidal mission to rid the cosmos of all traces of the Wraiths.'

'Of course those soft fools would deny knowledge of our actions,' Aquillon began. 'But they will—'

'They deny it because you're wanted by the Herdworld yourself,' the Doctor snapped. She turned to Masst and the other centaur-creature. 'Did your Legate tell you that you're all considered war criminals? That if you return to your Herdworld you'll stand court martial? That this is why your ship is run-down, ill-equipped – because the war is long over and the Astingir are moving forward in peace?'

Masst stared at his superior. 'This is why you denied me leave to return when my wife, my child—?'

'The war can never be over!' Aquillon snarled. 'We have all lost family. And we have all taken our vow. The Wraiths may be trapped but if they find a way to return, they will destroy us. Destroy us without mercy.'

'Like you tried to destroy me, and Graham?' The Doctor looked heartbroken now. 'Can't you see that you've become just like them?'

'We know what you did!'

'No,' the Doctor thundered. 'You inferred, and you were wrong. On your "Site of Mass Contrition", I was trying to make sure the Wraiths could be dealt with without a war if they ever escaped. Ace and I, we didn't mean to kill your soldiers. The ground gave way beneath them, we didn't know!' She wiped crossly at a tear in her eye. 'Our actions can have consequences we never imagined. Lost lives ...'

'And living on, lost,' Yaz added quietly.

Graham noticed the hum of the force-field generator begin to flicker. 'Er, Doc? I hate to spoil the moment ...'

'What?' The Doctor looked about worriedly. 'Ah. Force field's conking out a bit, it's not designed to stick out this far. Might be time to run.' She looked back up at Aquillon, then shepherded Yaz and Graham away. 'I think we're finished here in any case.'

Aquillon started forward, an armoured fetlock sparking against the force field. 'This isn't over, Doctor!'

'For you, it never will be,' the Doctor said quietly.

Graham looked back, haunted by the sight of Masst and his fellow centaurion staring down at the ground while their leader reared up against the force field. Then they rounded a sticky dark corner in the Wraith ship's corridor and the Astingir were lost from sight.

'Doc,' Graham said, as they hurried along, 'how are we going to find Ryan if he hasn't got his tag any more?'

'Each transit station holds the location of the next one in the chain,' Yaz said, 'so we just go to each in turn.'

'You mean it was just luck you were here when I showed?' said Graham.

'Course not!' the Doctor protested. 'The Astingir got hold of the same coordinates we had. We just pipped them to the post.'

She stopped abruptly, and Yaz and Graham almost knocked into her. 'What worries me is, how did they get hold of the location of that *first* Wraith station, in the chain, the one around the Moon?'

'Well if they locked up the Wraiths, there must have been records left behind of all their outposts, gear, what was being held where,' Graham reasoned.

'But the Wraiths didn't put the stations there, did they?' Yaz pointed out. 'The Ratts did.'

'Or whoever they're working for,' said the Doctor, as the pulsing of the energy field crackled and went out around them. 'Oops! Now there's nothing holding back our legion of the lost.' In the distance, a bloodthirsty yell and a scatter of hoof-falls sounded. 'We'd better get back to the TARDIS – and the next station – while we can. Come on!'

CHAPTER TWENTY-SIX

Chantelle sat on a filthy floor in the corner of a crowded holding area, hugging her knees. The suns burned in at the high, barred windows and the smell of sweat and unwashed bodies was stomach-churning in the heat.

There were no Ratts about; hovering robots, like the ones that had snatched her in the dark upon entering, were the jailers here. Jailers and something more sinister.

The robots were sleek, angular and faceless, like the posh hand-driers you found in good hotels but ten times the size and festooned with Doctor Octopus-like tentacles. There was certainly something medical about them – they had laid her on a metal slab surrounded by an array of machinery, like an operating table. There had been other people trapped on their own slabs all about her, shouting and pleading, pinned down and probed by fierce lights from above. One of the octopus arms had pricked her neck with a needle and after that she remembered her ordeal only in dizzy snatches. Floating in a tank of water. Something like a large metal bullet being pushed up her nose. Filaments like metal spider-legs forcing their way under her fingernails.

And when she had woken up again, here, she'd found herself wearing some kind of squishy, fluid-filled body suit, like a man-sized IV bag tailored to fit, limbs and body hidden by the dark red solution inside.

'Bet you never wore anything like that on a fashion shoot, huh.'

Chantelle jumped as if poked with a stick, and saw beside her— 'Kim!'

She tried to grab him in a hug but fell dizzily forwards. He tried to catch her but fell instead into her plasticky arms and they both went down with a squishy thump.

'Smooth, aren't I?' he said.

'You agreed the terms and conditions, then.'

'You charged right in. I've always been easily led.'

'And I've always led easily.' Chantelle's smile faded as she woozily disentangled herself. 'What have they done to us, Kim?'

'Classic alien abduction shtick. Medical tests. Mental scans. Implants.'

'Implants? I can't! People like me for my natural look …' Chantelle caught herself and snorted. 'You don't mean those sorts of implants, do you.'

'Not cosmetic. These are in us now for a purpose.' Kim held up his red fingertips, and Chantelle saw little metal splinters sticking out from under the nails. She looked down at her own nails, cracked and torn, and saw she had the same things, like the tips of tweezers pushing out from her flesh. She gingerly tapped finger and thumb together, afraid they would hurt. But she felt nothing. Numb. Anaesthetised.

'What have they done to us?'

'I have no idea.' Kim shrugged. 'You know I always dreamed of being abducted by aliens. It was kind of the Holy Grail, you know. The ultimate experience. You met them, you communed – just as we have.' He actually laughed out loud. 'God, I wish I had my recorder. The podcast I could do here.'

'Alien abductions ...' Chantelle had caught enough episodes of *The X-Files* to know about those. 'Thing is, they let you go after, don't they? All the people taken, they wake up back where they were taken.' She looked at him, willed herself to focus. 'You think they're going to send us back to Earth?'

He looked down at the squishy plastic suit, gave a small, apologetic smile that was very Kim, and shook his head. 'I don't think we're ever going to see our homes ever again.'

'Don't say that.' Chantelle put her knuckle to her mouth. 'Don't say that, all right? Ace and the Doctor, they'll find us. They'll help us. We're going to get out of here.'

Kim nodded quickly. 'Sure. You're right. I'm sorry. Feeling sorry for myself won't help anyone will it?'

A panel in the wall slid open behind them. Chantelle turned to find another hovering robot. It flicked out a metal tongue that caught around Kim, like it was a frog and he a juicy fly. In a single horrible second, before he could even react, it had jerked him clean away, out of the room even as the door slid back shut.

'Kim!' Chantelle shouted. She struggled over to the wall and banged her fists on it. There was no sign of a door. Had she imagined the whole thing? Was she still asleep on the slab with the robots all around, and dreaming? No, her anger was starting to clear her head now. 'Did you see that?' she demanded of the teen-aged girl beside her. 'Did you see what happened?'

The girl rocked on her haunches, hugging her knees through that horrible plastic suit, face barely visible behind a long black fringe. 'None of this is real,' the girl said.

'If this is a dream, what d'you think is waiting for us when we wake up?' Chantelle crouched and put both hands on the girl's shoulders. 'We could be next. Get away from the wall.'

The girl shrugged her off.

'Listen! Please.' Chantelle turned to address her fellow inmates. All creeds and colours were here; the Ratts must have been recruiting from cities all over the Earth. 'My friend was just snatched away from here and we could be next! We need to get away from the walls, link arms. Make it harder for them to take us.'

Slowly people were starting to look at her. An African man started speaking in a deep, guttural language she didn't understand. He held hands with a smaller man beside him, and reached out to Chantelle.

Chantelle crossed and sat beside him, crooking her arm into his, the gesture saying more than words. She linked arms with a Chinese woman beside her as well. Slowly, the chain was growing.

She thought of Kim and found she was too angry to cry. She'd survived a fair amount of hell in her life. She'd allowed herself to think that her predicament here was worse because it was so far removed from anything she'd ever known or even imagined. But seeing Kim get taken like that ...

You don't stop fighting, she told herself. *You just have to fight harder.*

Yaz was losing the fight against her own impatience. Each station they landed upon, she prayed it was the last link in the chain. But no, each time, there was another one waiting ahead of them through the gulfs of space.

It wouldn't be so bad but she knew there was nothing she could do. The Doctor and Squidget had their coordinate-cracking double act down pat. All Yaz could do was watch and distract with no-use questions: Can't you wipe the next set of coordinates from the station's data drive so Aquillon can't follow us? ('*Nope, data's deadlocked.*') Can't we steer this station somewhere else so Aquillon can't find it? ('*Nope, controls are dead-locked.*') Can't we check for a pattern in these first few stations and work out the last one in the sequence from that? ('*Nope, because there is no pattern ... and if there was, it'd be deadlocked.*') In turn she was distracting the Doctor who tried to make her feel better by setting her little tasks. She'd already called in her tag as a false alarm to the Peace Corps on Hondopel, and listened in on comms to and from the Astingir Herdworld for possible updates.

'Seven we've done now!' she cried, slumped against a wall in the TARDIS console room. 'Seven Wraith stations!'

'Yeah, I'd noticed,' Graham said, rubbing his eyes with tiredness.

'How many more can there be?'

'Don't matter, does it?' He crossed to Yaz, crouched beside her and squeezed her hand. 'We'll keep on going till we get to the end.'

They both jumped as a gabble of voices squawked from the TARDIS speakers, unintelligible.

'Something rattling them horsies' chains?' Graham wondered.

Yaz got up, grateful for something to do, and studied a readout. 'Translating now,' she reported, and Graham rose stiffly to join her.

The gabbling voice had been recorded, only now it spoke in strangely accented English. 'The activities of Legate Aquillon can no longer be tolerated. Hondopel outrage is … final straw. Squadron Triumphalis, under Section 9, Article 15 of Peacetime Enforcement Legislation, will proceed on seek and contain mission …'

'Aquillon's in trouble with the boss,' said Graham with satisfaction.

'About time something went our way!' Yaz agreed.

'I reckon this is just the start,' Graham said. 'The tide's changing. Here's where we come out on top!'

The Doctor burst in with Squidget, who was drooping in her arms. 'The next station in the chain.' She looked ashen-faced. 'It's been destroyed.'

'What?' Yaz and Graham chorused.

The Doctor plonked Squidget on the console and got busy at the controls, calling up the sky scanner, zooming in on a cluster of star systems. 'Yes … would've been just about there. Now it's burned up in the atmosphere of Obsidian Four …'

Graham groaned. 'How come?'

'The Astingir?' Yaz hazarded.

'Must've been. Aquillon's been hunting all trace of the Wraiths. And she's been using Wraith star charts, knows the wormholes they'd have navigated. The portal by Obsidian is actually closest to the Astingir's own system …'

'I don't get it.' Graham looked so bitterly disappointed. 'How'd they find the first in the chain after clobbering the last?'

'A chain doesn't have to be a line, does it?' said Yaz. 'It can be joined up too. Like this.' She reached for Graham's collar and gently fished out the frog necklace he wore around his neck. 'Circular, you know?'

'So the first in the chain is next to the *last* in the chain,' Graham concluded. 'Leaving us stuffed!'

'Maybe not.' The Doctor stood, a slow smile spreading over her face. 'At least we know the location of that final stepping stone.' She started fiddling with the console. 'Perhaps we can't find a sub-atomic needle in a hundred thousand, million, billion haystacks, but now the odds are reduced …'

'Ryan's lost his tag!' cried Graham.

'But Ace has found her bat. Ha!' The Doctor pointed up as a small red light began to pulse in the dark shadows above the console. 'There, you see? That's it! The energies that bled into the atomic structure of that bat are some of the oldest in the universe …'

'Shining like a star.' Yaz felt hope and excitement climb a helter-skelter inside her. 'Where?'

The Doctor squinted at the controls. 'Peerie Canto: an insignificant rock of a planet in an unremarkable triple star system. And if Ace was taken there … Ryan, Chantelle and Kim must be there too!'

CHAPTER TWENTY-SEVEN

Ryan felt kitten-weak and weary with the worst travel sickness he'd ever known. When the ground grew solid under his feet again he collapsed to his knees – and yelled as he realised how sharp it was.

The pain brought strength to his senses. He was kneeling in a desert, the light from three suns failing as they sank behind distant dunes. A large building, part factory, part citadel, stood dominant on the near horizon. No one else was around.

I'm not expected, Ryan realised. *Let's use that to our advantage shall we?*

He carefully stood up on trembling legs and started towards the citadel. The rugged soles of his shoes couldn't shield him from the stinging sands, but Ryan walked purposefully and as fast as he could. He hadn't gone too far before he saw signs of struggle in the sand.

He scanned the scene and his eyes widened at what he saw.

'Where the hell did that come from?' Ryan breathed.

Ace had followed Halogi-Kari down gloomy channels hollowed through the foundations of his citadel. She eyed each shadowed recess in the walls, her imagination peopling the darkness with monsters, poised to strike at her. Somehow, though, Ace knew it was the creature before her who was most dangerous, for all its calm conversation: the stumpy figure with curved horns rising from its misshapen head, and the thick, elephantine blister of its veiny hide. She knew that Halogi-Kari possessed a malevolence greater than any menace that might haunt those thick shadows. Ace felt it in her bones.

And just then she saw the bones of others, scattered around the tunnels. Some large and misshapen, monstrous, others like those of a human, or maybe a large rodent.

'Where are you taking me?' Ace whispered.

'To the heart of my sanctum.' Halogi-Kari peered back at her, black eyes flashing. 'You think it primitive, no doubt, as if you tread some ancient castle labyrinth. Stone and bone and crystals for light – what a place, hmm?' He tittered. 'And yet, no technology could function down here. Not so close to the energies contained in this space.'

'Energies?' Ace frowned. 'But I can't feel anything, hear anything.'

'That is good! It is because you understand those energies – unlike these poor creatures whose remains you see about us. You have felt these energies before and now they do not bother you.'

Ace wanted to shake him, but the incense she'd breathed still tripped up her thoughts before action could be reached. 'What do you mean, I understand the energies?'

Halogi paused before a huge metal door in the tunnel ahead of them, big as a bank vault's. 'You have entered the realm of the Quantum Anvil, have you not?' He looked back at her. 'You stand on the precipice of doing so again.'

'What?' Ace frowned. 'But … this isn't the planet of the Anvil. The gravity's different, there are too many suns …'

He shivered as if with pleasure, so smug. 'I have created a quantum borehole into the realm of the Anvil that joins it to my citadel here on Peerie Canto.'

'But … the Wraiths were trapped there for all time … for every time.' Ace felt fear balling up deep inside her. 'You can't have set them free.'

'No, indeed, I cannot. Were I to widen the 13 dimensional tunnel that bridges the Quantum Anvil's realm and our physical universe, the Astingir, the Shadow Proclamation, all the civilised races of the galaxy would rain down hell upon us to shatter that link. But this way …' Halogi-Kari smiled. 'Just as a fly can buzz around a room for hours before chancing on the window ajar that leads to freedom, so it is with these poor damaged creatures. Slowly, one by one, a number of Wraiths have found the way through. Do you wish to see? I think that you do.'

'I do,' Ace heard herself saying through gritted teeth.

Halogi-Kari placed his hand to the door and it swung inward, soundlessly – to reveal another door, this one with a blue hue to the thick steel. Again, it opened, to reveal another behind it. 'The safeguards are many,' he said. 'They have to be, do you see? Such energies I have released …'

Ace was starting to feel them now. A tingling inside, like little tongues dipping into her veins, a stirring in her senses, awakening higher senses she'd never known she possessed. Her limbs began to twitch. She felt dizzy.

As Halogi-Kari opened yet another door, one that was deep crimson in hue, powerful light and heat radiated out from inside. Ace knew that these sensations were just the tiniest, throwaway hints of the energies' true properties, the first clumsy taps of some unknowable creator's chisel on the dull stone of her human senses.

In the space beyond the door, Ace slowly perceived movement. A dark, skeletal shape, stalking through a white void, flickering.

A Wraith.

She heard the Doctor's voice echo in her head from long ago: *'One day the Wraiths may find a way out of this trans-temporal hell they've been caught in …'*

'These poor creatures,' said Halogi-Kari. 'Out of the Anvil, the Wraiths have no way to interact consistently with reality any more. Only here, in this no man's land I have built where the abstract and physical meet, can they function. But it is little more than the sticky paper that holds the fly stranded in mid-flight until it dies. In order to move on, to escape, reality must be re-imposed on the Wraiths.'

'You think they won't want revenge?' the Doctor had cried. *'That they won't wage war on the cosmos again?'*

Dimly, Ace perceived other shapes. Sharp, sleek robotic creatures, hovering, circling, flicking out tendrils of liquid metal into the Wraith's flickering, fragile form. One of them held something. Ace had the ridiculous image for a moment of an assistant in a clothes shop, hovering behind a customer with a new suit to try on. A blood-red suit, blurred and indistinct.

'As the Wraiths' cellular stability warps and wends, only living organisms can anchor them in reality.' Halogi-Kari smiled at her from beside the door. 'Living creatures have a fixed relationship with time, you see? They are born ageing, moving inexorably towards death. That steady tick, tick, tick of life's clock, the complex chemical kinetics of organic decay … with a certain amount of technical assistance, these can be absorbed by the Wraiths, helping to stabilise their fractured forms.'

With horror, Ace realised that it was no empty suit in the robot's clutches. It was a man, a man with a spider-web of metal filaments falling from his fingers, stitching themselves into the skeletal form of the Wraith. The robot draped the man over the Wraith's bony shoulders, strapping him in place like a backpack made of flesh. Slowly the figures grew clearer to her.

With horror, she saw it was Kim Fortune now piggy-backed on the Wraith, his eyes blank white, the fluid in his plastic suit bubbling, his fingers digging like needles into the alien's dark, mottled skin.

'Your friend feels no pain, at least,' said Halogi-Kari. 'Consciousness is suspended. The processed abductees are little more than organic pacemakers. Once conjoined with their Wraith, they are placed in cold storage until their forces are finally great enough ...'

'Why do this ...?' They were the only words she could form, and sounded so small and feeble in that storm of light and heat and horror.

'No one will be expecting the Wraiths to escape their captivity, least of all the Shadow Proclamation. So, at my direction, those dear do-gooders will be the first to be torn apart.' The imp-creature grinned, dimples deepening in the waxy veined cheeks. 'I shall be free from the Proclamation's scrutiny. Free to act exactly as I choose.'

The anger sparked deeper inside Ace now. 'You'll unleash a new war on the universe ... leave millions of worlds undefended ... probably kill billions ... because you can't handle your parole board?'

'What a comeback, mm?' Halogi-Kari was practically hopping from foot to foot. 'Wiping out the Shadow Proclamation. What won't people pay for my services then, mm?'

Ace felt her fingers curling into fists. Nothing could stop it. 'Why ... are you showing me?'

'Because you will help me, Earth-Child.' He laughed. 'So much!'

'No,' she hissed. 'Never.'

'Oh, yes, and very soon.' There was such craftiness in the dark eyes. 'The people I have taken, they die too quickly on the backs of the Wraiths. My systems distort the mismatch between our reality and theirs, sure, but life expectancy is badly compromised. To improve this, what I need is someone who has touched the Wraiths already and felt their touch. Someone who has ridden time and space the hard way. Who *knows* the Wraiths ...'

Ace felt cold to her core. She remembered the Doctor's words: 'Someone who can interact with them would make a useful ... emissary.'

But not yours, Professor, she realised, her anger building. *Halogi-Kari's.*

'No!' She tried to lunge for the little demon, but found her movements were hopelessly slow; Ace couldn't stop him as he stepped smartly back through the door of the vault and it slammed shut behind him. 'Let me out of here!'

Almost at once, a shadowy circle of darkness formed and grew behind the twitching Wraith who held poor Kim on its back. The blaze of light and heat was growing wilder. A portal was opening. It had to be Halogi-Kari's secret borehole into the realm of the Quantum Anvil.

Halogi-Kari's laughter carried above the maelstrom. He was trying to send her back inside.

'I won't!' Ace yelled.

But suddenly the newly anchored Wraith was looming over her, Kim's empty white eyes staring over its shoulder. Its scratchy fingers closed on her arms, its twisted ebony face pressed up against her own, as the portal opened like the mouth of hell and swallowed her.

Chapter Twenty-Eight

Chantelle was almost starting to feel better. She and her fellow prisoners had all piled in to huddle in the middle of the space, locking arms, proper Greenham Common spirit – *We Will Not Be Moved*. Even the girl with the dark fringe was held in the grip of fellow travellers either side.

While Chantelle didn't know how much resistance the group would offer – in all honesty, probably not so much – just feeling there was some way of standing up for themselves ... it helped.

Any cosy feelings snapped dead as the door in the wall slid open. Chantelle felt a stab of fear as the same faceless, hovering robot appeared again and lashed out its metal tongue. The flexible frond wrapped around the shoulders of the girl with the long black fringe with horrible precision. Her head jerked back, hair jumping over her wide blue eyes. Shocked by the sudden movement, the people either side of her recoiled, let go of the girl's arms.

Chantelle screamed, 'No—!'

But as the girl hurtled back towards the robot, wound in like a flounder on the end of a line, the faceless head caved in and spewed bright blue sparks like a firework. The girl fell sprawling

251

on the stone floor, shocked and dazed, as the robot clattered down beside her in the open doorway, smoke pouring from the blackened cranium.

'What the hell …?' Chantelle began to rise as a familiar figure stepped through the smoke.

'Whoa, this thing's got a hell of a wallop.' Ryan stood awkwardly in the doorway wielding a silver baseball bat. 'There's gonna be some rat-monsters not happy about that …'

Even as he spoke, Chantelle saw the Ratt coming up behind him.

'Ryan!' she screamed.

Ryan actually smelled the Ratt before he saw it. He turned round quickly, caught a glimpse of the shock on its face, watched it harden to anger. The noise must've disturbed it – it had food round its face and a bottle of something frothing gripped in its tail.

The creature pressed a gadget on its belt and lunged for him. Ryan brought up the bat to defend himself, tripped over the robot's corpse and fell hard against the wall – as the door to the holding area slid closed. The Ratt used its tail to break the bottle on the wall and swiped at him with the lethal glass edge. Ryan parried the blow with the bat, smashing the remaining glass to smithereens and causing the Ratt to howl with pain.

At the sound of its distress, more Ratts came running, their huge, hairy bodies filling the corridors.

I don't stand a chance! Ryan thought.

As the first Ratt closed to attack again, Ryan desperately pushed the end of the bat into the gadget on its belt. There was a flash of white sparks and the Ratt was thrown across the corridor, striking the wall with a colossal boom – as the door to the holding area slid back open.

The other Ratts had quickened their scurrying step and were almost on Ryan now. 'Little help?' he yelled.

Chantelle came tearing out through the door along with a big guy, who picked up the still-smoking robot and hurled it at the oncoming Ratts. It struck the two in front hard and they went down, sending the two behind them sprawling. Chantelle jumped on one and pulled a kind of glass and metal spike from its belt. She pressed it to the Ratt's head and its features contorted in pain as blue sparks arced from the tip.

'That's for Kim!' she hissed into its twitching ear.

Another handful of people came out from inside, all wearing the same weird suits that seemed tailored from blackcurrant squash pouches. Ryan winced to see them start going to town on the Ratts, taking their weapons and taking revenge. After all they'd been through, he supposed he couldn't blame them, even as he turned away.

As Chantelle stood up he took hold of her arm. 'Can't believe I've found you,' he said.

'Can't believe it took you so long,' said Chantelle, and she kissed him on the lips before breaking off and sniffing his skin. 'You smell like a stables.'

'Don't even go there.'

'Where did you get that bat? It's Ace's!'

Ryan shrugged. 'Found it lying in the desert. There were signs of a struggle, I should've known …' He eyed the prone body of the Ratt. 'You said that was for Kim. What happened to him?'

'He was … taken.' Chantelle's face clouded. 'You won't believe the stuff we've been put through.' She looked at her fingertips and shuddered. 'Come on,' she said, stepping over the fallen Ratts and squeezing past the purple alien, 'we've got to get out of here.'

'I don't reckon there's anywhere to go,' said Ryan, following her to a turn in the corridor. 'That means we have to try and take charge of this place. It's not gonna be easy. We'll all have to work together.'

'Against the Ratts?'

'Yeah. And, um – *them.*' Ryan pointed over her shoulder to the end of the corridor.

With metal tendrils snapping smartly, four of the streamlined robots were zinging through the air towards them.

Ace was falling through a nightmare of past, present and endless futures. The Wraith that had held her was gone from her gaze and she was rolling and tumbling in a thousand guises as each moment ripped apart into a million possibilities.

She saw herself emerging victorious, standing over Halogi-Kari's bloodied body. Then she saw him standing over hers. She saw the Doctor killed by the Astingir, a gold-shod hoof plunging down towards her face. Horrified, she turned away from the sight and found herself gazing out over the desert dunes as Wraiths rose up from the sands and into the free wilds of space ... then she saw the Astingir fleet blasting them relentlessly, the bodies dropping to earth like falling stars.

There were so many futures crowding her, too many to take in. Ace felt sick, felt she was drowning in a sea of shadows longing to be cast by the light inside her. Helpless, hopeless, she closed her eyes.

And when she reopened them, all around her was night-dark. A Wraith floated before her, its hand like the silhouette of a winter tree as it brought it down on her shoulder. It seemed to pass through her flesh and grip hold of the bone.

She felt more than its burning touch, though. Their minds brushed and she felt the Wraith's loneliness, the ache in its cells and its soul.

'What do you want?' Ace demanded. 'What do you need?'

Its mouth flickered open and it whispered into her, a voice like dead leaves trodden into thick frost:

'We ... need ... YOU.'

'No,' Ace said. 'No, please. You don't have to do this ...'

'But we do.'

Ace felt a flash of fear: flickering, moving close then darting away like silver fish in a dark, dark ocean, Ace saw one of the robots, identical to the machine that had joined Kim to the Wraith outside.

Now, she knew, it had come to do the same to her.

In quiet, intense concentration, Halogi-Kari sat cross-legged on the floor behind the first of his three great protective vault doors. With his mind fed both by psychic emanations from the Wraiths and by the hyperspatial sensors of his quantum-boring machines, he could almost catch the psychic whispers of the meeting of minds in the mouth of the Anvil.

The details were unclear but, still, every heartbeat of the encounter was being recorded by his robotic psychosurgeon, straddling a stream of realities as it stood ready to conjoin Wraith and Earth-Child.

He smiled. The girl's core had already been shredded at a quantum level; she would be better able to survive the Wraiths' cellular predation than the others he'd taken, even without a plasma suit. And, with the process recorded, even if the Earth-Child died in the process he would know exactly what strands of mutated genetic code made that better match possible.

'Master!'

The Ratt's nervous gasp was like a scream in the ears of Halogi-Kari. He rounded on the intruder, casting out his hands and with the force of his mind pinning the creature against the wall, spreadeagled and squealing.

'I'm sorry, Master,' the Ratt babbled, wide-eyed. 'The processed ones – some have gotten out of the holding area.'

Halogi-Kari closed his eyes for a moment. The Ratts were a motley, substandard race of work units, which was one reason the Proclamation took such little heed of them and their activities. The psychosurgeons had destroyed thousands in attempts to resurrect the Wraiths, but the Ratts' brain capacity was simply too limited to allow effective integration, even after he'd employed that fool Crozier to perform augmentation. He'd had no choice other than to incubate some of his surviving Ratts with limited time-storm powers in order to gather more suitable livestock. But the feeble-minded idiots couldn't be trusted to do much else on their own.

'How did the processed ones get out?' Halogi-Kari hissed, and as expected, the Ratt had no answer. 'They are unarmed and there is nowhere they can go.'

The Ratt squirmed in the invisible grip. 'But—'

'No excuses. You and your fellows must contain them again. Fail me and I will plant a time-storm in your feral hearts so that they burst in your chests. Now, go!'

He waved a hand and the terrified Ratt fell to the floor and scurried away on all fours.

Trusting that such incompetence would soon be rectified, Halogi-Kari resumed his meditations, probing with his senses through the outer frenzy of the quantum interface.

And he smiled as he heard the Earth-Child screaming.

CHAPTER TWENTY-NINE

As the four robots approached along the corridor, Ryan passed Chantelle the baseball bat and dug into his pocket for Ace's cylinder.

'You want a piece of me?' Chantelle raised the bat at the robots. 'Cos the day I've had, I'll give you more than you—'

A metal tendril zipped out and struck the silver, jarring the bat from her hands in a blaze of sparks. Chantelle yelled and recoiled as the tendril retracted, blackened and smoking. The other three robots stopped their advance, hovering suspiciously. Ryan caught Chantelle's arm and dragged her further back along the corridor.

Chantelle pointed to the bat, which was smoking. 'What about that?'

'Too hot to handle,' said Ryan, tipping a Nitro-90 marble from the holder into his palm. He threw it towards the robots. 'Speaking of which …!'

The ball-bearing hit the ground just in front of the robots with a ferociously noisy explosion. Flames and smoke leapt greedily to be free, as if trapped inside the tiny space for so long, consuming the corridor and billowing out in a sudden gale. Ryan and Chantelle were thrown backwards, tumbling over the stone.

'Whoa!' Ears ringing, Ryan choked on the smoke. He turned to Chantelle. 'The last boom was way smaller. You need to tell your mate to dial down her works in progress …'

Chantelle was sitting up, looking past him with a fixed expression.

Ryan frowned, shook her shoulder. 'You all right?'

'Are *you* all right, Ryan Sinclair?' boomed a familiar voice.

Like a miracle, striding through the smoke, with arms stretched wide and a grin even wider, came the Doctor. She wrapped up Ryan in a humungous hug and yanked him to his feet.

'Doctor, I was scared you'd really had it that time.'

'Trust me, I've had it enough times in my life to send it straight back again.' She stepped back from him, still beaming. 'Now are you all right? And you?' She hugged Chantelle too. 'We've been worried sick!'

Chantelle got up, looking royally baffled. 'We …?'

Ryan smiled as he took in the solid blue bulk of the TARDIS in the middle of the corridor between them and the remains of the robots; it must have materialised in the smoke and echoes of the blast. Yaz stepped out from behind the police box, carrying the fallen baseball bat.

'Nice flying, Doctor,' she said. 'You homed right in on this thing.' Then she ran up to Ryan too and grabbed him close. Ryan hugged her back.

Graham came out too, cradling the squirming metal Squidget in his arms. 'Good to see you, mate! Sorry I can't join in the hugs, got me hands full …'

Ryan laughed with happiness, but Chantelle was looking worried. 'Don't worry, Chantelle, that thing won't bite …'

The smoke was dissipating, and the reunion greetings were kept short as the big man emerged cautiously from the corridor junction, wielding one of the Ratt's weapons. His eyes flicked between Chantelle and the Doctor, Yaz and Graham. 'Are these ones on our side?' he said.

Chantelle gasped. 'I can understand you!'

Graham nodded at the TARDIS. 'Universal translator.'

'Course it is.' Chantelle smiled at the man. 'Yes. These are our friends.'

'The noise will bring more rat-things,' the man said grimly. 'We must prepare.'

'He's right,' Ryan said. 'We're gonna have a fight on our hands.'

'Where's Ace?' the Doctor said suddenly.

Yaz nodded, gesturing round at the ruined corridor. 'Ace's bat, Ace's explosives, Ace herself . . . ?'

'I haven't seen her,' said Chantelle, 'I thought she'd be with you.' Quickly she told them all that she and Kim had been through, as the Doctor crouched beside the remains of the robots and scanned them with the sonic. 'Programmed for psycho-surgery, live grafting and interspecies vivisection. Whatever they're up to, it's nasty. Very nasty.' She stood up. 'We need to get all the abductees into the TARDIS, keep them safe—'

She broke off as an energy ray whizzed past her and struck the side of the TARDIS. A squad of Ratts was scurrying down the corridor. The Doctor quickly scrambled behind the police box, and her friends did the same, sheltered by its cover as more gunfire sounded.

Graham groaned. 'Couldn't have parked this thing the other way round, could you!'

'Those things are hanging back,' Ryan realised. 'Must think we've set a trap.'

'We wish,' Chantelle muttered.

'I've got one more Nitro-90 capsule,' said Ryan.

'Save it,' said the Doctor. 'You could bring the roof down on us all this time.'

'So what *is* the plan?' asked Yaz, hefting the bat.

'Take Ryan and Graham. Follow that nice man back to the other abductees. Defend them. I reckon the Ratts'll be all "phasers on stun" cos they won't want to kill their victims after whatever's been done to them ... but please, don't take any needless risks.' She grabbed the silvery squid from Graham. 'Or Squidget.'

'I'll show you the way,' Chantelle told Ryan.

'No, you're with me, Chantelle.' The Doctor winced, as another blast of energy smacked off the TARDIS. 'I need to get a sense of the overall layout. That plastic sheet you signed just by looking at it opened the front door. With some help from the sonic and Squidget, maybe it can open a few more.'

'Sick.' Ryan nodded. 'But how are we gonna get anywhere with all them armed Ratts there?'

The Doctor put down Squidget, reached into her coat pocket and then pulled out something shiny and red with white stitching. Then with a high-pitched yell she hurled it over the roof of the TARDIS towards the Ratts. '*Incoming!*' she yelled.

The Ratts scattered ... as a cricket ball bounced its way along the shattered corridor.

'All these faces later, still got it!' Beaming, the Doctor shooed her friends away. 'Go on. I'll see you soon.'

Ryan looked at her, sad that the reunion was so brief. 'You'd better.'

With Yaz and Graham beside him, Ryan made his way back towards the holding area.

Chantelle trailed after the Doctor as she strode through the corridors of the Ratt palace. 'How do you know this is the way?' she asked. 'I can't tell, it was pitch dark, I was grabbed by one of those robots, it carried me ...'

The Doctor had Squidget tucked under one arm (Chantelle could swear it was sniffing the air like a hound with a scent) and was waving her sonic screwdriver with the other, like a buzzing torch. 'I'm following the trail of agitated air molecules those hovering 'bots leave behind. The trail is thick – really thick – along here ...'

'So, you reckon loads of robots have come and gone this way?' Chantelle reasoned.

'I do! And look.' The Doctor grinned as they came up short against cold pumice. 'Door in the wall! Combined with the strength of the trail, I reckon this is our way out.' She did something to the sonic and its whirr changed in pitch.

Suddenly the door slid open to reveal the sand and hard sunlight beyond, stinging Chantelle's eyes. The Doctor marched straight out, peering around. The Ratt's kiosk beside the entrance had been left open; well, thought Chantelle, it wasn't as if anyone was about to nick stuff here.

The Doctor picked up one of the plastic sheets and waved it under Squidget's virtual nose. Squidget sneezed out a slender nozzle, which stuck to the material, while the Doctor held it up to Chantelle. 'Look into this, can you?'

Chantelle did so, and with a beep the plastic turned green. Squidget made a low gurgling noise, and the colour of the sheet grew brighter.

'What's that thing doing?' she asked.

'Accepting these terms that granted you permission to enter before,' the Doctor explained. 'My clever Squidget is pushing those permissions through the entire system so now we should be Access All Areas.'

'Weren't you already?' Chantelle said. 'You've got your magic wand for opening doors.'

'If I'm right about what's going on here,' said the Doctor, 'there are gonna be some doors that no one can open without the most privileged access. But I'm guessing whoever's in charge won't be expecting …' She looked past Chantelle, frowning. 'Them.'

'What?' Chantelle turned and gasped to see a beautiful golden shape slowly, silently gliding into sight. It was roughly spherical, with spires and latticework contained within two spinning, interlocking circles. It looked like some gleaming gold ornament hanging from invisible strings, but she knew what it had to be. 'Is that a spaceship?'

'An Astingir War Chariot,' said the Doctor grimly. 'Legate Aquillon followed me here.'

I'm dreaming, Chantelle thought, scared but held spellbound by the eerie sight.

Squidget gave a squeak of alarm, jolting Chantelle back to the drama on the ground: two Ratts scuttling out from the shadows towards them, fleshy hoods pulled down over their faces. One held one of the glass-and-metal batons. The tip glowed bloody red and the Doctor shouted with pain, staggered and fell to the ground

The other Ratt started towards Chantelle but stopped at the sight of the War Chariot as it landed gently on the sand. 'What the frug is *that*...?'

Chantelle grabbed her moment, together with the nearest sharp stone to hand. 'Stay back,' she warned the Ratts, 'or...' She held the point of the stone to her squashy suit. 'I'll cut this thing open. Ruin it. Then what will you do?'

The Ratt turned to her, red eyes blazing in its scabrous face. Then with a cold hissing sound it exploded into nothingness. Only a sprawled shadow was left behind. The one beside it lifted its baton but a second hissing sound reduced it to a dark stain on the ground.

The stains looked to be twitching.

Shocked and revolted, Chantelle turned to find perhaps two-dozen armoured horse creatures with human arms and torsos jumping out from their outlandish craft. Two burlier horse-things had already advanced across the ground. They were carrying golden canopies on their backs, with a jewelled sceptre rising from each roof. The horse-things were looking at her...

'*Look out!*' The Doctor scrambled up and launched herself at Chantelle, dragging her to the ground as the canopy sceptres flashed and the air seemed to freeze about them. 'Astingir infantry... with organic vaporisers.'

'What do we do?' Chantelle cried in a panic. 'We're sitting ducks!'

But a plague of Ratts came pouring out through openings in the pumice-stone walls of their factory fortress – fresh aggressive targets that commanded the firepower of the horse-things as they galloped across the sand, armour dazzling bright in the sunshine.

'Get inside, now!' the Doctor shouted as the Ratts began to vanish in mid-charge.

Glad at least that her suit had protected her from the spiteful ground, Chantelle got up and darted into the black hole in the wall. The Doctor, clutching Squidget and her precious piece of plastic, dived in after her, scratched and dishevelled.

'Sonic,' she panted, patting her pockets. 'Need to close the door, where's the sonic …? Ah!' She held it up, but then stopped, agog, as the Astingir War Chariot was suddenly plucked up into the air like a child's toy in a tornado of sound and sand and light, the sky flashing crazily light and dark as if night and day were falling over each other high above the planet. The horse-things reared up, galloped about, nickering.

'Time-storm,' the Doctor said wonderingly. She pressed the sonic and the door slid down, shutting out the chaos. 'The powers-that-be here know they're being invaded and they're flexing their muscles …'

'So what do we do?' asked Chantelle.

The Doctor got up, put Squidget under one arm and marched off down the corridor. 'We get ready for war,' she said.

CHAPTER THIRTY

Halogi-Kari screamed as the last of the time-storm left his conjuring mind, panting for breath, his hide barely containing his pulsing, bulging veins. He'd been too slow, weakened by long years of inactivity. He had thrown the Astingir craft out across Peerie Canto's star system and twisted it hundreds of years into the past, but he knew a significant Astingir force must already be on the ground ...

The timing was damnable. Disturbance both within and without – and just as his joining of the Earth-Child with the Wraiths was nearing fruition. Petty unrest among the abductees was something his Ratts could deal with, but the Astingir heavy infantry? They would be wiped out, leaving their master isolated.

Well, then, he thought, a gleam stealing back into the dull black of his eyes. *Perhaps those Wraiths restored from the Quantum Anvil have lain in silent dark for long enough. Let them rise again and punish their would-be conquerors. Let their human batteries burn and boil away with the strain of fresh combat. Let the Wraiths sip vengeance – and let their hunger for it grow ...*

Wheezing with amusement, Halogi-Kari scuttled away to see to it himself.

*

Graham, Yaz and Ryan had done their best to build a barricade using parts of the dead robot, the jammed door and rubble smashed off the walls with Ace's supercharged baseball bat. In truth it wouldn't hold up for long, but it gave at least a bit of cover. Now Graham looked around at the stinking holding area, at the people cowering inside, and felt properly angry. It was bad enough to be told that kids from the streets of a dozen cities were being kidnapped and thrown through space, but when you *saw* them here, all bundled together in this dump, shattered, dressed up in God knew what …

'I'd like to get hold of whoever's done this,' he said.

'We will,' Yaz told him, peering out over the barricade, a Ratt zap-stick in her hand.

'I'd like to find Ace,' said Ryan, staring down at her baseball bat. 'And a nice safe way out of here.'

The zip and blast of energy weapons and metallic whip-cracks echoed from outside.

'Fat chance of "safe" around here,' Graham sighed.

'Robots,' came the frightened mutter of the crowd.

'And that's not all.' Ryan looked at Graham. 'Recognise the gunfire?'

He nodded with a neigh. 'All we need. Our horsey mates.'

But then a proper braying started up from beyond. It sounded like a bigger weapon had been brought into play. The sound of raucous Ratt laughter rose above the whickers and whinnies of the Astingir.

'I can't stand this,' Graham said, grabbing Ace's bat from Ryan. He scrambled over the barricade. 'I'm not having it.'

'Graham, wait!' Yaz vaulted the barrier to follow him. 'Ryan, you got things here?'

Ryan held up his remaining capsule of Nitro-90. 'Covered.'

'Come on, then,' Graham told Yaz grimly.

'And do what?'

'Something. Anything!'

It didn't take them long to reach the battle zone. The corridors had been bypassed; holes had been blown in the walls and four Ratts and as many robots were blasting at the Astingir with an enormous high-tech cannon across some sort of nightmarish operating theatre. The equipment was in ruins, and centaurion corpses lay in dark sticky puddles. More of the Astingir were firing hand-weapons from behind golden shields, or rearing up to loose disruptor bolts from their armoured fetlocks.

Graham saw one Astingir take a shot to the side, screaming as her armour melted and seared her hide. He ran up behind the Ratts and swung the bat down on the cannon. There was an explosion of coruscating sparks and the unprepared Ratts fell back yelping – where Yaz turned their own stick-weapons against them, stunning one after another, shocking them into submission on the floor.

The robots turned on Graham, then. With a yell of anger, he swung the bat and smashed one into another. The third whipped out a mechanical line towards him, too quick for him to dodge. He felt it tighten around his throat.

Then the robot was torn apart in a barrage of power from the Astingir survivors as they pushed forward. Graham fell to his knees, choking and grappling with the metal cord at his neck. Yaz knelt beside him, calmly working her fingers underneath the steel before finally ripping it free.

Then the centaur-creatures were looming over them, panting, their armour blackened, hides patterned with blood and scurf.

Graham looked up and recognised the head of the herd, Legate Aquillon. Her plaited mane had been half-burned off, her face scarred raw.

He cleared his aching throat. 'Maybe now you'll accept we're not your enemies?'

Aquillon snorted and turned to the centaurion beside her. 'Take them,' she hissed.

Ryan's cold sweat really kicked in when the gunfire stopped. The battle had ended, but which way had it gone? 'Yaz!' he shouted. 'Graham ...?'

'We're all right, son,' Graham called back.

'Sort of,' Yaz added.

Ryan caught a heavy, animal stench and felt his heart sink as eight Astingir clattered into sight. He hardly heard the cries of the abductees, the sound of their plastic suits scraping the stone as they tried to back away. All he could see was Graham and Yaz in the grip of the horse-creatures – and Legate Aquillon leading the way.

She swept her gory horse-head from side to side, taking in the scene, and her eyes came down hard on Ryan. 'So. The war criminal cowers here, defending Wraith assets.'

'They're just people,' Ryan said. 'Kids, mostly. Kidnapped. Terrified.'

There was a pounding of hooves behind her as two more battered Astingir charged up. With a quickening of his pulse, Ryan saw one of them was Centaurion Masst.

'No contact with the Chariot, Legate,' Masst said sullenly.

'Half our forces were still on board when it was thrown out into space,' said the second Astingir, his hide as dark as the scorch-marks on his armour.

'I am aware of that, Centaurion Elkon,' Aquillon whickered. 'And there are ten more fallen here.'

'We can help you,' Ryan said. 'Help you to stop this.'

'Oh, I can assure you that "this" will be stopped.'

'Legate, please.' Masst approached her. 'While scanning for our brothers and sisters, we detected a battle fleet on its way from the Herdworld.'

'On its way here?' Aquillon turned to him sharply. 'Finally! Our work is recognised!'

Masst hesitated, shifting from hoof to hoof. 'We are ordered to stand down.'

'We are deemed in breach of peacetime protocols,' Elkon went on. 'A Securing Force has been sent to apprehend us.'

'And you, Legate …' Masst looked her in the eyes. 'You have been relieved of your rank and right to lead us.'

Aquillon stared at her subordinates. Ryan held his breath, the capsule of Nitro-90 cold in his clammy fist.

'The Securing Force is not yet here,' Aquillon said, frighteningly calm. 'And messages from the Herdworld are hard to hear over such great distances …'

'Please, Legate …'

'You saw the detector readings yourself, Centaurion. The Quantum Anvil has been compromised. The Wraiths are freed.'

Masst tried again. 'We don't know for sure what the readings mean—'

'Which is why we must go on.' Aquillon gestured to her troops, who threw Graham and Yaz to the floor, still covering them with their weapons. 'Masst, you and Centaurion Elkon will eliminate the Wraith assets and hold this area, while I lead the campaign onward.' Without another word, she pushed past the centaurions and her gaunt, golden warriors trailed after her.

As they did so, Ryan realised just what she'd meant by 'eliminate the Wraith assets'.

Graham and Yaz had started crawling towards the barricade. Elkon raised a hoof and chunks of stone were blasted from the floor between them, and they both held still as statues.

'Masst,' said Ryan urgently, 'mate, think about this. You can't kill these people.'

'Legate Aquillon orders it,' said Elkon..

'You heard your herd,' Graham spoke up from the floor in front of the barricade. 'She don't have the right to give orders now.'

Masst nickered. 'The Wraiths must be destroyed.'

'Look at these people!' Yaz turned defiantly, looked Elkon in the eyes. 'They're not Wraiths!'

'It's almost over,' Elkon told Masst. 'You want it over, don't you?'

'It'll be over, all right.' Ryan held up the Nitro-90, trying to calm his breathing. 'You know what this stuff can do. Let go of my friends or I'll chuck this, I swear. It'll blow you to bits.'

Masst raised his gleaming crossbow at Graham. 'Raise your hand any further and I'll kill this man you love.'

'Do you hear yourself?' Yaz snapped. 'What are you, a soldier or a murderer?'

'Look at these people.' Slowly, stiffly, Graham stood up. 'They're different from you, but they're just as scared. They're longing for home, just like you.'

'They didn't ask to be here,' Yaz said. 'They've been used.'

'And you're being used now,' Ryan added, 'to fight a war that ended way back.'

Masst snorted. 'You don't know what the Wraiths did!'

'I know that these people have done nothing to you, it's all been done to them!' Ryan felt the ball of Nitro-90 so cold in his palm. Slowly he lowered his fist. 'I'm not gonna use this. You say you want it over? Well, open fire on these people, Masst, and it'll never be over. You'll hear their screams every time you fall asleep. You'll see their eyes whenever you close yours.' He swallowed hard, eyes locked with the centaurion's. 'Never. Ever. Over.'

The holding area was silent. It felt like time had stopped.

With a hiss of anger, Elkon raised his own crossbow and opened fire.

CHAPTER THIRTY-ONE

Chantelle was following the Doctor down a dark, shadowy palace passage. Suddenly the Doctor came to a halt.

'This pulsation of energy. I know what it is!' She was staring at the sheet of plastic, at the lines drawn upon it and pulsing circles of light. Squidget shuddered and made a mournful bleep. 'Someone's tapped into the power of the Quantum Anvil. The Wraiths will have a way back out into our world.'

'And that's bad, right?' said Chantelle.

'Bad? Yeah, you could say it's bad.' The Doctor went on gawping at the screen. Then Squidget blooped loudly, and she quickened her step. 'But it's not the worst of it.'

'What is the worst?'

'Huge energy surge up ahead,' she said. 'According to Squidget, something's been activated.'

'What something? A machine?'

'Maybe. But it's brought *that* something into being. A war-hungry creature I thought the universe was rid of ...'

The Doctor pointed ahead of them. Standing before a huge vault door, like a sentry, was a night-dark figure as tall as a tree with something draped over it ...

'A Wraith,' breathed the Doctor. 'Out of the Quantum realm, back in ours.'

'What the …? Doctor, look.' Chantelle felt recognition like a knife to the guts. There was a man spreadeagled on the back of the creature, his face contorted with pain. 'It's Kim. That thing's wearing *Kim* like a stole.'

The Doctor nodded gravely. '*Stole* is right.'

'What's happened to him?'

'Cellular predation,' said the Doctor, fascinated and revolted. 'The Wraith's own alignment with our reality is totally messed up, so it's having to feed off Kim's to inhabit this time frame.'

'You never speak English!' Chantelle groaned. 'Is Kim dead?'

'Not yet. You could say he's been turned into a sort of living metronome, setting the beat for that Wraith to live by … and to kill by, given half a chance.' The Doctor's lip curled. 'But that beat hasn't settled and steadied yet. Kim's still in there, and that must be throwing off the Wraith's own nature.'

'Then we've got to do something!' Seeing Kim's blank face, Chantelle wanted to cry. 'We've got to help Kim!'

The Wraith lurched forward. Kim's face, contorted with pain, seemed to look Chantelle's way: 'You … pretty …'

'Kim's consciousness must still be separate from the Wraith's.' The Doctor looked surprised but so happy. 'Chantelle, he's responding to you. Go to him. Try to keep him talking – we need Kim's consciousness engaged instead of the Wraith.'

'What if I can't?' Chantelle looked at the Doctor. 'What if the Wraith takes control and kills me?'

'I need you to try.'

'What are you going to do?'

'Get past him, and through that door.' The Doctor pointed to the huge vault door in the wall. 'Maybe then I can stop whoever's behind all this.' She looked at Chantelle. 'You got this?'

Chantelle tried to compose herself. 'Kim …?' She approached the huge, charcoal-black creature. 'Kim … can you come to me?'

272

'Pretty.' Kim's mouth slurred the word again. 'Pretty.'

'Um, thanks.' She swallowed hard. 'You, uh, you look well too.'

'Be ... co ... host ...'

'Co-host on your podcast?' Chantelle felt she could cry as she took a step nearer; Kim couldn't know what had happened to him. She didn't *want* him to know. 'Yeah, I can get my geek on, Kim. I'm down with that.' She beckoned the creature to come to her. 'You and me presenting your Strange World thing ...'

The dark creature took a step towards her, and Kim's mouth flapped open and shut. 'Mys ... myst ... myster ...'

'Mysterious World, right. Course.' Trying not to shake, she wagged a finger, pantomime stern. 'Just as friends, though, yeah? We can host it together but nothing dodgy ...'

'Together,' Kim said, blank-eyed, his lips twitching like they were trying to make a smile.

The Doctor gave Chantelle a big thumbs-up and circled round behind the horrible composite of Kim and the dark thing. She waved the sonic over the vault door. Nothing happened so she put Squidget to work and it cracked it. The door swung slowly open.

A moment later, the Doctor had detached her pet tool and was through the door, lost from Chantelle's sight.

That was when the Wraith lurched forward and grabbed Chantelle's shoulders, its huge, ebony face thrusting close to hers, eyes black. Kim's head had rolled back, and a sickening gurgle was building in the creature's throat.

The Doctor blinked to find herself in a kind of airlock with a further heavy, bronze door in front of her. 'Deadlocked,' she deduced, and looked down at Squidget. It threw out its trademark tendrils once more and, like a master safe-cracker, seemed to listen to the tiniest sounds coming from the lock. This took longer, and the Doctor was trying not to pace with impatience. But eventually the second door opened onto a small chamber containing a third. The Doctor could feel an increasing heaviness in the atmosphere, the hairs on the back of her neck standing on end. She knew she was drawing closer to incredible energies.

Squidget helped her open the third door and finally they were through.

A blaze of bright light blew into her face and the Doctor realized at once that she had reached the inner sanctum of whatever force was at work here. There were no details to the room; it was all glowing white, an '80s pop video of a place, gloss and shine but no coherent depth. Perspective changed with every look you took. The Doctor perceived menace bristling at the fringes of her sight, just outside her focus, but more worryingly she could sense a puncture in the reality of the room: a quantum borehole right through the space-time vortex ...

'Professor ...!'

Ace's voice burst from nowhere and roiled around the space and no-space of the chamber. The Doctor looked around, frantic. 'Ace?'

'Professor, please ...'

'I'm here for you. I'm going to find you, all right?' The Doctor knew where Ace was; the only place she could be. The same place she had helped push Ace into once before.

Ace was inside the endless prison of the Wraiths. Inside the Quantum Anvil. In those creatures' hands.

'And I can't get in. Can't get to you.' The Doctor looked down at Squidget. 'Or can I?' She waved the sonic, scanning for the precise entry point. 'Squidge, you can meld incompatible tech together, mechanical or otherwise. If you could link me to the quantum borehole, destabilise my own physical form long enough for me to survive a journey inside and get Ace back out ...?'

Squidget strained eagerly like a greyhound spotting a hare.

'Find me the interface,' the Doctor breathed. 'Find me the way in.' She set Squidget down and it wiggled, metal widgets probing the air. With a beep, it sent out a probe which seemed to disappear like a fishing line into water.

'Got it!' The Doctor clapped. 'Good boy. Clever boy!' She strode up to Squidget. 'Now if you can connect me to—'

Suddenly Squidget screamed as the air itself turned against it, spinning it round and lifting it up. Blue flame burst from its side and it shrivelled like a balloon.

'Squidge!' the Doctor shouted.

But Squidget was already gone, sucked inside the borehole like water down a drain.

The Doctor spun round. A short, bipedal creature, its thick, waxy flesh traced with dark veins, was standing between her and the closed vault door – a door that she knew she could no longer open. The same energy that had engulfed Squidget seemed to spark and flicker around the creature's hands and horns.

'A time-storm,' the Doctor realised. 'So, you're the monster behind all this.'

'Halogi-Kari. Bringer of time and distance.' The creature inclined his head, black Anime eyes shining. 'You are a Time Lord.'

'Yes.'

'You depend on machines for your mastery.'

'Whereas you – your powers are all natural. You're a Harbinger, aren't you?'

Halogi-Kari smiled. 'You know of my kind?'

'Very rare. Very powerful.' The Doctor regarded Halogi-Kari warily. 'To travel through time my way, to observe or stick an oar in now and then – that's one thing. To propel others through time at will is quite a feat.'

The creature chuckled. 'Perhaps, then, Halogi-Kari is the true Lord of Time?'

'I don't think you've done anything true in your life.' The Doctor stepped towards him. 'Why have you placed Ace in the Anvil?'

275

'For the same reasons as you.' Halogi-Kari smiled serenely. 'She is my emissary. Her unique cellular make-up leaves her able to inhabit the same unstable space as the Wraiths. She shall join with the Wraith Queen, give her body and voice in our coming conquest.'

'No.' The Doctor shook her head slowly. 'Nuh-uh. You're not unleashing the Wraiths on the universe again, to ravage, to kill, to destroy.'

'Oh?'

'And you're going to bring back Ace. And you're going to return the humans you took.'

'And you will make me?' He licked his lips with a grey slug of a tongue. 'Even though you know Halogi-Kari to be very rare and very powerful?'

'Even then.' The Doctor took another step closer.

'Even though you know I can destroy you?'

'With a time-storm?' The Doctor jeered. 'I was cooking those up in the nursery. Just try and turn a time-storm on me, I dare you. Go on, try.'

Halogi-Kari gave a malicious cackle. He lowered his horns and held out his arms.

The Doctor felt an awful moment of dislocation. She had a vivid flashback to challenging Morbius, a renegade Time Lord, to a mind-bending contest long ago. The resultant psychic shock had almost killed her. Now, as Halogi-Kari began to swill raw time around her and she rose into the air, she had to resist the same urge to panic, to run. The assault was strong and extreme; he was trying to push whole millennia through her, to diminish mind and body, whittle her away like old wood. A golden glow emanated from her skin as her essence began to boil off into the mad rush of the centuries spinning by about her.

CHAPTER THIRTY-TWO

No, thought the Doctor. *I can weather this.*

All Time Lords had a special relationship to time, existing as perpetual outsiders. She could shrug off the aggressive weave of the years that Halogi-Kari was spinning about her, if she only had the right locus to fix herself upon. And so she chose to focus on a single second, a syllable of Ace's cry from beyond the Quantum Anvil. Such a sad and heartbreaking sound; one that needed an answer in the here and now. The Doctor made it her anchor. *I'm coming to get you, Ace.* She would not leave this moment, wouldn't leave Ace alone. Not now.

And so she began to navigate the temporal riptide, using it to pull herself back down to the ground. Halogi-Kari hunched over, redoubled his efforts, energy radiating from his horns, his misshapen fingers. But now the Doctor was walking towards him, teeth gritted, moving onward through the storm. She felt her clothes start to tatter, felt her skin line and tighten, her face shrivel against her skull. But the Doctor endured, and glowed with golden light, and renewed, and inched closer.

Until, suddenly, she glimpsed movement behind Halogi-Kari. The vault had opened. A Wraith staggered in, Kim Fortune still strung about its neck, Chantelle powerless in its grip. As the Doctor's concentration wavered, Halogi-Kari got the upper hand and pushed her back, tossed her into the air like a doll and then twisted. She closed her eyes, fighting back through the maelstrom of energy erupting about her.

Then came a single shot that seemed to ring out for an eternity. Halogi-Kari's shoulder burst apart in a liquorice fountain. The storm around the Doctor howled itself out as if giving voice to his agonies as he fell, eyes creasing shut.

The Doctor tried to move but her body seemed caught in slow motion, her vision blurred and head splitting. She recognised Legate Aquillon, her laser crossbow freshly fired, as she reared up and struck at the Wraith that still clutched hold of Chantelle, knocking both to the ground. The Doctor shouted out, but the sound was caught in her throat and time was still distorting. She felt powerless.

Halogi-Kari, still bleeding, veins tracing black and swollen over his body, propped himself up on one elbow and emitted a sound like some sinister war cry. The blinding brightness in the chamber dimmed to reveal Wraiths in waiting around the outer walls, humans strapped to their backs, sparking, shaking and smoking as the creatures they rode staggered closer.

Trapped beneath the body of the Wraith, Kim's head lolling beside hers, Chantelle looked up at the approaching forces in terror. Aquillon reared up again, and her heavy infantry aimed their cannons.

'WAIT.'

Ace's voice cut through the chamber, and through whatever invisible bonds of time still held the Doctor. She rolled over, panting for breath – and saw a sight to chill her blood.

It was Ace, her body contorted and sprawled over the back of the Wraith Queen. Her hair hung down over its face as though they shared a fringe. Then the Doctor realised that the battle-scarred Squidget was pressed between them, its tendrils linking Ace to her dark mount, bridging the gap between them and keeping her conscious, though her face showed the most terrible pain.

'WAIT.' Ace's voice carried a deeper rasp; was it the Wraith Queen speaking through her ... or perhaps *with* her? 'WE WILL BE HEARD.'

Aquillon's eyes were wild, foam flecking her mouth. 'You will be *killed*!' she shouted and opened fire.

The Wraith Queen raised her hand and deflected the blast of light, struck it back at Aquillon. The Astingir turned her head but was thrown back against her troops by the force of impact. At that moment, the vault door was slammed open to reveal Centaurion Masst in the doorway. He saw the Wraiths and raised his weapons.

'Listen to me.' The Doctor got to her knees. 'All of you! Please, just lower your weapons. It doesn't need to be this way. You don't have to be warriors any more!'

'But that's just it, Professor,' Ace said, eyes half-closed, strain telling on her face. 'The Wraiths ... don't *want* to be warriors.'

The Doctor looked on, and Masst stared, incredulous, as the Wraiths around the chamber bowed slowly, fell to one knee in deference and held up their arms in surrender.

'The Quantum Anvil held us trapped,' the Wraith Queen intoned. 'And it showed us all possible futures. All ...' She paused, reeling back and almost overbalancing. Squidget glowed dark purple and it was Ace who spoke again. 'The only futures that brought eventual prosperity to their race were peace. A charitable peace. Making amends. Doing things ... differently.'

'No,' Aquillon hissed, rising up, shaking her gory plaited mane. 'It's a trick.'

Squidget's colour had deepened further. The Doctor felt a presence at the fringes of her consciousness, a mental projection.

The Wraith Queen spoke again: 'OPEN YOUR MINDS TO US.'

The Doctor gasped as through her senses flitted visions not of war, but of fellowship and rebuilding. Wraiths and Astingir and so many other races moving forward, colonising worlds together, creating an enduring legacy. Squidget was channelling the images from Ace and the Queen.

No, not just images. Hope. Belief.

'It's a trick!' Aquillon snarled. 'Wraiths cannot change. They have no right to. Our pain is deep, our vows are clear.' She nodded to her infantry. 'Kill them! All of them!'

'I wouldn't!' Ryan shouted, pushing out from behind Masst, a metal capsule held up between finger and thumb. Behind him came Yaz, still holding Ace's baseball bat, and Graham, who helped Chantelle up from under the fallen Wraith.

'It was holding me safe,' Chantelle insisted. 'Showing me Kim will be OK. They want to go back to the Anvil, go back inside!'

'You're pathetic!' Aquillon bellowed at Ryan but clearly including them all. 'You honestly believe that these beasts will change?' She spat at Ryan's feet. 'Ever?' Heedless of his threat, she turned back to her infantry. 'Open—'

She never finished her command. Masst shot her down with a bolt from his bow and her legs buckled beneath her as she fell, unconscious.

'I believe – I hope – that we can *all* change.' Shaking, Masst looked at his comrades in the rogue legion. 'Legate Aquillon has been stripped of her rank. To fight under her command is henceforth illegal. Any who try will be forcibly restrained.'

Slowly, the Astingir heavy infantry lowered their weapons and sank to their haunches.

The Doctor looked at her friends. 'The abductees …?'

'They're safe,' Graham confirmed. 'One of them horse-things opened fire—'

'But Masst brought him down,' said Ryan, and Chantelle grabbed him close in a grateful hug.

'I took no pleasure in doing so,' said Masst sadly. 'But we had received direct instructions from the Herdworld and Aquillon and Elkon would not obey.' He turned to Ace, and the Wraith Queen. 'I know you could be tricking us all,' he said quietly. 'I don't trust you. I've spent my whole life hating you. Which is why I don't trust myself either.' He paused. 'I will not start a new war between our peoples. A Securing Force from the Herdworld is moving into orbit. You must plead your case to my superiors, and we shall abide by the outcome.'

'WE SHALL,' said the Wraith Queen, as if she had known all along, and placed a hand to Ace's head. 'THIS CREATURE CAN SUMMON ME AGAIN.'

'But what about everyone who's been taken here?' Graham placed his hand on Kim Fortune's, and gestured round at the genuflecting Wraiths. 'They're being used ...'

'Used up, more like,' Yaz added. 'Look at them!'

The humans were still twitching feebly, imprisoned in their plastic skins.

'They're right, you know.' The Doctor crossed to the Wraith Queen. 'You can't use these people to secure yourselves in our time and space.'

'WE SHALL NOT.' The Queen bowed her great head. 'A SINGLE PULSE OF ENERGY ALONG THE CORRECT FREQUENCY WILL SEVER OUR BONDS WITH THE SLEEPERS. YOU WILL PROVIDE IT.'

'And revive them?' The Doctor raised the sonic screwdriver; Squidget beeped with quiet dignity and extruded a tendril to wrap around its tip. 'Yes, of course, he will know the wavelength. But you Wraiths will go back into the Quantum realm, trapped and intangible all over again. Perhaps forever.'

'WE HAVE SEEN,' said the Wraith Queen with what might just have been a smile. 'IT WILL NOT BE FOR EVER.'

Squidget pulsed, and the sonic glowed, and the sound filled the chamber like a choir ascending.

Kim was the first to buck and scream as his body fell away from that of the Wraith beneath him as it flickered into nothing. All around the chamber, the Wraiths were dissolving, the humans on their backs shucked off like old skins, left to crumple to the floor. Graham and Ryan ran over to check on them. Yaz dropped the bat and hurried to help.

Masst stomped a hoof on the ground as if spooked, as he and his comrades stared about in disbelief. 'The Wraiths return to the hell we made for them ... of their own accord?'

'People change. Hearts change. Minds change. Just look at you.' The Doctor spoke tersely, her eye on Ace and the Wraith Queen. Ace's whole body shook and contorted as the alien became a blur of shadow movement, shaking like a wet dog drying its fur. Ace toppled to the floor, and the Doctor rushed to her. Chantelle ran over as well.

'Ace?' The Doctor felt for a pulse – found a strong one – and stared down at her old friend.

'You'll be all right,' Chantelle said encouragingly.

'Tell that to what's left of my brain, will you?' Ace looked up at the Doctor groggily. 'She let me go. The Wraith Queen ...'

'Yes. It was her choice. She chose right.' When the Doctor looked back at the Queen, she had disappeared along with the other Wraiths that had been revived by Halogi-Kari.

Halogi-Kari?

He had disappeared too.

There were only black bloodstains now where he'd been lying on the ground, dripping away in a trail.

'That Harbinger,' the Doctor said suddenly. 'The thing behind all of this. Where did Halogi-Kari go?'

Ryan, Yaz and Graham stared around anxiously.

Ace used the Doctor's wrist to yank herself up. 'Don't worry, Professor.' Getting unsteadily to her feet, she scooped up the baseball bat from the floor and staggered off into the shadows after the spats of blood. 'I'll find him.'

'Ace!' the Doctor shouted. 'You're not thinking straight …'

'Go after her,' Yaz said, struggling to arrange an unconscious woman into the recovery position. 'We'll keep an eye on Kim and the others here.'

'Yeah, we're on it, Doc,' Graham added, helping Ryan with more of the fallen abductees. 'We'll do what we can.'

'Chantelle, give us a hand, yeah?' said Ryan. To his amazement, Masst came over to help too, while his infantry troops stood guard beside their unconscious commander.

'I'll be back!' And the Doctor ran from the room, after Ace.

It didn't take Ace long to find Halogi-Kari; she felt in a bad way, but clearly he felt worse. He'd crept out of a hidden exit in the Quantum chamber but was too weak from his wound to get far. Sobbing with pain, he had come to a halt in the corridor beyond, trembling in the middle of the flagstones.

'There you are.' Ace raised the bat and walked slowly towards him. 'Easy pickings.'

'Back!' Halogi-Kari pointed his bloodied hands at her as if about to tear up a time-storm. But Ace brought the bat down on the ground and, in a hail of sparks, fault lines cracked through the flagstones, running like a gunpowder fuse towards him. He squealed and fell back.

'Finally,' Ace said quietly, as the echoes of her strike faded. 'So much blood on your hands … now the blood's your own.'

'You think Halogi-Kari is finished?'

'Oh, no. You've got a long way to go.' Ace advanced on him, slowly. 'Give me one reason why I shouldn't kill you. After all you've done to me – stealing me away and throwing me into Fenric's game … hurting so many people … ruining so many lives just for status, power, greed. Give me one reason why I shouldn't smash you to a pulp right now?'

Halogi-Kari looked up at her. He didn't – couldn't – say anything.

'Ace …' The Doctor's voice sounded softly behind her.

'Stay out of this, Professor.'

'I only want—'

'*Stay out.*' Ace didn't turn round, her eyes still locked with Halogi-Kari's.

'So. You can't think of any reasons, then?' She took a deep, shaky breath, slowly raised the bat above her head.

Then she brought it down, and let it fall to the floor.

'All right then,' Ace hissed as the echoes rang on. 'I'll give you a reason. You're gonna go through that tally of yours – each name on every one of those pennants in your throne room – and find them again. Find them alive. You're gonna send everyone back to where you stole them from, and you'll put them back and you're gonna give them the chance of working things out for themselves.' She leaned on the bat, crouching over him. 'And then you're gonna face justice for all you've done here from the Shadow Proclamation. And I reckon this time there'll be no end to your sentence. You'll never harm another living soul for the rest of your life.'

Halogi-Kari shook his head fiercely. 'I will not go back into their putrescent hands. I'd die first.'

'Not on my watch,' said Ace. 'You'll clean up this mess you've made and serve the time you deserve.'

'And that will be for ever.' The Doctor stepped forward from the shadows to join her. 'Thank you, Ace. I couldn't have put it better myself.'

'Is that right.' Ace turned, exhausted, and looked at the Doctor. 'Did you really think I was going to kill him?'

'No,' said the Doctor. 'But thank you for not proving me wrong. You know how much I hate that.'

'I do,' Ace conceded. '30 years ago, Professor, when you started all this on the Wraith world … You told me then that I could be an emissary. Did you never think I could be up to that challenge?'

'For all my planning, and plotting, and rigging the odds, you were always there, beside me. So strongly there, I never stopped to truly imagine your future ... What you could really be.' The Doctor smiled. 'But I see you now. I see you so clearly. I really have changed, Ace. Just as you have.'

Ace found strength to smile. 'Older and wiser?'

'Nah.' The Doctor shook her head. 'Older and *brilliant.*'

CODA

'Lights.'

The dim emergency lighting in the deserted batcave came on as Will Buckland stepped through the door. He saw at once that nothing had changed from the last time he had been here.

He had gone through the same routine every week for over a month now, always hoping to find some sign of Dorothy or the Doctor, always disappointed.

He'd stopped telling Sam where he was going now. He was sure she knew in any case, and it wasn't like he had anything better to do. She had taken his old job now, while he had been quietly let go amid talk of mental breakdown and paranoid delusions that had led to him being granted indefinite garden leave. He knew his career was finished.

But he also knew his business here was not. If she were able, Dorothy would find some way to get in touch with him. Or the Doctor would. Surely there had to be hope?

He made a slow circuit of the workshop, listlessly rearranging items on the shelves, checking that the equipment was still working. Without the Squidget as a control, the alien power source that ran the batcave was silent and cold. It was only because he topped up the petrol generators outside each week that he still had light and heat.

Satisfied that everything was still in order, he was about to turn off the lights and leave when there was a knock at the door.

'Dorothy?'

Not daring to believe it, Will hurried to the door and flung it open. Sanaul was standing there, a silver box in his arms, a large white envelope taped to its lid.

The envelope was marked with a single word: 'WILL'.

Sanaul silently handed over the box, then turned and limped back to his Range Rover. The old man had recovered well from his ordeal – after seeing the remains of Dorothy's flat, Will had been amazed that anyone had walked away from it. A pair of green eyes in a black furry face suddenly appeared at the passenger window, and Will smiled. It wasn't only Sanaul who'd survived.

Will closed the door and set down the box on the workbench.

For a few moments he stared at the closed metal lid. Then he opened it up.

A happy electronic burble came from beneath some bubble-wrap, and the Squidget emerged, tentacles wriggling contentedly. The interface gripped hold of Will's hand as if to shake it, then zipped quickly away into its alcove in the alien pod, at home again.

Will looked back down at the envelope on the desk, apprehension building in his chest.

With a deep breath he picked it up, tore it open, and sat down on the bench to read.

My dearest Will

I'm writing to you from such a long way away. I don't know if you'll get this, I don't even know if you'll be waiting any longer. But Squidget knows his way home, and he knows to find you.

I'm staying here for a bit, Will. There's tons of work needed here to make things right. You know me, I'm no stranger to warzones, clearing up the messy aftermath, trying to bring sides together.

Well, the two sides here, the Astingir and the Wraiths, are more alien than you could ever imagine, but their hopes and needs are as human as anyone I've helped before. They have the key to losing the weapons they created and the hate that went with it, and I'm not going to leave until I know it's been sorted. I'm part of it. It was something the Doctor did to me a long time ago. I never understood back then, but now I know it's meant to be.

The Doctor and crew are taking home the people the Ratts stole, but don't worry – I'm not all alone out here. Chantelle has decided to stay on with me, and Kim too. They're as surprised about that as anyone, but I reckon Kim's already planning a new podcast about how things are in outer space. Listen out for him, you never know, right? That dish at Devesham's big enough to pick up anything!

So, to the point.

You once told me that the world doesn't work the way I want it to. You said, 'You might think that you can go it alone, that you don't need anyone else, but sometimes you do. Sometimes you just have to trust people.'

Well, you were right, you smug git. And I've always trusted you. That's why I'm asking you to take over from me at A Charitable Earth. I don't know when I'll be back, but I need to know things are in good hands while I'm away. You've already got Squidget and the keys to the batcave. Sanaul can show you how the organisation works from the ground up.

I know you're probably thinking, Hang on, what about my career? But running A Charitable Earth is more than just a job. It's a calling, and I know you're the right man to answer that call. Keep an eye out for the Doctor, she's threatened to drop in on you from time to time. If I can send word via her, I will. If not . . . well, I'm gonna have one hell of a story to tell you when I'm back.

I'll see you soon, I hope. Until that day, take care.
I'll be thinking of you, and I know you'll be Ace.

Dorothy

Will stared at the letter for some time.

Suddenly there was a hum of power as the lights returned to full brightness. Squidget had flexed his tentacles, linking all systems and bringing the batcave's inexhaustible power source back online. Will looked around at all the alien technology held here, gleaming in the diamond-hard light.

'Well, Squidget,' he said, smiling for the first time in so many weeks. 'Looks like you and I have got work to do.'

ACKNOWLEDGEMENTS

This book simply could not have been written without the joyful collaboration and consummate skill of my talented friends, old mucker Mike Tucker, and all round good egg Steve Cole. I cannot thank you enough.

There are millions of Classic *Doctor Who* fans (as us oldies like to call ourselves) who kept the flame alive in the 1990s. For your loyalty and love, I thank you.

Hats off (or fezzes if you prefer) to the new era fans who have taken this amazing adventure series to their many hearts.

Huge thanks also to JNT (executive producer 1980–1989) whose instinctive casting 33 years ago changed my life forever; Russell T Davies whose genius caused the Phoenix to rise again and gave Ace A Charitable Earth; the lovely team at Penguin Random House including Albert, Nell, Becky and Patsy for their enthusiasm and support; my agent, the patient, humorous and hard working Rebecca Singer; the distinctions and transformational work of Landmark; my brilliant and loving family – all of you; and last but by no means least, my debt of gratitude to 13 extraordinary men and woman (and in particular Sylvester McCoy) whose unique talents and personalities have shaped and caused what is without doubt The Greatest Show in the Universe.